The
HAND
Of
MAUD

Patti A. Pierucci

INKSPIRE™
PRESS

The Hand of Maud

By Patti A. Pierucci

ISBN #: 979-8-9994463-6-7

Book cover design: InkSpire Press

Creative Consultant: Donalyn Powell

Editor: Teresa Crumpton

Author's Note: This is a work of fiction. Names, events, and characters (including real-life historical figures and events) are either entirely imaginary or are used fictitiously.

All biblical references are from the New King James Version, Thomas Nelson publishers, 1982.

Dedication

To my father,
Dr. Louis Pierucci, Jr.,
my biggest fan,
with love and gratitude.

PROLOGUE

Bouvines, France

1214

Eleanor's eyes fluttered against a bright sun. A sudden sun. It was dark one moment, and bright the next. Strange noises chittered all around.

How did I get here?

I was at the medieval fair with my friend Carol. July. The fair commemorating the Battle of Bouvines. That's right; I remember now. My name is Eleanor MacLean. The year is 1964, and I was watching a magic show at the fair. I stepped into the magic tent. The strange magician looming in the shadows. The curtain wrapped around me like a shroud. His dead, black eyes, bottomless, staring. The air thickened. Dizzy …

… The world began to tilt.

Eleanor's head—or the ground, she couldn't tell—spun in wild, frantic loops. Arms outstretched, flailing, she grasped at nothing as she fell. Then she realized she was already on the ground. Her stomach lurched, and she vomited in the dirt. She rolled onto her back, waiting for the spinning to stop, eyes closed. Stretched out, pale, sweating, panting, she slowly began to recover and turned her attention to the sounds around her.

She opened her eyes. To her right, several men were lying on the ground, re-enacting a battle scene, typical of medieval re-enactments. Horses in the distance charged at each other, swords clashing, and one knight fell to the ground. So realistic. She watched with fascination, lifting herself sluggishly onto one elbow to see better.

How real it looks. But how did I get here? Why am I on the ground?

I was in the magician's tent. I don't remember walking to the jousting arena. Where's Carol? Something must've made me sick. I must've fainted.

A noise to her left. She rolled over onto her other elbow to view the re-enactment from the other side and gasped in horror. She was lying next to a dying man. She corrected herself: a man pretending to be dying. He moaned and cupped his hands over his wound. It looked so convincing that she recoiled from the gruesome scene. He was lying on his back, a huge gash on his side oozing red, seeping between his fingers. How did he make it look so real? And why was she on the ground in the middle of this re-enactment? What had happened to the fairgrounds? Looking around, she could only see the battlefield where the re-enactment was taking place, not the fair that should have been visible all around with its flags and tents, the vendors, the booths, the salesmen hawking medieval garb and trinkets, the girls dressed as wenches. They were all gone.

What's happening? It was as if the world had tilted off its axis and she couldn't find her footing.

The dying man looked at her with an imploring, pleading look. Ragged breathing. His face was pale gray, and his eyes were moist, shadowed with red streaks. Great acting. But the man would not stop staring at her as he played out the death scene. Finally, he stopped groaning and panting and appeared to stop breathing altogether. His eyes ceased to see her, although they were still open. He didn't blink. Please blink. Please, please blink. But he didn't. I must be imagining it.

She struggled to her feet but wobbled and slid onto her knees. She was dizzy and weak again and wanted to get back to the hotel where she and Carol had been staying. If I could only lie on the bed for a while, I'd feel better. She could not look at the battle re-enactment without feeling queasy, so she covered her face with her hands, crouching into a small, round ball, while the battle, the mock battle, raged about her.

Think, Ellie, think. Try to remember how you got here. Think ... Her mind swirled, like water running down a drain, gaining no traction.

Then the ground began to shake in rhythmic beats, like a subterranean drumbeat rising nearer and nearer to the surface. She looked up toward the noise. A man on a white horse—a huge white horse with powerful hindquarters and a broad chest—was galloping toward her. He stopped only feet away with a quick, sharp jerk of the reins. The horse reared up on its hind legs.

The man dressed as a knight and the horse were covered in chain-mail armor. He was a tall, powerful man, well built with broad, muscled shoulders. He was sturdy and well seated on the horse. His head was also covered in a helmet of chain mail, but his face was visible. His hair, sprinkled with gray, created a fringe at the front of his helmet. He had a gray close-cropped beard and brilliant eyes set in a weathered but handsome face. He was an older man, imposing. He carried a shield and a sword, which he held in the air poised as if he would slice down on her neck at any moment.

"Woman," he said, addressing her in a deep, forceful voice, "what are ye doing here in this place of battle? It's no place for a young woman like yerself. Get up, get up now, I say!"

What language was he speaking? It sounded like French, which she could speak but only with difficulty. She vaguely grasped his meaning yet couldn't find the words to reply. Why was one of the jousters trying to draw her into the re-enactment, especially when she was obviously so sick? Did he think she was part of the show? Looking up at him, his fearsome tone, his angry eyes, and the snorting horse that looked like it could stomp her head into the ground with one strong kick, she felt dizzy and fainted.

Some time later—she could not tell how much time had passed—her mind came swimming back to consciousness. She was bouncing along on the back end of the galloping horse, slung over sideways, face down toward the ground. The knight's woven armor dug into her bare flesh. She started to scream and finally found her voice. "Stop! Where are you taking me? Stop, please!"

The knight reined in the horse quickly, and with one arm reached around, gripped Eleanor by the waist and swung her up into a sitting position behind him astride the horse. "Hold on," he commanded in English. "We need to get away from here."

She obeyed, and wrapped her arms around his broad waist, clinging to the metal armor. It scraped her exposed skin again, and she winced. His sword had been holstered in its scabbard, on the left side of his body, so she gripped its handle to help steady her as he led the horse into a full gallop.

As the horse and its two passengers raced away from the battlefield, Eleanor cast a look back at the scene she had just escaped. Dozens of bodies, maybe hundreds, were writhing and moaning on the ground. She had never witnessed such a vivid, frightening re-enactment. As the field grew smaller with distance, the fallen reminded her of insects caught on flypaper, wriggling and fighting for their lives, a ghastly pantomime of the moments before death. This was real, she thought. If I'm not dreaming, this is all real. But she quickly put the thought out of her mind as she, the knight, and the horse raced away from the battlefield and into the forest edging the field of carnage.

PART ONE

Present Day

"But, beloved, do not forget this one thing,
that with the Lord one day is as a thousand years,
and a thousand years as one day."

2 Peter 3:8

.

Chapter One

Eleanor was thinking about her granddaughter when the power went out.

It was almost time to go to bed when the TV made a zizzing sound and went black. The lights flashed a few times, then stayed off.

She was in the kitchen shuffling around in her slippers and old bathrobe. She had just put the water on for a cup of tea when the power died. "Darn it," she muttered. The kettle's whistle faded away like a dying siren, but the water was hot enough, so she poured it into a cup and let the tea steep while she hunted for candles.

There they were, in the back of the junk drawer. Placing some candles around the house, she walked back into the kitchen and turned on her radio—the fancy radio her granddaughter, Donna, had given her.

"Grandma, you can listen to the radio on the internet now," she'd told her. "Or on your phone. You don't need to have a separate radio."

"Dumplin', I can't be bothered to turn on the computer every time I want to hear the news, and it sounds too small and too tinny on my phone."

She turned on the radio, and the Beach Boys started singing "Help Me, Rhonda." Eleanor began to move with the music, bopping up and down, side to side. Then she caught sight of herself in the dining room mirror—her 80-year-old self—dancing in her frayed pink bathrobe and fuzzy slippers, sipping on a cup of old granny tea, and she laughed.

She took another sip and tuned the radio to local news. There was no information on the power outage. Then she tuned the dial to her favorite news station, BBC. She had a keen interest in news from England.

While the announcer droned on about the latest excesses of the Parliament, Eleanor continued pondering her granddaughter's future. What will Donna do when she graduates from college? And when I'm gone, what will happen to her? She'll have this house, but I hope I live long enough to see her find someone, get married, have children, and live on her own. I want her married and safe before I die.

That thought made her laugh again. Safe? Back then? Not even remotely. And yet, here I am.

Donna would be home soon from the campus library. I'll try to wait up, tell her about the power outage. Make sure she eats something. This was their routine when Donna worked late.

Suddenly her ears perked up. The BBC announcer was saying something that made her stop dead. Scalding water sloshed over the side of her cup as she halted mid-step, burning her skin, but she didn't flinch. She stood motionless, like a statue—like one of Pompeii's doomed, frozen in the middle of an ordinary moment.

"The long-lost treasure of King John, who lost the crown jewels of England in 1216 as he attempted to cross marshy ground off the coast of England, may have been unearthed by a metal detectorist who has scanned a farm in a Lincolnshire village," the announcer said. "Peter Foster Hughes, sixty-three, says he is one-hundred percent certain that the 800-plus-year-old artifacts he has located at an undisclosed site did, indeed, belong to the former king of England—who was often described as the evilest monarch in British history. Hughes's equipment has isolated what he calls high-value items he believes include gold, silver, emeralds, sapphires, and rubies."

Then the voice of metal detectorist Peter Foster Hughes crackled over the radio. "People have been searching for the lost crown jewels for centuries, and I'm certain we've located them." He spoke in a rapid, breathless tone. "If we can bring them up, we may finally recover some of the spectacular crowns and jewelry worn by the royal family, including magnificent relics like the Hand of Maud."

What was wrong with her feet? Eleanor could not move. Her breathing became rapid, like that of Peter Foster Hughes breathlessly recounting his discovery. She started to pant. She forced herself to snap out of her trance, lunged for the radio, and cranked up the volume.

Grabbing a pen from the half-open junk drawer, she began writing down details of the news report on her tea-stained napkin.

She sat on the sofa in the dark living room minutes later. The only light came from the flickering candle on the coffee table. The napkin with her scribbles lay on her lap, as her mind raced in circles, reliving a horrifying event from her past. The wet, musty smell of mud, mingling with the sound of men screaming and gasping for breath. The horses, shrieking and flailing their legs, their large nostrils flared, desperate for air. Her thoughts clawed at her mind, like an undertow dragging the past into the future. She pressed both hands to the sides of her head and closed her eyes, as if trying to squeeze out some semblance of calm and reason.

They found them. They really did. After eight centuries … they're finally found. What do I do? Should I call this man in England and tell him what I know? Should I tell him …

The lights flickered and came back on.

Chapter Two

Something's off with Grandma.

When Donna came home last night from her job at the library, her grandmother was still awake. She found Eleanor sitting in the living room, staring at a blank TV. All the lights were off, but candles were burning throughout the main level of the house. In the kitchen, a candle had melted onto the countertop, leaving a hardened puddle of wax.

When Donna walked into the living room and asked, "Hey, Grandma, what are you doing sitting in the dark?" Eleanor looked at her with wide eyes, then stood and went straight to bed, refusing to be questioned.

"Yes, yes, I'm fine," she told Donna with a wave of her hand, as she disappeared into her bedroom. She hadn't hugged her and said, "See you in the morning, dumplin'"—her favorite endearment for Donna— or even a terse, "There's food in the fridge." No, she'd padded off to bed quickly, as if trying to outrun something.

It was the following afternoon, and the mood in the house was still strained, discolored, as if a storm had passed right through the front door and out the back, leaving the air damp and heavy. The bright sunlight streaming through the living room window was incongruous with her grandmother's edgy mood.

Donna perched on the edge of the sofa, her brows drawn together. Beside her sat Doctor George Ellis, a professor of antiquities at the university where Donna worked and took classes. Eleanor had called him that morning in a state of agitation, pleading with him to come to her home that day to examine her "treasures"—treasures from medieval England, she told him. George was fiddling with his pen, his fingers tapping an off-beat rhythm with it against his knee.

Eleanor paced the room, her hands wringing a worn handkerchief. "I don't know how to begin," she murmured, her voice shaky.

Oh no, what's coming. The weird behavior last night. The moodiness that hung like a blanket over the morning. Her grandmother was behaving like a penitent confessing her sins to a priest. Maybe she's ill and got bad news from her doctor.

"Just tell us, Grandma," Donna finally urged. "You've been acting strange since last night. What's going on?"

Eleanor exhaled slowly, as if bracing herself. "There's something I need to tell you. Something I never thought I'd say out loud."

Donna gave a nervous laugh. "Grandma, you're scaring me."

"I called George and asked him to be here because I want him to hear this, too. And I want him to examine my treasures."

All eyes turned to the box on the table labeled 1216, which Eleanor had produced from somewhere inside her bedroom and set on the coffee table.

"I've been somewhere neither of you would believe." She met their eyes. "I lived in medieval England."

Silence, then, "lived?" Donna repeated. "You mean, you studied it, right? When you were in college? When you did those old-timey re-enactments?"

Eleanor shook her head. "No, sweetheart. I was there."

George leaned forward. "You're saying you—what? You time-traveled?" He was smiling, as if he wanted to be let in on the joke. His voice was a smooth baritone, yet it carried the measured detachment of a scholar.

"Yes." Eleanor's voice didn't waver. "I went back. I lived among them. And I have proof."

Donna rubbed her temples. "Grandma, please, this isn't funny—"

But Eleanor was already reaching into the pocket of her cardigan. Slowly, deliberately, she withdrew a small, velvet pouch. Sitting opposite them, she placed it on the coffee table and loosened the drawstring.

She pulled out a large ruby ring. The gold was thick and aged, its surface covered with intricate carvings of leaves. But it was the stone that caught the light—deep, wine-red, and huge—a ruby, dazzling in the light and the size of a marble. The ruby was surrounded by tiny diamonds and pearls.

George's breath hitched. "Is that—"

"It's a ring originally belonging to English royalty," Eleanor finished for him. "It was given to me."

Donna blinked rapidly, her mouth opening and closing as if the right words might eventually come. "That's not—is it real?"

Eleanor turned the ring between her fingers to catch the light. "It is."

George hesitated before reaching for it. Then, delicately, he turned it over, inspecting the ruby and craftsmanship. He looked up, his face pale and eyes wide. "This looks genuine."

"It is," Eleanor insisted. "It was worn by Queen Isabella of England. She was the wife of King John." She screwed up her face when she said "King John," like she'd just tasted a raw lemon.

Donna shook her head. "No. No, Grandma. Did you inherit it? Maybe you found it? Maybe … Grandma, last night when I came home, you were upset about something. What was it? Did it have to do with this ring?"

Donna shot George a resentful look then, wishing he wasn't intruding on such personal conversations that didn't involve him. "Maybe," Donna said, turning to her grandmother, "maybe you and I should be discussing this in private."

"No," Eleanor said. "I want him here." She was firm. She stood and began pacing again, her gaze flickering between them. "Last night I heard on the radio that a man in England may have found the lost crown jewels. They've been buried in quicksand in England for more than 800 years. That's why I called George."

George became animated. "Yes, I heard about that," he said. "I read an article that a man claims to have found the jewels lost by King John in the Wash off the coast. That's what they call the quicksand," he added, turning to Donna.

"I was there." Eleanor's words hung in the air.

Then Donna's voice cracked a little, and she stood, moving to embrace her grandmother. "It's impossible, Grandma. Come sit down, please."

Eleanor held Donna at arm's length and met her granddaughter's gaze. "I thought it was impossible, too. Until I woke up in the thirteenth century. I can describe in detail what King John's court looked like, the ladies and courtiers, the smells of the King's kitchen, the rough fabric I wore, what it felt like to walk through the halls of Windsor Castle in the Middle Ages, the dark recesses ..." Her voice caught for a moment. "I lived it for two years."

Donna stared at her grandmother, torn between worry and disbelief. "Grandma, this is ... it's not possible." She punctuated every word.

Eleanor leaned forward and placed a hand on Donna's shoulder. "I know it sounds impossible, Donna. But I need you to trust me. And I need you both to help me figure out what to do about this ring."

Eleanor swallowed. When she spoke again, her voice was softer. "There's something else ... I was married."

Donna's breath caught in her throat. She didn't think she could absorb many more surprises from her grandmother. "What? You mean, before Grandpa?"

Eleanor blinked rapidly and let out a shaky sigh, as if her memories were threatening to strangle her. "His name was Thomas. He was ..." She clasped her hands together and began to smile. "Oh, he was a wonderful man, brave, stubborn, handsome. I never thought I'd see this ring again. I never thought I'd be sitting here, in this century, trying to explain something that shouldn't be possible." She glanced between Donna and George. "But it happened."

Donna closed her eyes as if to shut out the reality that was raking its way into her brain—that her grandmother was losing her mind. Dementia. It was a terrifying word, and it ricocheted around her head until she thought she would go mad with worry. She didn't want to open her eyes and let reality seep back in, but even through her eyelids she could still see—the little veins in her eyelids, the moving shadow of her grandmother, gesturing to George. Then the movement stopped. She opened her eyes and realized they were both looking at her.

Eleanor spoke, barely above a whisper.

"If I went back once, what makes you think it can't happen again?"

In that moment, Donna knew her quiet life had been shattered, and her adult life had begun.

Eleanor leaned against the partially open front door eavesdropping on Donna and George. They stood on the front porch, locked in a heated argument, more like they were an old married couple than two people who had just met an hour ago.

This was not at all how Eleanor expected it to go, even knowing her story would be hard for them to hear. She caught most of what they were saying from where she was hiding along the inside edge of the door.

"I assure you, Donna, I have no ulterior motive in taking these objects." He was holding the box marked 1216 that contained Eleanor's treasures.

"Look George, I didn't speak everything that was on my mind in there. I listened to all the crazy stuff my grandmother said, but now I need to say a few things without her hearing. You're leaving with a valuable ring that belongs to my grandmother. She's confused, she shouldn't have given you this stuff, and you shouldn't have taken it."

"Donna, I understand ..."

"No, you don't!" Donna snapped.

Eleanor sidled over to a front-facing window near the door and peered through to get a clear view of the two of them. George was registering a look of shock at Donna's outburst.

So, she thinks I'm crazy. Maybe he does, too.

"You don't understand anything," Donna said. She was leaning forward toward him, one arm motioning backward toward the house, presumably gesturing toward Eleanor. "My grandmother is clearly not well. I've been living with her since I was a little girl; I moved in with her after both my parents died when I was just eleven years old, so I know her better than anyone else in the world."

Eleanor rolled her eyes. You really don't know everything, missy.

"I'm sorry about your parents, Donna," said George. He was frowning slightly and his eyes softened.

"Okay ... I mean thank you." His sympathy seemed to rattle her. "My point is that the ring might not even be hers," Donna said. "It might be stolen. She said it belonged to the royal family, but I'm not sure I believe it. Her story has a lot of holes in it, not the least of which is that she says she got the ring—and those other items in that box—in medieval England."

Eleanor saw George wrap a protective arm around the box which contained the ring and the other items her grandmother had handed over to him—her other treasures from England. He backed away a little as if Donna might lunge for them.

"Donna, with all respect, this is your grandmother's decision," he said, addressing her slowly, as if she was a child. "They belong to her, and she said I could take them with me to examine them and get opinions from some colleagues. I think DNA testing and maybe some carbon dating will help determine their true ages. I assure you again that nothing bad will happen to them. My colleagues see valuable antiques all the time." He paused for a moment. "Although the ring … they might spot that as unique, as an authentic piece of royal jewelry. But nothing bad will happen, alright?"

Donna had both hands on her hips. "I want to meet with you after you and your pals have done your research—before you speak to my grandmother again. Okay?" Donna said.

Eleanor could tell that Donna was angry. She's only being protective, but I hate the way she talks about me when she thinks I can't hear her, like I'm a doddering old crazy woman. If she thinks that's crazy, wait till I tell her the rest of my story.

"That's fine, Donna," George was saying in a strained voice. It sounded like his veneer of professorial calm was beginning to crack. "But I'm working on behalf of your grandmother. Not you."

Ooh, that was the wrong thing to say to her hair-trigger granddaughter. She watched Donna bristle with anger, her posture stiffening like a dog with its hackles raised. With a low mutter that Eleanor could not hear, Donna pursed her lips and stomped inside.

Eleanor scurried to the kitchen just in time.

Chapter Three

Donna and George met on campus the following week.
In the days leading up to their meeting, a strained silence
hung between Donna and her grandmother. Eleanor remained
aloof, refusing to discuss her stories—more like hallucinations, decided
Donna—about her life in medieval England until George completed his
research.

"My library shift ends at two o'clock," Donna told George over the
phone. "I can meet you afterward."

"I'll come to the library at two," he responded. "That will be a good
place to talk."

They sat at a table in the rear of the library, a private spot where
only an occasional student wandered by.

"Donna, first, I want to apologize for … for any tension that I may
have caused between us the other day," he began. "I only want to be of
help to your grandmother. It's not for me, or any of my colleagues, to
decide what happens to your grandmother's items."

He was behaving in a more congenial manner today, but he was still
talking like an academic—polite, careful of every word he spoke, and
a little nervous, too, she noted. The pen tapping and the hand he kept
running through his hair were dead giveaways.

Donna had been ashamed of her emotional outburst on the front
porch and breathed a sigh of relief when he broke the ice by mentioning
it first. Her internet search of Doctor George Ellis convinced her he

was, indeed, a genuine expert in antiquities. He'd even written a book about medieval England titled, *The Kingdom's Shadow*. Still, this man didn't belong in the middle of the sad drama unfolding in Donna's life. Her grandmother was breaking with reality, and Donna was responsible for her care. She had to figure out what to do about her grandmother's mental state.

And there was the enormous ring, possibly a stolen ring, that Eleanor had in her possession, hidden in her bedroom for who knows how long. What was she going to do about that?

"I apologize, too," she said, looking down at her hands and not wanting to meet his intense gaze. "I'm just worried about my grandmother. I guess I've got some decisions to make soon about her care."

George said, "I understand, Donna. You've got your hands full. But let me show you a few things that might shed some light on what your grandmother told us. She may be more clear-headed than you realize."

Donna cocked her head and looked at him directly. *He can't possibly believe a word of her story.*

He opened his backpack and pulled out a computer printout of a painting. "This is Queen Isabella, the queen your grandmother mentioned. The wife of King John."

Donna noticed it right away. The printout showed a color image of a queen, painted in the style of medieval paintings, flat, lacking depth and perspective, like a paper doll. Queen Isabella was seated on a throne, wearing a red gown with a red cape draped around her shoulders and a crown on her head. On her right hand, which clutched the ties of the cape, was a large ruby ring. *The* ring.

"George, I can hardly believe it. Where did you find this picture?"

George shrugged. "On the internet. It looks like your grandmother's ring really did belong to the royal family. And my colleagues believe it's genuine, not a reproduction. They date it back to the Middle Ages. It has all the characteristics of belonging to the Plantagenet ruling family— which is exactly when Isabella was Queen."

Donna tapped her fingernails against the table and breathed deeply. Her grandmother really did have a piece of jewelry that once belonged to the royal family of England. Did she and her husband, this Thomas person, find it? Did they steal it?

George said, "Remember this parchment sketch that your grandmother gave me? And this tunic?"

He opened his backpack again and pulled out a charcoal drawing and a roughly made, worn garment, laying them on the table—two more of Eleanor's "treasures" from the mysterious box. Eleanor had explained that the drawing was one she made of Thomas. It depicted him leaning on a farm tool, like a hoe, wearing a tunic—the garment now lying on the table. Donna nodded. Yes, she remembered these.

"My colleagues don't believe this parchment sketch is older than fifty or sixty years. There's not enough degradation of the leather parchment."

She felt a wave of relief. If the DNA had confirmed her grandmother's "treasures" were truly ancient—dating back to the 1200s—Donna would've faced a difficult dilemma: what to do with centuries-old artifacts in her grandmother's possession. Still, the test results brought cold comfort. Learning her grandmother was wrong about their age only confirmed what she feared most—Grandma's grip on reality is slipping.

George said, "Something did turn up in the DNA testing of the parchment that puzzled me. The skin used to make this parchment is from a breed of sheep that became extinct centuries ago."

That hit Donna's mind like a bolt of lightning, sharp and disorienting. "What? What does that mean?"

"I honestly don't know. The leather doesn't show the type of age it should if it was eight centuries old, but the DNA testing of the leather confirms that it's from a long-extinct breed, so it should show much more age than it does. Hopefully, Eleanor can explain it."

"What about this clothing?"

"We were able to extract some DNA from this tunic, but there are no matches yet. It's hand-made, but it's not 800 years old. Like the parchment, it's only about fifty or sixty years old."

He then placed a letter on the table, its words written on rustic handmade paper. It was a letter from Thomas to her Eleanor, in flowery language.

"Let's go through this letter," George said, and he began to read:

"My heartily beloved Eleanor, whose name is most dear to me and reminds me

of our beloved Queen Eleanor."

George paused and looked up. "I believe the reference to Queen Eleanor is Eleanor of Aquitaine, not your grandmother. She was, by the way, King John's mother." He continued reading.

"I pray you accept this token from me, a ring of royal heritage, fit for the queen of my heart, thee! Although, as thou knowest, it be not mine at first, it be mine now that I hath rescued it after that unforgettable flight from the Wash, eternally separated from its original owner."

George looked up again. "Obviously, the reference is to the ruby ring. It was part of the crown jewels, and therefore 'eternally separated' from its owner, King John, when it went down in the Wash, the quicksand, with all the other jewels."

George continued to read:

"I know, as none other does, the woes and tribulations thou hath endured at the hands of that monster, the Tyrant, now dead, thanks be to a merciful God. Wouldst thou grant me my greatest desire: To be thine husband? Say yes, my love, my life, my sweet Eleanor. Say yes! Forever Yours, Thomas"

George said, "The tyrant would be the king, King John. He was known to be a nasty piece of work."

"I really don't know who he is, George," said Donna.

"Remember the Robin Hood tales? He's the bad king from those stories."

"Oh," said Donna. "So, he was a real person."

"Yes, very real."

"So, then what?" asked Donna. "My grandmother got some of the facts right, but she made up the time-travel story?"

"I don't know, Donna. We need to get ..."

Their conversation was cut short by the bubbly, high-pitched giggle of a young female student. "Oh—hi, Dr. Ellis. I didn't expect to see you here." The girl tucked a strand of hair behind her ear, then untucked it, fumbling with her words and tittering nervously.

"Hello Miss ..." George said, standing up politely.

"It's Ashley, professor," she said, directing a coy smile at him. "I'm in your class Courtly Love and Troubadour Traditions." She gasped, causing Donna to jump a little in her seat. "Oh, I just love it!"

Ashley leaned against the bookshelf behind her, casually, a dimpled smile playing on her lips. "Do you always haunt the philosophy section?" Her voice was a little breathless, like a stale imitation of Marilyn Monroe, and she clutched her books to her chest and tilted her head.

"Well, I didn't … is this the philosophy section?" he said, turning around to eye the shelves. "Uh, we're just having a meeting here, so if you …"

"Oh sure." Ashley walked closer to George and almost whispered, "Dr. Ellis, I need to meet with you to discuss the writing assignment. I'm struggling a little." She fluttered her eyelashes at him in a shameless display of flirtation.

Donna rolled her eyes.

"Alright," he said, sitting again. "Make an appointment with my office. But the assignment is still due on Thursday."

The eyelashes fluttered again like butterfly wings as she walked away, then she cast an icy glance over her shoulder at Donna.

Oh, come on. Blondes, seriously? "Better be careful, professor," Donna said with a smirk.

He laughed playfully, casting an appraising look at Donna, then said, "Don't tell me you're jealous, Miss Westbrook."

His comment made her suddenly feel lightheaded, as if she had too much air in her lungs. Composing herself, she began to gather her books. "Hardly. You're way too old for me, *doctor*."

George reached across the table and took her hand, stopping her cold. "Donna, I admire you for being so protective of your grandmother. I'm glad she has you, and I'll help in any way I can."

She wanted to pull her hand away but seemed powerless to move it. She looked down at his hands, so warm on hers. She could smell a pleasant scent coming from him. Was it aftershave? Soap? Him? She looked at him. Look at that—he has little flecks of gold in his eyes. He shifted his weight and leaned toward her slowly, almost indiscernibly, like there was an electric force drawing him toward her. For a second, she thought he would kiss her. Would she allow him to kiss her? Right here in the campus library? Would she kiss him back? But he was only shifting his weight, nothing more.

Very lightly, his finger on her hand moved, stroking it. Did she imagine that? Her head began to swim, and her breath quickened. She had to break the tension before she passed out.

She pulled her hand away, stacked her books quickly and stood. "I better get to class."

"May I walk you, Donna?"

"No, no I've got to go."

Feeling like a coward, she bolted away.

Chapter Four

E leanor rested her head back on the sofa, her eyes closed and her hands on the small Book of Psalms given to her by the preacher all those years ago. She tried to still her racing thoughts, but her memories were having none of it.

The preacher's handwritten inscription inside the book in her hands echoed in her mind: "Deliver me, O my God, out of the hand of the wicked, out of the hand of the unrighteous and cruel man."

As her memories drifted in a twilight haze, her mind replayed the desperate escape from the battlefield. She was back there—*then*—being rescued by the pretender knight. Or was she being kidnapped? She glided through the forest on the back of his horse. Once in the dense woods, they slowed to a trot and Eleanor had drifted into a dreamlike state, nearly falling asleep behind the imposing knight.

I'm in a play, she had told herself, floating through the moment. It's not real. I'm the princess being rescued from … let's see, who was she fleeing from? An evil magician who wanted to force her into marriage or imprison her for the rest of her life in a tower. Her fairy tales were getting all tangled together in her mind and confusing her dream, with reality seeping in around the edges. She was being rescued by a strong knight who carried her away into the forest for safekeeping. He had with him a glass slipper that he tried to place on her bare foot.

She had glanced down at her feet then. They were both bare …

A knock on the door jolted Eleanor back to the present.

"I'll get it," called Donna from upstairs.

Donna tore down the steps, sounding like a one-woman stampede. Eleanor heard her stop for a moment at the door before opening it, then George and Donna exchanging a few polite words before entering the living room.

Eleanor noticed they did not sit side by side on the sofa, as they had last week, and she caught the glance they exchanged—was it embarrassment? Unease? Something between them felt off. What was going on? Donna sat rigidly, casting furtive glances at George every few minutes.

George placed the box on the coffee table and cast an inscrutable look toward Eleanor. She couldn't read him, so she guessed he was preparing to give her bad news.

Clearing his voice, George said, "I've shown the tunic, the parchment, and the letter from Thomas to several colleagues. I'm sorry, Eleanor, but none of them are more than about sixty years old."

Eleanor drew back, stiffening at his comments. "With all due respect, George, you're flat wrong. And so are your colleagues. How can your science contradict the facts? How can you say they're not as old as I know them to be?"

George explained the basics of carbon dating and DNA testing. "We were able to carbon date the parchment and the linen tunic," he answered. "I'll grant you; they look old. They're made to look old. But there is no way they're older than sixty years." Then he added, "We obtained DNA from the parchment, the tunic, and the letter and fed them into the national database, but we haven't had any hits yet."

Eleanor's eyes narrowed, and a flicker of disbelief passed over her face. She knew that all his so-called experts were wrong, but how could she prove it?

"You said the ring was authentic."

George said, "Yes, the ring is the only one of your treasures that I, and my colleagues, believe dates back to the Middle Ages. We didn't determine this through carbon dating," he added, "which doesn't work on inorganic objects like jewelry. We determined its authenticity by investigating archives of royal jewelry belonging to the Plantagenets. So, yes," he scratched his chin absently while he spoke. "Yes, the ring is genuine, but … there is another mystery."

Eleanor cocked her head, eyes fixed on him, waiting for his next words to drop.

"The DNA test we conducted on the parchment, with the sketch of Thomas, revealed that the skin comes from an extinct breed of sheep that used to live in England. But the parchment itself is no more than sixty years old. Can you explain that?"

A relieved smile broke across Eleanor's face, and the tension melted from her body. "Yes. Yes, I can," she said with a short laugh. "But … you're not going to believe it."

Eleanor rose to her feet and began to pace. Her old bones creaked with the effort, but her memories were young and unburdened by time. She had lived in medieval England, more than 800 years ago, she told them. Yet when she came back to the present with her treasures, it was 1966.

"All my treasures were practically new when I came back about sixty years ago," Eleanor stressed. "What other explanation makes sense?"

George, tapping his pen, looked perplexed, clearly turning over her explanation in his mind, trying to make sense of it. Her granddaughter looked at Eleanor with an expression of deep concern—skeptical, sorrowful, as if she was watching the Titanic go down in slow motion.

Donna said, "Grandma, you know this sounds impossible, right? Help me make sense of it. I mean … how did you get there?"

"You mean, *then*," Eleanor corrected her.

Donna just heaved a heavy sigh. "Okay, *then*."

"I'll tell you everything—because it's the only way to make you believe. But before I do, there's something else I need to tell you: I know where more of the crown jewels are. One of them was mentioned on the radio by that fellow in England. The Hand of Maud."

—◆—

"Alright. I should start with your grandfather."

They sat on the back porch, iced teas in hand, the summer air thick with silence. Eleanor had set out a tray of cookies, a small attempt to soften the weight of what she was saying—to make the setting feel less terrifying than the story itself.

At the mention of the Hand of Maud, George became more alert, his excitement evident as he leaned forward, encouraging Eleanor to continue. In stark contrast, Donna remained on edge, her tension unrelenting, with worry etched across her face.

"We were planning to marry as soon as I finished school. Your grandfather was just starting his medical practice, and I had one year left at the university."

Eleanor smiled at the memory, amused at how clever she'd once thought she was. Back in college, she believed she knew everything about history, about life in medieval times from her studies, about good and evil, about life in general—but oh, how wrong she'd been.

"There was a famous battle in Normandy," Eleanor continued, "when the English lost their territory in northern France. The battle was in a small village called Bouvines, and every year they still hold a medieval fair on the battlefield to commemorate the event and the lives lost.

"In 2014 they celebrated the 800th anniversary of the Battle of Bouvines," Eleanor said. "Wish I could've gone. After all, I was there for the original event."

Donna's eyebrows rose. Eleanor ignored it and took another sip of her iced tea.

"Anyway, it was summer, so I decided to go with my friend Carol and spend a couple of weeks in Europe. We were going to start at the festival in Bouvines, then travel to France, England and Italy. It would've been a great vacation … but I missed most of it."

"This was the year 1964?" George asked.

Eleanor nodded. "Yes, it was in July. So, Carol and I flew to France and went to the festival. I always dressed up in costume when I went to one of these festivals. Some people wore goofy things, like dressing as wenches with corsets and low-cut dresses. Believe me, women would not be allowed in public looking like that in real medieval times. Well, maybe in brothels. Some women dressed as witches."

Eleanor let out a short, brittle laugh. "People accused of witchcraft were not treated well in medieval days, but what did they know? They thought it was fun to dress up like that."

Eleanor remembered the dress she was wearing that day—a long dress made of burgundy-colored silk. She had braided her hair in two long braids and wound ribbons through them to the end, then attached a veil. How happy she'd been walking around the festival in her beautiful costume. How innocent and unsuspecting.

"The fair was better than most," she continued, "because it was centered around a real historic event—the Battle of Bouvines. In some ways it was like a carnival, but this one included an ax-throwing contest and a crossbow shoot. And jousting." She paused and swallowed, without taking a drink, like something was caught in her throat. "Finally, toward the end of the day, Carol and I stopped to watch a magic show."

Eleanor's mood changed abruptly, and she stopped speaking. Condensation ran down her glass and dripped onto her shirt, but she didn't notice.

The magic show. The magician. She felt a little sick to her stomach and breathed heavily. After a long pause she put her head in her hands and closed her eyes, squeezing them tight.

No, no, please God. I don't want to relive this … That man, that horrible man. I don't want to talk about him. I don't want to remember him.

"Grandma … Grandma."

Donna was leaning over her, stroking her arm, petting her gray hair. Donna's face was tight with concern and fear.

Eleanor looked down at the worn Book of Psalms resting in her lap, and a sense of calm washed over her. She carried it with her everywhere, because the mere presence of it comforted her. This little book is more evidence that my memories are true, she reminded herself, but I can't tell them about it. Not yet.

"I'm okay, dear," she said. She sat up straight and took a sip of her tea. "Really, I am. It's hard to remember some of this. I want to go on; just give me a minute."

George, watching Eleanor's composure waver, leaned forward with concern creasing his face. "Take your time," he said softly, his voice gentle.

After a deep breath, Eleanor said, "Carol and I were walking around the fair, having a great time, people-watching, when we spotted the magic act up ahead. There was a large crowd, so we pushed our way close to the stage to see what was going on. The stage was raised off the ground a little, and it looked like a theater setup, with curtains drawn around the sides and back. On top of the stage stood another platform with something that looked like a chamber, with more curtains around that.

"When we walked close to the stage, the magician—the name on his sign was Simon the Seer—was performing a few tricks. When he saw me in the front of the crowd, he stopped and stared at me. It felt odd.

He looked at me as if he knew me; that's what I remember thinking. I thought to myself, do I know him? Later I understood this was not the only time we'd seen each other, so he did recognize me. But I'll get to that part of the story later.

"Simon had a long, black beard and black eyes—lifeless, inky eyes, like the eyes of an animal, stuffed and mounted on the wall.

"I didn't believe in magic. As a Christian, I knew magic was fakery; it was a gimmick, so why should I be afraid of it? I thought the magician was just … well, creepy. He held out his hand and asked me to come up on the stage to volunteer for his next trick. He made me feel a little uncomfortable, singling me out like that, so I turned to Carol and asked her, 'Should I?' She shrugged and said, 'Might be fun.' So, I let him help me onto the stage.

"He said, 'Ladies and gentlemen, for my final act of magic, I will make this lovely young woman disappear. I will need your help with this difficult act of magic. It is the most difficult one I perform, and your incantation will be the charm that helps this young lady—that helps Eleanor—disappear from this Earth.'

"Now, how did he know my name? I figured I must've told him. I was afraid, then. That chill running up my spine was sending a message to me. 'Just walk away, Ellie,' it was saying. 'He's scary.' But I didn't. Simon asked the audience to repeat an incantation of nonsense words over and over again.

"The audience chanted the words, while his assistant helped me onto the platform and behind the smaller curtain. In the floor of the platform there was a door, like a trap door. I figured they wanted me to crouch down and disappear through that door so it would seem like I had disappeared. That maybe there would be a space below the stage for me to hide.

"Just as I was expecting the assistant to give me my instructions, the magician appeared at the back of the curtain. 'Go up front,' he told the assistant, 'and keep them reciting the words.' He drew the curtains around me, leaving a small opening where we could see each other. He slowly reached his hand toward my face, but he didn't touch me. He hovered his open hand in front of my face, his black eyes boring into mine, and that's when I thought, 'Ellie, he's trying to hypnotize you.' I tried to look away from his face but couldn't. I remember looking at his black eyes, and suddenly the skin around his eyes started to darken. He began to have dark circles around his eyes, like a watercolor soaking in the deepest, darkest ink. The darkness spread across his face.

"Again, I thought I was being hypnotized. I had no power to fight it.

"His face was dissolving, turning black, until I could see only the whites of his eyes. He kept his hand stretched out toward me, like he was attaching me to himself.

"Inside, I was screaming. Terrified. I prayed, 'Dear Lord, he's going to kill me. He's hypnotizing me; he's given me a drug to paralyze me so I can't run. Help me!' My brain was in overdrive, racing.

"Everything went black. Then, from the darkness, brilliant light. Feeling dizzy. Spinning—my head, the ground, the bright light, the platform I was standing on. My ears ringing, buzzing so loudly in my head I thought I'd go deaf. I thought I was going to fall from the spinning, so I braced my legs. Simon's awful black face hovered in front of me, the nonsense chanting echoing in my brain like a demented chorus. I thought he said something. 'Go get them, Eleanor, get the ghouls.' Or did he say, 'Get the jewels?' But neither one made sense. I didn't know what he meant. Had I been struck in the head, or was it only the spinning?

"I blacked out … and that's when the real nightmare began."

PART TWO

Eleanor

1214-1216

"I felt a nightmare sensation of falling; and, looking round, I saw the laboratory exactly as before ... Then I noted the clock. A moment before, as it seemed, it had stood at a minute or so past ten; now it was nearly half-past three!"

H.G. Wells, "The Time Machine"

Chapter One

The battlefield. Had she dreamed it? Now she was on the back of a large, white horse sitting behind a knight, and they were trotting briskly through the forest. She looked down at her feet, and they were both bare. Was she dreaming this, too?

She straightened up; she'd been asleep or passed out on the horse with her head resting against the back of the knight and her arms dangling at her sides. She'd been lost in a dream, a tangled blend of fairy tales. The knight was not a dream; he was a real person—an actor—but not a young prince like the rescuer of her fairytale dream. He was a powerful older man with a formidable presence. And he was now riding his horse at a slow trot through the woods and into a large clearing up ahead—a clearing filled with tents and men milling about. Soldiers dressed in medieval uniforms and armor, re-creating a medieval encampment.

As their horse slowly stomped through the camp, muddied from a recent rain, the men stopped what they were doing and stared at her. She clung tightly to the knight again and took stock of her surroundings.

Dozens of tents were staked out in a field as massive as two football fields. Chickens clucked and pigs grunted in a pen. Nearby were several men and women who attended a large pot of simmering stew. Eleanor, the knight, and his horse, rode on. The horse's huge hoofs pounded into the ground, spraying mud with each powerful stride. A few women, dressed like ones she had seen at many medieval fairs, poked their heads out of the tents. One looked Eleanor up and down and smirked at her as she and the knight rode through the camp.

"Welcome dearie," she crowed at Eleanor with a toothless grin.

"Hush, woman!" barked the knight. "Get back in the tent and don't let me see ye again." He was speaking in a colloquial form of English now. This knight was in a stern, no-nonsense frame of mind. Or acting like it.

"Please let me down," Eleanor said. "I'd like to get back to my hotel and get some rest. Please. I'm not sure where my friend is or even where I am. None of this looks familiar. Can you tell me where we are?"

The knight pulled up on the reins and stopped, turning his head around to look at her. "Ye speak English then, lass?"

"Yes," she answered, forgetting they were in northern France.

He looked at her more closely as they sat on the horse. She watched him survey her clothing, her bare feet, her hair that had fallen loose and tumbled around her face and shoulders like a filthy mop. The veil and brass circlet, which had been on top of her head, were now tangled in her hair. Eleanor, seeing his assessment of her state of dishevelment, ran her fingers through her hair and retrieved the circlet and veil that had been part of her costume.

"Put them on, lass," said the knight, and he turned around and continued until they arrived at a larger tent at the outskirts of the camp. A squire ran up to the horse to assist the knight, then he saw Eleanor and gasped.

"Help her down, Alfred. And close yer mouth."

Alfred helped Eleanor down, and her legs immediately buckled. The knight leaped from the horse and lifted Eleanor in his arms like she was a child, carried her inside the tent and laid her on a rough bed in the corner. She had not fainted, but her legs barely worked. What a relief to lie down for a moment. Why am I so tired? But even as she thought it, she drifted into a dreamless sleep on the uncomfortable bed. Her brain whirling, she heard the knight address the squire.

"Let her sleep, Alfred, but watch her carefully. She may be a French spy for that liver-eatin' Philip."

———

She awoke later when it was fully dark outside. The tent was lit by candles. She saw the squire, Alfred, seated in front of the bed, staring at her intently. Eleanor sat up in the bed. She swayed back and forth, eyes darting around the unfamiliar tent.

"Who are you? What am I doing here?" In a few moments she remembered the trip on the knight's horse. That wasn't a dream, then, because *here I am in the same tent. Can you wake up from a dream inside a previous dream?* Her mind continued to race around in circles, like a squall had taken up residence in her brain and would not settle down.

Alfred jumped up and ran outside the tent. "Quick, boy, find the Marshal and tell him to come here. The girl has awakened." Several men stood outside the opening to the tent, peering inside to get a look at Eleanor.

"What are you looking at?" she yelled and was surprised to see them scatter with looks of shock and fear on their faces. Even Alfred looked shocked. He poured her a cup from a small pot that hung over hot coals within the tent. "Here, miss, I mean lass, drink some tea."

She took the cup and sipped.

"Please," she pleaded, "What has happened?"

The tall, older knight, whom the squire had called "the Marshal," strode commandingly into the tent. He was no longer dressed in his armor but wore a tunic and rough hose.

"Well, lassie," he began in English. "Who are ye, and what were ye doing on that battlefield? Where do ye come from and who brought ye there? Were ye layin' in wait for me? Tell me the truth, for I'll know if ye're lyin'."

She blinked at him for several seconds, not knowing what he was talking about. She looked around, thinking there must be an audience for all this playacting.

"I ... I don't know how I got there," she began. "I'm an American, I was attending a fair in Bouvines, and I passed out and woke up where you found me."

Already Eleanor was beginning to work out in her mind that she should give out as little information as possible. Perhaps she had been taken captive as part of the re-creation. If so, she should not reveal too much.

The knight pulled up a chair and sat in front of her, a stern look on his face. "What is this talk? What is ah-mare-ikan? Is that yer trade, girl? What does a-mare-ikan do?"

She began to speak, but he interrupted her.

"I'm not finished, girl," he growled.

"But you asked—"

"Don't interrupt!" he thundered.

She recoiled in fear.

"Let's start with this question: What's yer name?"

She hesitated, not sure if it was safe for her to speak. "Eleanor MacLean." This would soon be her married name.

"Ahhh," he responded, and he leaned back on his chair and stroked his beard thoughtfully. "So ye're Scottish?"

Eleanor responded, "My mother was French; my father was Scottish." This was only partially true. Both of Eleanor's parents had Scottish blood, but Eleanor reasoned that she needed an explanation for why she was passed out on a French battlefield re-enactment.

He looked at her with an unyielding gaze for a long time.

"And what were ye doin' on that battleground that I had to rescue ye from yesterday?"

Yesterday? How long have I been asleep? She looked outside, beyond the gaping men at the entrance to the tent, and saw dawn emerging through the far trees.

"Sir," she began, understanding that this man would tolerate only respectful treatment from her. "Please tell me where I am. What place is this camp? And what day is this?"

"It's July, girl, the 28th day; 'tis Monday."

"What year, please?"

His eyebrows came together. "Ye don't know what year ye're in? Did ye come to some harm in the head on that battlefield?"

"I ... I don't think so. Well, yes, maybe. But I'm telling you the truth when I say I can't remember how I got there. I'm confused, sir, and I'm not sure of my surroundings or what year it is."

"It's the year of our Lord one-thousand two-hundred and fourteen."

Her eyes widened. "What did you say?" He repeated himself, watching her intently. She sat for a moment while her mind hopped from thought to thought, trying to make sense of what she had just heard. If she was a captive in some kind of macabre re-creation, then this was taking it too far. Her temper flared.

"Sir, I would like to go home." She sat up on the bed with her back straight and head held high. She smoothed her tousled hair. "To France," she added, realizing that mentioning America again would only raise more questions. He was playing his role too well.

The knight smiled at her. "No lassie, ye're not going back to yer masters in France. Ye're stayin' right here, with me, and I'll decide where ye go next." There was an edge to his tone.

Eleanor stood. "So, I am your captive, is that it? Sir, I do not have any masters in France. I heard you say I was a spy, but I am not. Not for this Philip, whoever he is, not for anyone. I was out walking around, and then I felt sick, I fainted, and I woke up right where you found me. That is the truth. I was staying near—I mean I live near Bouvines, and I don't remember much else. I must have hit my head, blacked out. And you're right, I may have injured myself and it affected my memory. My parents will be worried about me. But if you'll help me get back to my hotel ... I mean my home, I'll be happy to pay you for your help."

"Lass," said the knight, also standing now and towering over her. "Don't ye understand? We just lost a battle to the French, and I'm not takin' ye back there. It's not safe for us to go back. Right now they'll be combin' the countryside lookin' fer stragglers to slaughter."

"That was not a real battle!" she snapped. Hot anger washed over her. "Stop this nonsense, now. I want to go home."

She thought the knight might strike her, but he sat again wearily in the chair before her and appeared to soften, possibly sensing her fear and confusion.

"Girl, the battle I dragged ye from yesterday was real. It was a big loss for the crown. Do ye understand that? Yer French king, Philip," he said, spitting out the name with a grimace, "massacred us. We don't even know how many men we lost, but it was a bloody rout. They've taken hundreds of our men into captivity, parading them through the streets toward Paris, slaughtering them along the way, so I've heard. God knows what he'll do with those who survive. Lass, ye could have been among the captives if I hadn't found ye there."

The knight hung his head and sighed, as if weary from the battle, weary from explaining it to her, and weary with life in general. Eleanor recalled that the Battle of Bouvines in 1214 was significant in the war between England and France. The medieval fair she and Carol had flown across the Atlantic to attend was strategically located in Bouvines as an homage to those who fought and died there. But she really didn't remember much else about it or what it meant for England.

Reluctant to show too much ignorance, she asked, "Sir, why was the Battle of Bouvines so important? As a woman, I ... I haven't kept up too well with events between England and France."

"What do ye mean, girl?" he exploded at her. "It's over for England, and for John's holdin's in France. We've lost it all, and now we're in retreat and need to get across the Channel quickly before we're all captured or killed."

He stood, rallying himself and speaking with authority. "Get yerself presentable, lass, we're headin' out. I'll get ye some shoes and some food, but get ready. We're headin' north in about an hour."

Moments later, Squire Alfred brought her some bread and cheese, along with a tankard of ale. He slipped out of the tent to give her privacy while she tidied herself. She slipped on the leather shoes that Alfred had brought her, lacing them up so that they fit snugly. Then she ran her fingers through her hair, braiding it again and securing it beneath her veil and circlet. Her dress was filthy, but the mud had dried, and she was able to wipe off most of it with a rag that she'd dampened from the basin of water left by Alfred. She looked rough but presentable.

The food was surprisingly refreshing, and the ale, though unpleasantly sour, left her with a welcome buzz, relaxing her enough to prepare for the trip. If they were going to England, perhaps she could get some help there and find her way back home.

Good heavens, what will become of Carol, waiting for me in Bouvines?

Chapter Two

O ne hour later, they were quickly making their way north on horseback. The Marshal had provided her with her own small horse which seemed to glide along these rutted dirt roads. Wouldn't want to spend another minute on the back of his horse; it's nearly the size of a Macy's parade float.

Clad once again in his armor, as were the hundreds of other knights, the Marshal was an imposing, majestic, sight. He admonished her to stay close behind him.

"Keep up with me, lassie. We're in a hurry."

In less than five hours, the entire army had arrived at Calais. The trip through the French countryside, despite its speed, left Eleanor convinced she was still in a dream state, or in a state of confusion, because this was not the France she and Carol had arrived in two days before with its modern homes and cities, its bustling highways, and commercial districts. Before her was a barren countryside with small clusters of rough homes with thatched roofs scattered in the distance. The Marshal's forces carefully avoided these villages on their dash to the English Channel, and they saw few people along the way. Eleanor spotted several castles in the distance that looked not at all like ancient ruins, as she expected, but like recently constructed structures. If she had been transported to the past, this is what she would have expected the landscape to look like.

Oh, this is so confusing. Her theory was that she was dreaming everything. But the flaw in that theory was that her dreams rarely developed on a straight timeline, as this one was doing. Going back to the fair in Bouvines, she could account for everything that had occurred sequentially, including the magic show, stepping onstage, entering the curtained platform, then ... right there, that's where she lost time. She'd become dizzy and sick, but once she awakened on the battlefield, time picked up again in a linear progression.

At the port of Calais, the army and all its horses and equipment boarded several primitive-looking ships. The Marshal kept Eleanor close by his side on the smallest vessel. Wherever she went, she drew attention. Although there were a few women on board, the crew and passengers were mostly men, knights in full armor, armor quickly shed upon embarking.

At all times Eleanor was protected by Alfred. She looked out over the vast English Channel as they sailed away from France. Where on earth am I going? France, growing smaller by the minute, never looked so barren or so beautiful. The coastline was dotted with small seaports, not the mammoth port cities teeming with modern ships, speedboats, and commercial activity. It reminded her of Venice, with small boats paddling around in the water, like gondolas, merchants with food and fish stalls—all growing smaller by the minute as they sailed away from France and toward England.

The Marshal said the winds were ideal for their trip across the Channel, with a warm, refreshing breeze providing a few moments of calm for her.

She closed her eyes, breathed deeply, and listened to the hum of voices around her. I'll just have to go along with this—whatever "this" is. I'm a prisoner aboard a ship sailing across the English Channel, so, Ellie, you'd better start figuring out what comes next.

She heard a voice address the Marshal. "Sir William," he called with alarm, "there's a French vessel comin' up southeast fast."

"I see it, Peter," called the Marshal, looking out across the Channel. Eleanor saw it, too. It was approaching rapidly. Looking north, she saw the first hazy impression of the coastline of Dover, where they were headed. The white cliffs were a stirring sight, impossible to mistake for anything else in the world. The harbor at Dover was also becoming visible, and it looked much like the port of Calais, like a painting from another time.

"We're going to make it," called the Marshal. "The sun will still be risin' when we make port." He looked at the fast-approaching ship thoughtfully, stroking his beard as he spoke. "They're showin' a lot of cheek, though, coming this close to England."

The man Peter called the Marshal "William." Something is ringing a bell in my memory, but my mind can't quite land on it. Marshal William. No, that's not it. She reversed the order in her mind, William Marshal. Much closer. William Marshal, William *the* Marshal. That was it! William the Marshal, the famous English knight, the most famous knight in history, who served four English kings, including Richard the Lionheart. Her studies in medieval history had not prepared her to recall every detail of life in England during the Middle Ages, and her recollection of the details of English royalty during the early reign of the Plantagenets was murky. But the name of William the Marshal was legendary.

Her eyes widened, and she said out loud, "William the Marshal." Both the Marshal and his companion, Peter, along with Alfred, who had not left her side, turned to look at her.

"What's that, lassie?" asked the Marshal. "Did ye address me?"

Oh no. If this is really William the Marshal of medieval fame, and this is the year 1214, then the king he is serving now is King John; that's the John the Marshal mentioned. John has the reputation as the vilest king in English history and was the model for the evil, usurper king in all the Robin Hood stories and films. I hope I don't run into him. She ignored the quizzical looks of William the Marshal and his companions. She quickly reminded her confused brain that she was a woman from 1960s America, living out a re-enactment—either in a long, vivid dream, or for real. Either way, if she met the evil king, he would not be real. But ... the thought nagged at her and would not let up its constant drumbeat in her head: This all feels so real.

"They're gainin' on us!" yelled Peter. An arrow struck the side of their ship. Then another. Eleanor shrieked and crouched low to the deck, shielding her head with her hands.

"We're in English waters now," said the Marshal. "Calm yerself, woman. They'll be turnin' around any minute." He shook his head and actually laughed at her.

One of the ships in the English fleet maneuvered east and sailed toward the approaching French ship. It looked like another battle, this time on water, but as the Marshal had predicted, the French ship turned around and headed back to the port of Calais.

"I'll be lookin' after ye, miss," said a short, round woman with apple cheeks who approached Eleanor as they prepared to disembark. "Sir William asked me to stay close, make sure yer fed and help ye with all yer needs."

"Thank you," said Eleanor. "What's your name?"

"It's Sarah, miss. I been workin' for the Marshal for many years now, and a better man than he ye won't find. I told him I'd not let ye out of my sight, I did." Sarah flashed a toothy smile that instantly put Eleanor at ease.

"Where'd ye get that lovely dress?" she asked. "I've seen silk before, but none so beautiful or richly colored as that."

Eleanor thought quickly, then answered, "It came from France."

"It's lovely," cooed Sarah. "I've never seen such perfect stitching. And those long, flowin' sleeves, how perfectly lovely and unique. I'll get it mended and cleaned for ye when we're done travelin.'"

"Where are we going?" Eleanor asked. "Do you know?"

"Oh, miss, it's not fer me to say. Ye never know where the King will want to go next, but I expect we'll end up at Windsor."

"The King? Do you mean the King is with us right now?"

"No miss, he left Bouvines before we did, once he knew the battle was lost." Her bright smile vanished. "He'll be waitin' for us once we're ashore."

―――――

Their arrival at the port of Dover was solemn. They were the losers, so there were no cheering throngs to greet them. More soldiers on large war horses joined the Marshal at Dover. After a brief period of consultation, he ordered the horses loaded up with their supplies, along with some waiting wagons, and they mounted up to continue their trip north.

They traveled east along the English coastline atop the cliffs for about an hour, keeping a more leisurely pace than their dash from Bouvines to Calais. But they traveled with a purpose. They turned north along a dirt road and left the coastline, and France, behind them.

Soon they were met by another contingent of men, a hundred or more. Royal flags flew among this group, emblazoned with the red lion she had seen so often in history books. Her heart beat faster, thrumming in her eardrums. Were they going to meet the King himself? I mean the man pretending to be the King in this elaborate charade or dream. The sun was low in the sky as the men dismounted. William the Marshal led a small group of knights forward to meet the royal party. In the front was King John himself.

Sarah, still on her horse beside Eleanor, put a restraining hand on her arm as Eleanor began to dismount. "Stay where ye are fer now," she said. "Let the Marshal speak with the King first. The King won't be happy with the news he's about to hear."

King John was not at all what Eleanor had expected. Kings were supposed to be tall, majestic, commanding—even a king history reviled. John was short and plump. More than ordinary. Repugnant. Like a lumpy pillow, covered with gaudy jewels on his head, his waist, his shoes.

I mustn't laugh.

King John surprised her and strode boldly toward the Marshal. The Marshal bowed deeply before the King, bending on one knee, then stood; he was two heads taller than King John. "Your highness," began the Marshal ...

"I know!" thundered John. "We lost. What of our allies?"

"Fled."

"And Aquitaine?"

"Still yours, Your Highness," William answered. "The duchy of Normandy is in French hands now, it grieves me to say. But Aquitaine is still your fief. One more thing—Philip demands a peace treaty. It must be signed soon, Sire, else they will launch an invasion."

King John lowered his head. His shoulders flexed and tightened. He balled up his hands and began to quiver.

Eleanor saw the men around the King glance nervously at each other and back away from him. Only the Marshal remained unmoved. The next moment, John exploded in a tantrum that Eleanor never thought she would see thrown by a grown man.

He flung himself to the ground and beat his fists against the dirt until bloody patches emerged on his knuckles. The onlookers gawked at him, exchanging nervous glances. Head down in the dirt, he pulled at his hair, knocking off his crown, bleating curses at the French.

"Lost," he moaned. "Lost, lost, lost."

What a selfish baby he is.

Eventually King John rose, collected his crown, dusted it off, and placed it on his head. He stood panting, eyes closed, fists clenching and unclenching, like he was trying to grasp something. His sanity? He opened his eyes.

"We're off to London, William," he said, as if the tantrum had never existed. "I want to see you there in two days. Don't fail me again, Marshal." He spit out the word "Marshal" as if he was uttering a filthy word.

The Marshal had stood ramrod straight during the King's tantrum, pasting on a poker face. He bowed and said, "Yes, Your Majesty." He turned to the horses behind him and signaled the dismount.

Sarah tapped on Eleanor's shoulder and whispered, "Dismount, miss, and curtsy to the King."

The entire contingent of knights and squires, soldiers, cooks, and servants, along with Eleanor and the whores who traveled with the army, dismounted and bowed or curtsied to the King as he walked away.

Curtsy? She had no idea how to curtsy, but she mimicked Sarah as best as she could and displayed a passable sign of obeisance to King John, bowing her head and curtsying as low to the ground as she could manage. She glanced up furtively. King John turned to join his men, his face splotched with red and covered in dried spittle and dirt. He paused for a second and glared directly at Eleanor with a look of hostility mixed with curiosity. There was something else in his look—something intense—frightened her.

He turned away abruptly and joined his men. Once they had ridden off, the Marshal gave the order to mount up. One large group of knights and soldiers split away from them and traveled behind the King's men, while the Marshal kept about a hundred soldiers and the wounded.

Once their travels were under way again, the Marshal hung back and rode beside Eleanor for a few minutes. "Lass," he said, "our king has lost much in the last few weeks. As a Frenchie, ye may not understand how much pain that causes the English." He cast a sly glance her way. "But we've lost nearly all the lands and the people who kings and brave knights before us fought hard and died to hold."

"Sir," she answered with an edge to her tone, "I'm not a Frenchie. My mother was French, but I spent only a little time in France." She was making up a history for herself and knew she had to be careful. She understood well the antagonism—hatred would be more precise— between the English and French during the Middle Ages. "I've spent most of my life with the English." In America, she added to herself, trying to make it partially true.

"Is that so?" said the Marshal. "And where did ye spend all this time with the English? What village, lassie?"

Eleanor had traveled to England and Scotland before, but she was stumped. Where could she say she grew up without raising suspicion? She blurted, "Richmond." She had grown up near Richmond, Virginia, so this was as true as it could be. "On the outskirts," she added. "And when I was little we lived in Scotland, in Glasgow, but briefly."

This was a lie. Be careful, Ellie. Don't elaborate too much or your lies will trap you.

The Marshal eyed her warily for a moment. "Somethin's not right about yer story, lass. I don't know what it is, but I caution ye to take care with yer behavior and yer words. Ye talk funny, ye have little manners and show little respect for yer superiors." At that Eleanor bristled, but the Marshal continued. "Ye seem to be from another world altogether. Not from France, not from Richmond, not from Glasgow, I'll wager."

Eleanor didn't know how to take his words. It sounded like a threat, but this imposing knight, who seemed to be carrying the burdens of all of England on his broad shoulders—pretending to, she corrected herself—was immensely imposing and even likeable. She felt she was in protective hands when he was around, even if she was his prisoner. She wanted him to be her ally in this nightmare she was living through.

"Sir," she said, lowering her eyes and her tone. "Forgive me if I have been short tempered. It is inexcusable, but I have suffered an injury of some type which caused me to black out. I have lost a portion of my memory. You have been kind to me, and I am deeply grateful. But, Sir Knight, I am not a French spy. Would the French use a woman such as me to do their work, a woman so easily captured by you on the battlefield? I don't think so."

She paused for a moment to gauge his response. "Sir, I implore you, please help me get back home. My parents will need me." This was true.

She also longed to see her fiancé, Patrick, again.

"Tell me about your father," said the Marshal. He ignored her pleas to go home. It was easy for her to tell the truth about her father.

"He was born in Scotland and is a ... physician," she said. This was almost true. Her father was not born in Scotland, but his grandparents were from Glasgow. Her father had been a family doctor who loved his practice. She missed both her parents deeply, and her eyes misted with tears.

Looking at her, the Marshall softened his tone slightly. "Tell me about your mum."

Her mother was also in the medical profession; she was a nurse, specializing in labor and delivery. Eleanor quickly said, "My mother is a midwife."

"Very good," said the Marshal. "Did ye learn any of her skills? We always have need for midwives."

Eleanor did not know how to respond, but she calculated it would benefit her if she could boast of some skill to appear useful to her captors. "Yes, some," she said. But she did not want to stay here and work as a midwife; she couldn't even if she wanted to. She wanted to go home.

"And I take it ye're not yet wed," he stated.

How does he know that? "No sir, I'm not, but I'm betrothed to a physician. If I can get back home, we'll be married." She was beginning to feel like Dorothy in *The Wizard of Oz*.

William the Marshal did not respond. "Ye're a little old to just be gettin' married, lass."

"Yes sir," she responded. She gave no explanation, but the comment irritated her. She knew women in the Middle Ages married at very young ages, as soon as they were able to conceive.

"And yer rich clothin'," he continued, "where did that come from?"

"The cloth was a gift to my mother, in France, after she delivered the baby of a noblewoman," she lied. "She had it made into a dress for me." Totally made up.

"We'll make camp at sundown," he said, pulling his horse away from her abruptly. "Stay close to me, lass. Sarah, stay by her side."

"Yes, Sir William," said Sarah, riding up next to Eleanor. She had been trotting at a respectful distance behind them. She reached out a comforting hand and gave Eleanor a squeeze on her arm. "Don't worry, young miss. Ye're in good hands with the earl. He'll not let any harm come to ye."

"The earl?" asked Eleanor. "Who is the earl?"

"Why, Sir William is the earl!" she answered. "He's the Marshal of England, that's his official position within the realm, but he's also a nobleman in his own right. He's the earl of Pembroke, that's in Wales, miss. His lovely wife is an heiress. He's one of the richest men in all of England."

The sun was going down, so they found a spot to camp. Eleanor's tailbone ached from all the riding. The wounded men had been taken in by villagers along the way, and with fewer men in the contingent, the camp was faster and easier to set up. The Marshal had a comfortable tent pitched for Eleanor and Sarah. Sarah put a small bed together on the ground next to Eleanor's more elaborate bed of straw.

This is roughing it, but at least they're treating me with kindness, whoever these imposters are.

Food was brought in by Alfred for both women. It consisted of dried meat, dried fruit, cheese, spiced wine and dark bread—horse bread, Sarah called it.

"Lovely meal!" exclaimed Sarah. And she was right. Even the low-quality bread was delicious. She covered it with honey and gobbled it up.

Outside, William the Marshal was speaking with his squire, Alfred, in hushed tones. Eleanor picked up a few words here and there, but paid little attention until she heard Alfred say, "That's right. Did ye see the way he looked at the Frenchie girl? It concerns me, Sir William."

"Aye, I noticed," said William, so low it was hard to hear every word. But what she did hear alarmed her. "We'll have to keep her away from the King, so she comes to no harm."

Chapter Three

I have to escape.

Sitting in her tent, thoughts darted through Eleanor's mind like fireflies in the dark. This strange world may be my new reality, if it is real at all, but I have to get out of here. I need to figure out a way to escape. Maybe I really am living in medieval England. Maybe—could it be?—that my old life in the 1960s is the dream?

If the King was a danger to Eleanor, although she hadn't a clue why—perhaps he, too, suspected her of being a spy—she had to come up with a plan. She could not rely on anyone in the camp, not even the Marshal, to help her. She was his prisoner. But how will I escape? How will I find my way back to France?

She formed a vague plan: I'll sneak out of camp at night, head south through the woods, and make my way back to the port of Dover. Would she even be able to get a boat to Calais, now that the Battle of Bouvines was lost? She had to try. She had to get to Bouvines. I know it won't be easy, but it's the only way I can think of to get back. Even if I can't get across the English Channel into France, I've got to get away from my kidnappers. Anything, any place, will be better than this.

That was it, the whole pathetic plan. But if she was going to try it, Eleanor knew it needed to be tonight, before they traveled any further away from Bouvines and her friend Carol, who was probably frantically looking for her.

She had no money, no food, no weapons, no extra clothing, only an iron will to get out of this military camp and away from her captors.

She was still confused about where she was or, more precisely, *when* she was, but she pushed this nagging incongruity out of her head. One thing was sure: She was alive, and she needed to continue living so she could get back home.

That night, Sarah curled up in a blanket on the ground inside the tent beside Eleanor's bed. Sarah fell asleep quickly and began to snore, her plump cheeks fluttering with every breath. Eleanor was exhausted, but too afraid and nervous to fall asleep. Eyes wide open, thoughts tangled up in her mind, she heard the camp quiet into dead silence. There would be sentries posted, but since they were in friendly territory she doubted they would be watching carefully. Behind her tent stood a thicket of woods. As soon as she thought it was safe she could slip beneath the tent and hide in the woods until morning, she would be able to get her bearings and head south. There was a brilliant moon tonight, which would aid her escape but would also make her easier to detect. She would have to be careful, quiet, and fast.

It's time to go. Must be about two in the morning. In a few hours the camp will be waking, and I needed to be long gone. She slowly slid out of bed, grabbed the last crust of bread and the knife beside it, wrapped them in a piece of cloth, and tied it around her waist beneath her dress. She moved as quietly as possible. Grabbing the shawl that Sarah had given her, Eleanor tied that around her shoulders and slowly crawled beneath the tent.

Poking her head out first, she looked right and then left. No one was there. Wriggling on her belly, she slid her entire body outside of the tent, then painstakingly crawled toward the woods about a hundred yards away. Suddenly, a shadow appeared. A sentry had stepped between two tents about fifteen yards to her right. She flattened herself to the ground, tasting dirt, arms and legs outstretched. The sentry walked a few yards away from the tents, never looking toward Eleanor, lifted his tunic and relieved himself on the ground, singing a quiet tune.

"Think well of me, dear mother, if I should die in battle," he sang cheerfully, as if the lyrics were a love poem instead of an ode to death. *"Think well of me, my lassie, if I should ne'er come home. Think well of me, my laddies, should enemy cause me to fall. Where'ere I travel, or where'ere I fall, remember my heart is with ye in England."*

It touched Eleanor to hear this young soldier sing of his death and his loved ones.

"Shut yer trap!" yelled someone from inside a nearby tent. "Ye'll be fallin' right where ye're standing if ye don't shut it!"

The sentry finished and skipped back between the tents. He had never known she was there. Quickly, still slithering on her belly like a snake, she made her way to the woods and stood. She was covered in dirt. The food and knife were still tied around her waist in the cloth beneath her dress, and the shawl wrapped around her was intact. She jogged in the direction she believed to be south, but found it slow going in the woods, even with a bright moon. The treetops, in full summer growth, blocked out most of the light.

After about thirty minutes of slow progress through the woods, she decided to wait for first light to aid her, then she could travel more quickly to make up lost time. She sat beneath a large oak tree, leaned against its trunk, and pulled out the bread to take a few bites. She unwrapped the shawl from her waist and wrapped it around her shoulders. She said a quick prayer. "Lord, please forgive all my lies today, please help me get home again, please keep me safe, please ..." She didn't know how to pray for her situation. "Lord, please give me a clear mind and help me understand where I am, what time I'm in. Please, please, wake me from this nightmare. Amen." Then she promptly fell asleep.

"Well, well, looky this," came a voice in her head.

Eleanor thought she was dreaming. Dreaming within a dream? Was that possible? She struggled to wake up. She was asleep in her comfortable bed in Lynchburg, Virginia, but something felt out of place. Her mattress felt hard and uncomfortable.

"Ain't she a purty thing, golden-haired like a Plantagenet queen, she is." Her eyes fluttered opened with a jolt of adrenaline, and she was looking into the face of a dirty young man dressed in rags, inches from her face. With a toothless grin, he was leaning over her, staring at her. The few teeth he did have were brown and reeking. His face was gaunt with round, protruding eyes. He was bone thin.

She gasped and tried to scream, but the man slapped a grimy hand over her mouth. Behind him, she saw two more men but couldn't make out any details. They snickered and urged on the scarecrow, who was restraining her against the tree. She bit down hard on the palm of his hand, and he shrieked in pain, jerking his hands away from her and examining his bloody palm. Eleanor scrambled away from them, still on her back, running backward like a crab, but her assailant, now with a face red and contorted with rage, leaped on top of her and pinned her down. Her arms were pinioned by his forearms and elbows, and her lower half was covered with his putrid body.

"Git 'er, Archie," called one of his companions with a laugh. She noticed that Archie's companion was munching on the remains of her bread, which had fallen on the ground while she slept. When she thought of her food, she remembered the knife she had taken from the tent before she sneaked away. It should still be wrapped in a cloth around her waist beneath her dress. How will I get my hands on it while he's got them pinned down on the ground?

She realized that Archie was grinning at her and beginning to fumble beneath his tunic. She knew she was about to be raped by this filthy, undernourished man, who was barely more than a boy, and she began to panic. She fought, screaming and writhing beneath him, but he struck her in the face to shut her up and pinned her down with the weight of his body. While he fumbled at his tunic, he lifted one hand away from her right arm. His gropings were beginning to bring him closer to the knife hidden around her waist, so she seized the opportunity. Eleanor quickly slid her free hand down on the ground along her right side, reached beneath her dress, grabbed the knife, and with a rapid arcing motion brought it down at an angle into Archie's neck.

He screamed again, this time a gurgling, high-pitched wail that sounded like a dying animal. Archie clutched at the knife sticking out of his throat. He pulled it out with a quick motion and blood sprayed onto the forest floor, coating the dirt and dried leaves and running down his neck and torso. Crouching on his knees, he cried, panted, coughed, and looked at Eleanor with a desperate, searching look.

Eleanor was horrified. What have I done? She scrambled away from Archie, and this time he didn't follow her. The ground quaked. What is that? What new calamity is about to befall me? An earthquake?

The galloping charger of William the Marshal tore into the clearing. Archie's companions were already disappearing into the woods. The

Marshal quickly surveyed the scene on the ground. The look of terror on Eleanor's face, her dress hiked up to her hips, Archie,still on his knees, clasping his throat as blood continued to pump out.

The Marshal slid off his horse, pulled out his sword, and swung it across Archie's already bloody neck. Archie's miserable, dirty, toothless head flew from his neck and rolled beneath the tree where he had first attacked Eleanor.

She could not move. The scene that had just unfolded before her had short-circuited something in her brain; she could not think clearly. Had a man been beheaded in front of her? A man she had stabbed in the neck?

"Are ye hurt, girl?" demanded the Marshal.

Eleanor was frozen. She shook and could not answer. Archie's headless body, still jerking and gushing blood, lay on the ground a few feet away. His head had mercifully landed face down in a pile of leaves. The Marshal strode over to her quickly and pulled her to her feet, examining her from head to toe for any injuries.

"Did he ... did he violate ye?"

She shook her head.

"Look here, lass," he said, gripping her by the shoulders and looking into her eyes closely, "We must leave these woods and get back to camp. The entire camp is waitin' for me to return with ye." He spoke with some anger, but she could tell he was trying to control it. "We should be on the move by now, girl. So I need ye to pull yerself together. I'm going to hoist ye up onto my horse, behind me, just like before. Do ye understand?"

Eleanor looked into his knowing eyes, surrounded by weathered and lined skin, and saw kindness and worry there. She nodded. He quickly mounted and deftly pulled her up behind him. "We'll talk about this later, lass. For now, let's concentrate on getting' out of these woods where we're unprotected and back to our people."

Eleanor began to cry lightly and, as she did, with her arms wrapped around the broad waist of William the Marshal, she laid her weary head on his back and let the tears flow.

Chapter Four

When they arrived back at camp all eyes surveyed her with unrestrained hostility as she slipped off the horse, splattered with Archie's blood.

"Well, well," hissed one of the whores, "Runnin' away to yer French masters?"

The Marshal guided her into her tent, where Sarah stood wringing her hands. She flung herself around Eleanor's shoulders. "Oh miss, it's glad I am that ye've been found. But dearie, what happened to ye? Let me tend to those scratches and clean ye up. Why, yer covered in blood!"

"That'll do Sarah," said the Marshal sternly. "Give us some time alone, will ye?"

She scurried out of the tent and closed the flap behind her.

"Sir Marshal ..." began Eleanor.

"Not a word," he said forcefully, holding up a finger before her face. "I'll do the talkin'. Ye're not safe in these woods, and ye learned that the hard way. Now a ragtag ruffian is dead because ye chose to run, instead of staying with yer protectors who can guarantee yer safety. Do ye understand the serious nature of yer behavior, girl?"

"But Sir Knight ..."

"Hush." He waggled his finger. "Ye'd best get used to the idea that, fer now, ye will be the guest of the English. We don't know who ye are, so we're keeping ye close. There will be no returnin' to France, at least not now. Do ye understand? Don't speak, just nod."

Eleanor nodded, her eyes lowered, contrite.

"Ye'll be given as much freedom to move about as I think ye deserve. Ye behave, ye don't run, and things will go well for ye, lass. Ye misbehave, ye try to run, and ye'll end up in chains. Do ye understand?"

She nodded again, eyes wide. Her breath came in ragged spurts. Images filled her mind of a dark, moldy, rat-infested medieval prison.

"Now, here's what I'm goin' to do with ye." He told her he would bring her to stay with a "good family" he knew, a short ride north, "for a while, until I know what to do with ye."

"May I speak now?" Eleanor asked meekly.

He sat and leaned back, crossed his arms and nodded. "Go ahead, girl."

"Sir Knight, I am deeply sorry and deeply saddened by what happened. In my defense, I was attacked by that man, and he would have raped me, probably killed me, if you hadn't saved me. I am so grateful to you. You saved my life. Again."

He said nothing, just continued to look at her.

"In my defense," she repeated, "I want to go home, and I have a right to go home."

The Marshal opened his mouth to protest.

But before he could speak, she continued. "I won't try to escape again, though. Once you see that I am not a spy, I am asking you, pleading with you, to help me find a way home. It's clear that I don't belong here and ... and ..." Tears stung her eyes, and she bit her tongue to keep from crying. "And I'm so unhappy here, Sir Knight. I'm afraid—"

The Marshal laughed, shocking Eleanor into silence. "Unhappy?" he roared with laughter. "What does happiness have to do with anything? This is war, girl. Do ye not understand that we're at war with the French? Yer own kinsmen? And ye have no rights here. Rights!" he blurted and laughed again.

She could argue the point no longer.

He softened and put a hand on her shoulder. "Lass, I can see how upset ye are. Ye must obey me now, and things will go well with ye. I am in charge here," he added firmly. "The family I want ye to stay with is a good one. They'll care for ye and make ye ... happy." He smirked. "Only fer a time, when the tensions between us and the French ease up bit." He patted her hand. "Ye'll be fine, lass."

Soon they mounted again and were on their way. They came to a fork in the road after about an hour of rapid travel. Her body ached from the movement of the horse, but she said nothing. The Marshal conferred briefly with his men, and they parted ways. Alfred stayed with the Marshal, never leaving his side, but Sarah trotted behind the departing army, throwing a wave toward Eleanor with a worried look on her face.

The three of them rode in silence on the path leading to the family who would host her. How long will I have to live with a strange family? What will they think of me? And how will they treat me, a "Frenchie"? That's the deepest cut. I'm as far from being French as the Marshal, but they had her pegged as a French spy. The absurdities of her new life made her smile for the first time in days.

"Ye're feeling a bit better, are ye?" the Marshal asked.

She nodded. "But I'm dreadfully tired."

"We'll be there soon. Let's keep goin', and ye can rest when we're there."

"Do they know we're coming?" she asked.

"No," he replied, "but they'll be happy to take ye in. They're a good, hard-workin' family, merchant folk, with plenty of people and young ones buzzin' about. They've got seven children, maybe eight, I can't remember, so ye'll fit right in with their large brood."

Soon homes dotted the dirt road, most of them small wooden structures with thatched roofs, big enough to have two rooms at the most. People hurried outside to watch the Marshal pass with his odd companion and his faithful squire. They all bowed and curtsied to the Marshal, including the children, some of them prodded by their parents with a rap on the head. The Marshal, in turn, inclined his head toward them as he passed. "God bless ye, Sir William!" many of them yelled, and they bowed and curtsied.

Her red silk dress, filthy and tattered, stained with Archie's blood, still looked out of place among these simple people. Presently, there were storefronts, a baker first, then a blacksmith. They slowed in front of a large building that surprised Eleanor in its size and complexity. It sat on the edge of the street, but it was surrounded by smaller buildings with thatched roofs and smoke appearing from the tops. People buzzed, as the Marshal had put it, around all these buildings, carrying items in and out, hammering, chattering, and laughing with each other. They all stopped to gaze at the Marshal and Eleanor.

The home was large with at least six or seven windows along the front, and a gabled roof that appeared to be made of wood covered in thatch. The entire home was made of stone. It seemed a marvel of engineering, considering the year was 1214. She snapped back to reality. Is this really happening? It's not 1214, she corrected herself. It's 1964.

The front door had a sign above it that read "Adelfrid Stonework & Grainery." As she was reading the sign, a woman rushed outside to greet the Marshal. Her face lit up with a wide smile when she saw him.

"Sir William, how good it is to see ye," she gushed with a quick curtsy. "Get down, get down, and let me tend to ye. Who have ye here? Who's this pretty lass with ye?"

"Mistress Beja," he began as he dismounted, "this is Eleanor, she's going to need to stay with ye for a little while, if that's agreeable to ye."

"Oh, of course!" Beja was a middle-aged woman, well dressed in a long, brown gown topped with a full-length embroidered tunic, a kirtle. Cinched at her waist was an embroidered belt, on which hung a small sack filled with items that poked out at odd angles. Beja was no peasant, but obviously not a noblewoman either. She looked busy and prosperous.

The Marshal dismounted and helped Eleanor slip awkwardly from her horse. Her back ached from riding.

"Lass, this is Mistress Adelfrid. She and her husband Richard own this store and all the land and buildings ye see around it. And these are a few of her children." The doorway had filled with children ranging from about age six or seven to teenage, all gawking at Eleanor.

"Ye spoke rightly, Sir William," said Beja with a laugh. "These are only a few of 'em. Two married, ye know, and several are out and around the town, probably getting' into mischief." She laughed again heartily. "Come in, come in. Ye're welcome here, Miss Eleanor. Please sit and let me tend to ye.

"Pour some drinks for our guests, Mary," she said to a young servant girl who had appeared at her elbow. Mary scurried off. Beja then led them through a large room at the front of the house filled with merchandise, into a large back room with a massive stone fireplace, arched ceiling with beams, and whitewashed walls. A massive pot bubbled in the fireplace. Along one wall was a sort of serving bar. It was a clean, bright room with a long table and bench chairs in the center. Beja shouted some orders to the servant, Mary, as she entered with drinks, and Mary scurried off again. Beja shooed the children away. "Out with ye, dearies, leave us alone for a bit. Go get yer father."

She turned to the Marshal and smiled. "Oh, Sir William, we've missed ye these months! It's a pleasure to see ye looking so fit." Mary emerged with a tray of ale, bread, cheese, and sweet cakes. "Please miss, refresh yerself. Drink up, all of ye. You, too, Alfred, eat eat!"

They relaxed under Beja's care and drank the ale and ate the food laid before them. Alfred swiped a handful of food and retreated to a corner of the room, where he gobbled it up with gusto. Within minutes the ale was making Eleanor lightheaded, so she pushed it away, but she found the food delicious.

"Thank you so much Mistress Adelfrid," said Eleanor, butchering the name, she was sure. "You've been so generous. Thank you for allowing me to stay with you for a while."

"Oh, dearie, it's no trouble at all," replied Beja.

Beja asked no questions about why Eleanor needed to stay with her family. "There's nothing I wouldn't do for the Marshal of England. He's the greatest man what ever lived, he is." She paused, then added, "Save for my own husband, of course. We go back a ways, don't we sir?"

"We do at that," said the smiling Marshal. "And how's yer brood farin'? How's yer husband? And how's young Thomas makin' out at Windsor? How's the work goin' there?"

"Richard's fine," she answered. "Workin' harder than ever. We can hardly keep up, but that's good, eh? He's in one of the fields now, I reckon, but he'll be along soon. Thomas pops in every now and then. He says the work is slow but progressin' at Windsor." She turned to Eleanor and explained. "Thomas is my oldest son. He's a stone mason, the best there is in the land, I'd say." She winked at the Marshal. "He's working on the King's castle at Windsor."

Windsor Castle, the sprawling royal home of British royalty since not long after the Norman conquest. It was the center of entertainment for Queen Victoria, the refuge for the royal family during the bombings of World War II, and now the weekend retreat of Queen Elizabeth II. In the 1960s, she added to herself.

The Marshal and Alfred spent the night, and in the morning, they prepared to leave. Eleanor awoke from her small but pleasant upstairs room after a long and undisturbed sleep in the first comfortable bed offered to her since arriving ... since arriving wherever or whenever she was. Her mattress was rough but soft enough, and one of the servants had left her some watery ale, more bread and cheese, and a basin of water. She heard the Marshal and Beja and another man speaking in low, hushed tones downstairs. She crept to the door, cracked it open slightly and listened.

"Yes, sir, we'll keep a keen eye on her, Sir William. Don't ye worry."

"Put her to work," said the Marshal. "Let her help out. Keep her busy, and she won't have time to lay any more escape plans. I warn ye, this girl is wily and determined to head south again to her people, but she's also a little fool. She doesn't understand the dangers of a young lass runnin' through the woods and the English countryside during times like these. I tell ye, Mistress Beja, I never thought to see such a foolish thing as that."

Eleanor's face flushed with anger. What did he expect her to do? She'd been kidnapped, held prisoner, and called a spy. Who wouldn't want to escape? She noticed that her filthy red dress was gone, and in its place was a plain linen dress with a kirtle and belt. She washed up in the basin left for her, dressed, and headed downstairs. As soon as they heard her on the steps, the conversation stopped.

Beja rushed over to her. "Good morning, young lass. Come and sit down and refresh yerself. Look, food and drink for ye."

She was introduced to Beja's husband, Richard, who nodded politely to her but said little. Alfred sat in the corner, once again eating a mountain of food on his plate.

"Good morning," Eleanor said. "I'm sorry I slept late, but it was such a comfortable bed and room. Thank you both so much for your kindness."

Beja rushed over to her. "Oh dearie, ye're welcome here. And later ye can have a bath, eh? We'll get ye feeling fine and fit! Come and sit. Eat, eat!"

After eating the Marshal rose from his seat. "We'll be movin' on, lass, so walk outside with me for a spell so we can have a talk." Uh-oh. This doesn't sound good.

"I want ye to heed what I said before," he began as they strolled through one of the fields at the back of the house. The wheat was up to her shoulders. "If ye try to run, I promise ye, ye'll end up dead ... or worse."

This gave her a jolt. His meaning was clear. "I won't Sir Knight, I gave you my word."

"Girl, despite all yer troublemakin', I've taken a likin' to ye, and I want ye to feel welcome, but I don't believe hardly a word ye've told me. Do ye understand?"

She nodded, saying nothing.

"Ye're not from France, ye're not from England, although ye speak both languages. But ye speak them like ye're from somewhere else. I don't know why ye're not telling me the truth. Perhaps ye've got good reason. But since ye're not speaking the truth, I must keep ye confined a bit. Remember, ye'll have as much freedom as ye earn."

Eleanor paused and then spoke. "Sir Knight, you must believe at least this one thing: I don't know the truth myself. I really don't know where I am or where I belong, but I remember where I came from. My story is as true as I can tell it, Sir William. I really don't know, don't understand, what has happened to me."

Every word she had spoken was the truth, but it was still cagey, and she saw understanding in the Marshal's keen eyes.

"Miss Eleanor," he said, using her name for the first time, "I want ye to be of help to Mistress Beja. She's one of the kindest women on this earth, and her husband's a good hard-workin' man. The entire brood will care for ye, but I ask ye to show them gratitude and respect. Rein in that tongue of yers, lassie. If what ye're saying is true, it won't do any good to have the entire village know ye came from France, and it won't help ye if people think ye've lost yer mind."

She winced, but perhaps it was true. Perhaps she had lost her mind, thinking she was from another time, thinking she was living in medieval England, thinking she could ever get back home to America, a continent which wouldn't be discovered for centuries. Yep, she was a little bit mad, so the Marshal spoke correctly. She would have to be careful about what she said.

"Tell people," he continued, "if anyone asks, that yer family is from Scotland. Ye've already said that, and ye can say ye've got some kin in

Richmond. Tell them the Adelfrids are distant kin. Mistress Beja has agreed to go along with this little lie. Be careful lass, don't say too much. Fer yer own safety."

She nodded. "Yes sir, I'll do everything you ask." No, I won't, because I have to work out a way to get back home. She would not run away as before, she had promised that, but she would never stop planning to get home, to her time. There had to be a way.

When the Marshal left with Alfred, they took her little horse with them. She was hobbled, as the Marshal intended.

Chapter Five

For the rest of the day Eleanor stayed close to Beja, helping in the kitchen and in the storefront, which filled up quickly with villagers eager to gawk at the stranger. Beja introduced her as a relative from Richmond, "distant kin," she told them, and Eleanor just smiled and nodded.

She liked these people. They chatted with her amiably about anything and everything. "Missie, ye'd best be prepared for the weather; the rain's a comin', I can feel it," said one older woman. "Do ye have a cloak? It's just July, but ye'll need it!"

"Mama, let her be," said her daughter, who had three young children in tow and apparently another one on the way any day. "Mistress Beja will care fer her; don't fret about it." The tots peered at Eleanor from behind their mother's skirts, and Eleanor winked at them. They giggled. All of them had heads of blonde curly hair.

"You have beautiful children," said Eleanor.

"Oh, thank ye, miss!" she exclaimed with a curtsy.

"What's your name?" Eleanor asked the young mother.

"I'm Heloise, miss, and this is Lucan, Sigrid, and Trea." She extricated the children from her skirts.

"Pretty names," Eleanor said with a smile. She knelt down and held out her hand to Heloise, who had no idea what to do with it, so she stroked Eleanor's fingers. The children did the same, grabbing Eleanor's hands and rubbing their tiny chubby ones over hers. Eleanor laughed.

Later in the day Beja's older daughter, 15-year-old Lavinia, gave

Eleanor a tour of the property in a carriage drawn by one horse. It reminded her of a chariot. The lands were vast, dotted with small homes, people bustling in and out, acres of cropland getting ready for harvest, beautiful woodland with mature trees that touched the sky, streams and ponds, and what looked like a river that bordered the northern boundary of the property.

"That's the River Dour," said Lavinia. "It flows to London, I hear, though I've never been there. I'd love to see London!"

"And what is this village that we're in? What are we near, Lavinia? I'm sorry, I should know, but I've forgotten."

Lavina eyed Eleanor with some skepticism. "Why, our village is called Graston, and we're not far from Canterbury, miss. The cathedral there is the most magnificent sight to behold in all of Christendom, no doubt," she said with great enthusiasm.

"So, you've seen it, then?" asked Eleanor.

"Oh yes, Ma and Pa took us all there about five years ago. What a wonderful day that was. It's only a few hours by horse, miss."

The grounds owned by the Adelfrids seemed to go on forever. Lavinia said they managed about eighty furlongs, "more or less," whatever that meant. "We have tenants, as you can see, and some of the land is left just for hay for the livestock." She pointed to a field of sheep, and another fenced in with horses.

"It's beautiful," Eleanor said, and she meant it.

"That high point over there," said Lavinia, pointing to a tree-covered peak in the far distance, "is about where it ends. Our overlord is thought to be a decent man for the most part, as long as we're earnin' for him. A good part of all our earnings go to him, Lord de Malet."

Eleanor knew the practice of feudalism dominated England in the Middle Ages. That meant that most land was owned by either the Crown or nobility, worked by the lower classes, merchants, and, at the bottom, the serfs.

"Our family has worked this land for centuries," continued Lavinia with pride. "Since before the Conquest, so we've had to fight to keep it. But it's still ours, in a manner of speakin'. Someday, when I'm married, Ma and Pa said I'll get my own piece of it as part of my dowry."

Eleanor liked Lavinia. She was smart, devoted to her family, and always had a smile on her face. It would do Eleanor good to spend more time with her, since Eleanor's mood was now one of perpetual gloom and ill humor. At some point she would have to accept her fate. She was no longer her own master, as she had been in her old life—attending college, going where she pleased, enjoying dinners out at restaurants with her fiancé, traveling, spending time with family, and taking advantage of all the opportunities modern life had offered her. That included attending medieval fairs. Now that was all gone. She was trapped in the past, a prisoner held by a long leash, but still a prisoner.

After several weeks living with the Adelfrids, Eleanor settled in comfortably. She happily helped with many of the chores, which began at sunrise and ended long after sundown. Although her thoughts of escape were crowded out by the many tasks that overwhelmed her during the day, at night she put her tired head on her feather pillow and dreamed of her old life. She knew it was real. No one could have such clear memories of another life, beginning with her childhood and running through all her formative experiences, up to her college days and engagement to Patrick. She remembered it all, the colors, the smells, the music. The time she fell off the swing as a little girl and cut her chin on a metal piece of the swingset. It left a scar along her chin. Lying in bed, she ran a finger over the thin scar. Still there. When her future disappeared, it was 1964 and the Beatles were a global sensation with "I Wanna Hold Your Hand." Would she ever get back home and live the life she had dreamed of? She wanted to complete her degree, get married, have children, work in her field of study, probably as a teacher, the wife of a doctor.

She had to get home. Again, she thought of Dorothy and repeated, "There's no place like home." So, she committed herself to working hard every day, not only because she wanted to help the Adelfrids, who were the kindest people she'd met in this new world, but because she could contemplate her future as she worked. She could plan, and she could think about the possibilities that right now eluded her.

Chapter Six

The pigpen was at the rear of house, close enough that toting the heavy slop bucket was manageable for the housemaids, but far enough away to keep the odor out of the kitchen. Eleanor was panting with the effort. She had just dumped the slop into the trough when she heard shouting from the house.

"Come quick, Miss Eleanor!" It was Mary, the kitchen maid. "Please come now!"

Eleanor followed the kitchen maid. Mary spoke haltingly as they ran.

"It's young Heloise, the tenant's daughter. The lass with the three babes. Ye met her, miss, she's strugglin'. The babe isn't comin'. We need yer help."

"But ... but what do you expect me to do?" Eleanor stopped running and stood frozen in the back field.

Beja ran out to meet them. "Eleanor, dearie, quick now. There's no time to waste. The Marshal told us ye had birthin' experience, and we fear for Heloise's life. She can't seem to get this babe born."

"But ... but, isn't there anyone else?"

"No, no one else!" Beja barked at her. "Now, wipe yer hands and take off that apron. Mary, help her straighten up, and both of ye meet me out front. Quick now." Eleanor's mind raced. How could she help? She tried to recall some of the stories that her mother had told her of the pregnant women she had attended at the hospital. Why had she told such a lie to the Marshall?

"Mary," Eleanor said, rousing herself, "please gather some twine, a knife or scissors, some alcohol, not ale or wine, we'll need something stronger, some strong spirits. And I'll meet you downstairs."

Richard drove the carriage for the three women—Mary, Beja, and Eleanor. Heloise's cottage was pandemonium; all the children were playing in the center room, with Heloise in the only other room in the back, laboring noisily. A young man, probably Heloise's husband, greeted them with a look of panic on his face.

"She's in here," he said, pointing the way.

Eleanor entered the room and quickly assessed the situation. Heloise lay on the bed, a straw mattress on the floor, with her head propped up on a pillow. She was panting hard, and her face was flushed red with the effort. She was drenched in sweat. She looked at Eleanor with wide eyes filled with pain. "Oh, Miss Eleanor," she began, but she was gripped with another pain and could not speak. She groaned and panted as the pain reached a crescendo.

Eleanor knelt at the foot of the bed, lifted Heloise's nightgown, and examined her closely. It was obviously a breech birth, bottom first instead of head. But what was she supposed to do? Fear gripped her. In her own time, a breech birth often required caesarian surgery. At least, that's what she recalled from some of her mother's stories. Was she equipped to perform such a procedure? Absolutely not. She had no idea what she would do if Heloise's baby could not be turned.

"Mary, please give me the alcohol you brought."

Mary handed her a bottle of yellowish liquid. She uncorked it, took a whiff, and poured it over her hands, rubbing them together vigorously. Bracing herself, she gently tried to turn the baby by pushing on Heloise's abdomen. It was beginning to work. She knelt again and could see the baby's back begin to show. But Heloise tensed again, uttered a deep moan, breathed quickly, and bore down with a hard push.

"No, no, Heloise, don't push!"

It was too late. The baby quickly slid back into the breach position, bottom down.

"Heloise, try not to push. Your baby is bottom first, instead of head first, so I need to try to turn the baby around. But if you push, the baby is going to turn the wrong way."

"Yes, miss, I'll try. It's easing up right now, please save my baby, Miss Eleanor!" Tears streamed down her face.

"I'll do my best; now don't push. I'm going to try again."

Standing above Heloise, Eleanor again massaged the woman's abdomen until the baby turned nearly around. Eleanor knelt and saw that the baby had, in fact, moved into the proper position.

"Here it is!" exclaimed Eleanor. "Now push! Push hard!"

Heloise pushed with all her might, and the baby's head appeared.

"Push again! Push, Heloise!"

The shoulders appeared, and in a fluid movement, the baby was born. A girl.

Eleanor had taken full possession of her nerves and was acting on the limited knowledge she had. She reached her little finger into the baby's mouth to clear it out and held it upside down to clear its lungs. In a few seconds, she heard a loud wail and saw a red-faced baby begin to breathe for the first time.

Eleanor tied a piece of twine tightly around its navel, then she cut the cord. She was shocked at how calm she was, delivering her first baby, cutting the umbilical cord, clearing out the lungs. This was no dream.

"Let's wipe her off and wrap her up," Eleanor said, pointing to a small, clean blanket neatly folded in the corner.

While the baby continued to wail, Eleanor handed her over to an exhausted but smiling Heloise. She had tears in her eyes as she gazed lovingly at her little girl. She looked up at Eleanor. "How can I ever thank ye, miss? Ye're an angel, that's fer sure."

Eleanor's eyes filled with tears, too, and she smiled at Heloise. The husband entered and raced over to Heloise. Beja and Mary busied themselves cleaning up.

"Ye haven't met properly," Heloise said. "This is my husband, Eldon."

"Mistress Eleanor," he said, and bowed to her. "We're mightily grateful to ye. We can never thank ye enough." He turned back to his wife and kneeled next to her and the baby, kissing Heloise sweetly while she nursed. Once Eleanor had cleaned up and was sure that both Heloise and the baby were safe and thriving, she prepared to leave with Beja and Mary.

"Gad! That were something to see, Miss," exclaimed Mary.

"She's right, Eleanor," said Beja. She had dropped the "miss" from her name, endearing herself to Eleanor. "You did a wondrous thing. But why did ye pour my husband's good liquor all over yer hands?"

"It's a way to steril—," Eleanor began. "I mean, it can remove more of the … bad humors. That's what I learned from my mother," she added.

As they were leaving, Heloise's husband came up to her and once again bowed and thanked her for delivering their new baby girl. "Mistress Eleanor," he said. "Heloise and I want to name her Eleanor. That's how grateful we are to ye." Eleanor was astounded. She glanced at Heloise, who beamed a brilliant smile at her and nodded. She was surrounded by her other children, all of whom cooed over their new sister.

"I would be honored," she said to Eldon, taking his hand. "God bless you, Eldon. And if Heloise has any difficulty, please let me know."

"Oh, I will, but she knows what to do with a babe once it's in her arms. She'll be fine, mistress. Give me one moment, please miss." He ran outside and returned with a chicken, holding the flapping bird upside down by its legs. "For you, as our payment."

As they traveled home, the chicken securely tucked away in a sack, Eleanor could not help but notice the look of admiration on Beja's face. *That's helpful. I want them to like me. Who knows what I might need from the members of this family to help me get home.*

She was satisfied and somewhat astounded that she had just delivered a baby. But all in all, *I'd rather be slopping the pigs.*

Chapter Seven

Eleanor's life in the village of Graston took on the everydayness of her life back in Virginia in the 1960s, like putting on a new suit of clothes as comfortable as the old one. Comfortable, yet different.

Every day she thought about the things she missed, like electricity, lipstick, a good book, a bottle of Coke, her parents, listening to her records, and, of course, her fiancé Patrick. But she was content in her new life in surprising new ways. Meals with the boisterous Adelfrid clan—often consisting of hearty bread and cheese, fish, and delectable sweets and cakes—were fun and spirited. The children scrambled for food hungrily, reaching across the table and snatching up the delicacies, while Beja swatted their hands and scolded them to show manners. Every meal began with a prayer and ended with another one, thanking God for the excellent meal.

She also enjoyed the physically demanding work that caused her to fall into bed at night exhausted and wake with a sense of purpose the next morning. She was becoming fond of the Adelfrids, especially Lavinia, who, although younger, had a winning disposition and wisdom beyond her years. Beja, too, had become a companion to Eleanor, like a stand-in for her own mother. That thought always made Eleanor yearn for home and piqued her sense of melancholy.

Eleanor became the go-to midwife in the village of Graston, and within a few months she had delivered four babies with no complications. Each time she feared a disaster; after all, she was not a doctor and had only a basic understanding of pregnancy and childbirth. But to the simple folks of the region, she was, as they often told her, a gift from God. And as her successful deliveries grew, so too did her reputation and standing among the villagers.

One day, William the Marshal stopped by to check on Eleanor. She suspected he was being regularly briefed on her behavior by Beja, but if so, she was not aware of any messages going back and forth. She had learned a lot more about the remarkable Sir William while living in Graston because he was the most famous knight in England, probably in the world at that time. At any time, she corrected herself.

After excelling at tournament competition as a young man, William eventually entered the service of the famous Queen Eleanor of Aquitaine. "She was the most beautiful Queen in the world!" gushed Lavinia as she and Eleanor kneaded bread dough in the kitchen. "Course I never saw her, but that's what they say. Oh, how I would've loved to see the Marshal as a young man! So handsome was he, so they say."

Eleanor smiled at the rapturous look on Lavinia's face. She was a true romantic. But when it came to the Marshal of England, she had a right to be. He had already served four kings, and she knew from her history studies that when King John died, William would briefly serve a fifth English king, John's son Henry, who would become Henry III.

But Eleanor's memory was still fuzzy when it came to English history. When did King John die? She knew he did not live to a ripe old age, and she recalled some of the circumstances, but would it be soon? Would she still be living in this time when it happened? She couldn't answer any of these questions, but they plagued her, swirling about in her head day in and day out. There was one grave fact that stood out in her memory about King John: He was a bad king and a bad man. Although it was a crime punishable by death to criticize the king, she could not help overhearing the grumblings about him that drifted from door to door. His taxes were onerous and back-breaking to the common folk of England, and his war with France had vastly diminished the holdings of the crown. She learned this from the Marshal himself. King John was now being called in secret "John Lackland," having lost so much of the English empire to the French.

The entire brood, including Eleanor, rushed out to meet Sir William when he arrived at their front door, as well as many of the villagers. He met her glance and smiled at her. How good it was to see him smile at her instead of scowling at her recklessness. Eleanor dressed as a member of the family, dirt caked on her shoes from working outside, and an apron covering her dress. Her hair was braided, and she wore a cap, beneath which unruly ringlets of hair escaped. She fit right in with the Adelfrid family.

"Look who I met on the road, Mistress Beja," William said, motioning to the horseman behind him. In addition to the steadfast Alfred, with them was another young man.

"Thomas!" exclaimed Beja, as she ran to the young man and flung her arms around him as he dismounted.

"Ma!" he laughed, "I can't breathe, ye silly woman!" When he extricated himself, he glad-handed and backslapped his brothers and sisters, who surrounded him with questions and laughter. "What'd ya bring me, Tom?" "What's it like livin' in the palace, Tom?" "Tell me about the King, Tom." "Oh, tell me about the Queen, Tom, and what her clothin' and jewels look like." chimed in Lavinia.

Thomas noticed Eleanor standing in the doorway. "This is Miss Eleanor, Thomas," said Beja, still hanging on his arm as she led him into the house. "She's stayin' with us fer a bit, at the request of the Marshal, and what a great help she's been. Eleanor dear, this is my oldest son, Thomas. He's a stone mason workin' at the King's castle at Windsor. He's been there for, what, nigh on two years now."

Thomas stopped in front of Eleanor and nodded wordlessly to her. She gave him a slight bob of a curtsy, not knowing what else to do. He raked her entire body with his eyes, fluidly looking her up and down, then he locked on her eyes. It was not a lascivious gesture; it was almost shy, but it pierced through her, and Eleanor suddenly felt exposed. She blushed and wrapped her arms around herself in an irrational protective gesture. Then, to hide the burning in her face and neck, she looked down, unable to stand up to his keen gaze.

Beja said, "Come in, come in, Sir William, and you, too, Alfred. Let's get you somethin' to eat and drink." She led Thomas inside, and they all sat at the table. Mary, Lavinia, and Eleanor busied themselves in the kitchen preparing some food, while the siblings poured ale for the visitors. For reasons she didn't understand, Eleanor's face was still hot from her meeting with Thomas. There was nothing really special about him. Okay, he is pleasant looking, in a rugged kind of way. But not nearly as handsome as my Patrick. He wore a tunic and leggings, but from the corner of her eye she saw him strip off his hose with the help of one of the servants.

"Gad! I'm roasting," he said. "That was a hot and dusty trip, but much better once I met up with Sir William here. He's always a great companion, ma. You can't believe the stories he tells."

William laughed. "I've got plenty more, too," he said. "But I better save some for the next time I see ye, or I'll run out of 'em. Then I'll have to start makin' 'em up."

"That won't happen," chimed in Alfred. "He's got enough fer two lifetimes."

Eleanor carried in a tray of food and set it on the table. Behind her, Lavinia and Mary carried some small cakes and dried meat. As she set down the tray, she glanced quickly at Thomas.

"Thank you, miss," he said, looking at her intently.

She nodded.

"Sit down with us Eleanor, and you too, Lavinia," said Beja, and the two obediently sat at the table.

"Well, yer lookin' fine, missy," Sir William said, turning his attention to Eleanor. "I heard about yer birthin' adventures. That was a grand thing ye did fer the young lass, savin' her baby. I'm proud of ye, girl."

Eleanor was so deeply flattered to receive praise from *the* Sir William the Marshal, especially after the numerous dressings-down at his hands, that she could not respond for a moment.

Finally, she did. "Thank you, Sir William. It was … it was not much, just a baby turned the wrong way."

"Well, ye did good, lass," he added with a twinkle in his eye, and he patted her arm affectionately. She glanced at Thomas, and he was smiling at her. Alfred, too. Then Alfred spoke up.

"Speakin' of good stories, William, tell 'em about the time ye unhorsed the Lionheart hisself, Sir Richard."

"Ye've all heard that one," William declared with a dismissive wave of his hand.

"No, no!" said Beja, "I've never heard it from you, Sir William! Please tell it."

"Nor I," chimed in Lavinia.

"Nor I," added the maid Mary from the kitchen, then she bobbed a curtsy. "Beggin' yer pardon, Sir William."

"Well, alright, alright," he began, leaning back in his chair with a tankard of ale in his large hands. "It was about twenty, no at least twenty-five years ago, during that difficult time when Richard and his, well some others, were rebellin' against their father, King Henry."

Eleanor knew what he was referring to. Henry's sons, Richard and John, the current King John, before either of them had become king, rebelled against their father and actually waged war against him, seeking more power in their father's kingdom, power that their father, King Henry, would not grant them. Their mother, the famed Eleanor of Aquitaine, sided with the sons, prompting Henry to imprison her for sixteen years to keep her out of mischief. Because it was a crime to speak ill of the king, so she understood why Sir William chose his words carefully and did not mention John by name.

"I had, as ye all know, sworn my fealty to King Henry, so I could not at that time swear allegiance to those who had taken up arms against him, even if they were Henry's own sons, who would someday become kings themselves. And who, I might add, I eventually did serve and still serve with loyalty."

They all nodded. "We were in Normandy, engagin' with Richard's men, tryin' to prevent them from advancin' into Henry's territory. We had just come from a small skirmish with some of the rebels near Anjou, where we'd killed a dozen rebel knights and run off a dozen more. We had might and we had right on our side," he added with some pride. "Well, I was ridin' on ahead of my men when I met Richard hisself sudden-like in the woods. 'Drop yer sword!' I yelled to him. I recognized him right away, though he was in plain knight's armor at the time. He did not recognize me, though we'd met many years before.

"'No, Sir Knight,' was his reply. 'You shall drop yours and dismount to the rightful king.'

"Well, that got my blood up, I tell ye," continued William. "I drew my sword against him, but I could not kill, nor even fight, the son of my king. I would not. And, if I'm bein' honest, I knew Richard to be a masterful swordsman and warrior. So, I engaged with a quick parry toward him, and he right fast began to draw his sword. While he was unsheathing it, I grabbed the reins of his horse, a magnificent black-and-white destrier, it was, and I pulled its head sharply toward me, causin' the beast to lose its' footin'. It fell over with Richard still astride and wavin' his sword in the air like a turtle flipped on its back."

They all laughed. Eleanor had never heard this story and was glued to her seat, waiting to hear what happened next.

"Like I said, I would not have harmed a hair on Richard's head, but he was an ungrateful, disobedient, and disloyal son," said William. "At that time," he added quickly. "So, I could've easily skewered him while he thrashed on the ground with one leg trapped beneath his horse. Instead, I kicked the sword out of his hand and held up my own trusty sword ..." He glanced over at the pile of weapons sitting in the corner by the fireplace. "And I held it over his neck—then plunged it into the neck of his horse before it could regain its footin'."

Eleanor's eyes widened. "Oh!" exclaimed Lavinia and Beja together. "What happened next, Sir William?"

"The poor beast died a pitiful death, thrashin' and whinnyin' as its lifeblood poured out. I said to Richard, 'I kill yer horse instead of ye, Prince Richard. Bein' an heir to the throne and the son of my king, I will not harm ye. T'would be a grievous sin, but I warn ye this: If ye get close to yer father, to whom ye owe everything, Sir Prince, and threaten his life, then I will run ye through with this sword that I hold in my hand, this sword that still drips with the blood of yer faithful steed.' And I was still holdin' the sword up in the air.

"Now, Richard was one of the bravest men I would ever know, and much of that bravery he displayed later as king. It was not lightly that I threatened him like that. But my fealty was to his father. So, I glowered at him, standin' on the ground, me on my horse with a sword raised above his head, sayin' a silent prayer that he would refuse to fight me.

"And then, bless me, he started to laugh. He rocked back and forth laughin' like he'd bust open. And finally, when he stopped laughin', he said, 'Well played, Sir William. I recognize you now. You've served my father well, and I urge you to go on your way and keep serving him, and I'll be on my way. I'll not allow any harm to come to you from my men, so move on, and let's both pray to God that we don't come upon each other again. Who knows if the circumstances will be different, and one of us takes the other's life. Second only to me, Sir William, you are the best swordsman I know of.'

"Well, I couldn't help laughin' myself," said William. "'Ye got the order mixed up, young prince,' I said to him. 'Ye're second to me, but we'll not argue that now. And I pray I never have cause to prove it to ye.' I bowed my head to him, which is due a prince of the realm, and off I went."

William's audience was mesmerized listening to the story. "Did you meet him again?" asked Eleanor naively. The others looked at her with some surprise, including William.

"Of course, lass," he answered. "'Twas just a few days later that King Henry died, God rest his soul. On his deathbed, he named Richard his heir. That was one of the squabbles between them. King Henry could not decide who it would be. Richard should have been the logical choice for Henry. But, well, I sometimes think Henry liked keepin' his sons all stirred up. As soon as I could, I requested an audience with my new king, Richard, and swore to him my fealty to the death. Which, sad to say, was only ten years later when he was struck by an arrow that turned putrid and festered, and quickly took the life of the great Richard Coeur de Lion."

They were all silent. These stories, told for centuries, had happened merely years before for Sir William. What an amazing life this man has led.

"If there was one great thing that the Lionheart did for me, it was to grant me the hand of the beautiful Isabel," he added as a postscript. "Never has a man had a lovelier, more amiable, and wiser wife than my dear Isabel. Except for you, Richard," he said to Beja's husband, who had entered the room quietly while the story was being told.

Beja laughed and gave her husband a quick peck on the cheek, while he pinched her through her skirts. "Stop it now, husband, and behave yerself, or I'll have Sir William unhorse ye like he did the other Richard!"

Truly, Beja and Richard were deeply in love, and Sir William obviously loved his wife, too. She glanced at Thomas who was watching her intently, and a shy smile bloomed on his handsome face.

Chapter Eight

"Would ye like to see the cathedral at Canterbury, Miss Eleanor?"

Thomas stood above Eleanor as she tended to the small kitchen garden in the rear of the main house. Using a rudimentary hand shovel, she was digging up some vegetables she couldn't identify, and some she could, like carrots and cabbage. Kneeling in the dirt, she was filling a large basket when Thomas appeared in front of her.

"What did you say, Thomas?" she asked.

"The cathedral," he repeated, stammering nervously. "The one in Canterbury. It's, it's, well, about, perhaps a two-hour ride, uh, maybe a little more." He stopped and looked at her anxiously. "Ma asked me to invite ye."

A smile broke out on her face. "Oh, I would love to see it!" she exclaimed, growing excited at the thought of an outing that would take her away from the village, even if only for one day.

Thomas smiled, too, and relaxed. A generation earlier, Canterbury Cathedral had been the site of the murder of Thomas Becket. This brutal assassination was rumored to be on the order of King Henry II, the father of King John, father of the Lionheart. Becket was considered a saint for his martyrdom. In modern times, thousands of pilgrims still flowed through the cathedral to visit Becket's shrine.

"We're plannin' a trip in the morning," Thomas said. "Ma will be comin', Lavinia, and a few of the young'uns. We'll go on horseback and be back before nightfall. I have to return to Windsor in a few days, so we all thought it would be nice to have a family outin' … and of course, ye're invited, Miss Eleanor."

She stood, her face streaked with dirt. "Thank you, Thomas. Thank you for treating me like I'm part of the family."

He frowned. "Well, yes, ye're like family. But, not family actually," he said. "But very much like family." He was beginning to stammer again.

Eleanor laughed. "I know what you mean, Thomas. And thank you again. I'll be ready early in the morning."

Later that day, with her daytime chores completed, Eleanor took a walk with some sticks of charcoal and several pieces of parchment given to her by Beja. She sat beside a tree and began to sketch the meadow in front of her. She heard a noise behind her and started.

"Beggin' yer pardon, Miss Eleanor, I didn't mean to frighten ye." It was Thomas. He had what looked like a hoe in one hand. "I was workin' in the garden and saw ye wander off. I wanted to be sure ye're safe, miss."

Eleanor smiled. "Oh yes, Thomas, I'm having a rest and doing some sketching." She held up the partially finished drawing of the meadow and trees to show him.

"That's fine!" exclaimed Thomas. "Ye've got a real talent there, Miss Eleanor."

"Thank you," she said. It flattered her that he liked her drawing.

Thomas stood before her, one hand resting on his hip and the other leaning on his garden hoe. Eleanor could not help noticing how well built he was. His shoulders were broad, his arms and legs were rugged and muscled, and he had a casual smile on his face, as if he were savoring the warmth of the sun and Eleanor's company.

"Tell me about yourself Thomas," Eleanor said, and as she did, she pulled out a fresh parchment and began to sketch him.

"Oh, there's not much to tell."

"How did you end up at Windsor Castle as a stone mason?"

"I had to apprentice, miss. A mason does a lot of travelin' and goes wherever the work is and where the guild sends him. I was called to Windsor about two years ago; I reckon I'll be there another few years with all the work there is. We're replacin' all the old wood with stone, miss. It will be a formidable castle when we're finished. I hope ye get to see it one day."

She thought of Windsor Castle today and realized that the work accomplished by this young man helped the castle stand for all these centuries. "Yes, I'd like to, Thomas. Thomas, do you have a sweetheart?"

Thomas turned to look at her and answered quickly. "Oh no, Miss Eleanor. Never."

"I'm surprised Thomas, a handsome and talented man like yourself." She was flirting. Stop it, Eleanor. "I mean, you must certainly be of age to marry."

"Yes, Miss Eleanor, I'm eight and twenty. Ma and Pa have been pesterin' me to marry one of the young lasses from Graston. They want to see some grand babes, but I'm not here long enough to meet anyone. Besides …" He paused, and a shy, pensive look passed over his face. "I haven't met anyone who catches my fancy, the girls in Graston, I mean. Some of them are downright silly creatures. Some of them are too fast for me. I reckon I'll know the right lass when I see her." And he directed his gaze toward her and held it there.

Eleanor grew unsettled. She looked down at her drawing and put final touches on it. She held it up to Thomas.

"Miss Eleanor, it's a marvel, it is!" he exclaimed. "May I keep it, miss?"

"Yes, Thomas, of course." She rolled up the small parchment and handed it to him. He tucked it into his tunic, and the two of them walked back to the house.

The next morning Eleanor was in the kitchen helping to prepare food to take on the trip to Canterbury. She was dressed in a traveling outfit supplied by Beja. She wore a long linen dress overlaid with a kirtle and belted at the waist. A small leather purse was attached to her belt, and she wore her best leather shoes, also supplied by Beja. She had washed and braided her hair and wore a clean cap which covered the top of her head. Considering where and *when* she was living, Eleanor thought she looked quite fetching.

About an hour into the trip, the group stopped along the road to refresh themselves with some food and drink. "This is delicious," said Eleanor after tasting a delectable baked pie. "What is it?" she asked Lavinia.

"Oh, that's a beaver tail tart," Lavinia answered, nibbling on one as she spoke. "It's not easy to catch one, either," she added. "Thomas caught this yesterday along the river. Delicious, eh?"

Eleanor quietly put her tart down, unfinished.

Then Thomas spoke. "Miss Eleanor, what's the mood in France right now. I mean, the French defeated the English at Bouvines, and I hear they're gathering forces in the south to march against King John again."

Eleanor didn't know how to answer. "I really don't know, Thomas. I was never privy to any information about the French king's battles and troop movements. We heard rumors, you see, but it never had any impact on our daily lives." Lies, she thought, more lies.

"Gracious!" exclaimed Lavinia. "It has an impact on our lives every day! The King and his men are constantly movin' about the country engagin' in skirmishes here and there, sometimes not even with the French, but with our own barons and clergy. Why he's in a terrific row right now with the Archbishop of Canterbury! Always levyin' more and more taxes on the people. And while they're movin' about, they're quartering their soldiers in many of our villages, eatin' our food, and wenchin' with our women."

"Lavinia!" injected Beja with a light smack to her head. "Watch yer words, girl, and keep yer voice down. Ye don't speak such things along the road where people might hear ye, and ye don't speak with such vulgarity. It's unbecomin', 'tis!"

"And then … and then," Lavinia continued, sputtering out her words angrily, "the interdict! Mama, ye know it's true. We have no peace anymore. I miss the old ways."

"Oh tish, girl!" exclaimed an exasperated Beja. "Ye're a child yerself; what do ye know of the old ways?"

Lavinia sulked.

"Thomas's work at Windsor has put a hand of protection on our family," said Beja. "Hasn't it, Thomas?"

"Yes, I believe so," he said quietly. "The King is happy with our work, and I'm learnin' more and gettin' better at my craft all the time. The King likes loyalty and generosity, and he rewards it. Remember, sister," he added, lowering his voice, "it's dangerous to speak ill of the King."

"'Tis true, Lavinia," echoed Beja in a hushed tone. "Between us, I grant the truth of what ye're sayin', but ye must be careful what ye say and who ye say it in front of." They all cast a wary eye toward Eleanor. She knew they still thought she might be a French spy, but a spy against the King of England? That was preposterous.

Eleanor walked off and let them comfort the distraught Lavinia.

When Thomas walked up to her a few minutes later, she asked, "What did Lavinia mean about the interdict? What is that?"

"I'm surprised ye haven't heard, Miss Eleanor," Thomas replied. "Pope Innocent placed all of England under an interdict when King John refused to accept the Archbishop of Canterbury, Stephen Langton. Langton is Innocent's chosen representative. The King wanted his own man, so the King has been ragin' about it ever since, threatenin' the clergy and forcin' Langton to run for his life for a time."

"But what does it mean?" asked Eleanor.

"The interdict was grave, indeed," Thomas said, but added quickly, "It's just been lifted, so things are gettin' back to normal. But when it was in effect, it meant that all church services were cut off for a couple of years, no one could hold Mass, no babies could be baptized, no one could be buried in consecrated ground with a church service. No one could be legally married in the church. We had to practice these rites secretly, without church sanctions. So yes, Miss Eleanor, the interdict has been a punishment laid on the backs of every Englishman and woman. A terrible burden for all of us to bear."

Thomas added, "Pope Innocent even ex-communicated King John for his defiance to the church and has thrown his support to King Philip of France. He's been encouragin' the French to march against England." Thomas surveyed her with caution. "That's one reason the French trounced us badly at Bouvines; they had the Pope's blessin'. And it's also why I asked ye about the mood in France."

"Thomas," she said, "I may have spent some time living in France, but you must know, you must believe me, I'm no French spy. I'm just a simple woman who, right now, wishes she could be back home with her family." Her throat tightened and she fought tears. Home, in America.

"I believe ye, miss," Thomas said, and he patted her hand sympathetically. "But ... there's nothing simple about ye." He smiled when he said it, and Eleanor looked down at his hand on hers, a warmth spreading across her neck. He said, "Things may soon be coming to a head. The interdict has been lifted, and Archbishop Langton has recently returned to Canterbury, so we may see him there today. But the King still despises him. 'Twas wrong of Rome to hurt us so." He looked around to make sure no one else was listening.

Eleanor spoke. "I didn't know how difficult times have been here in

England for your people. I'm sorry for you all. Your family has been so kind to me and kept me so sheltered and comfortable, that I had no idea of the troubles you've all been facing."

"'Tis not so burdensome," Thomas replied. "As Ma said, our family has much to be grateful for. Bad times don't last forever, Miss Eleanor." He smiled at her, and Eleanor smiled back. What a beautiful smile he has. She was aware that his hand was still on hers, creating a delicious warmth that caused her cheeks to redden.

"Miss Eleanor," he began, studying her hand intently as if it held the mysteries of life, "have ye a sweetheart or an intended back in France?" He did not look up.

"I did," said Eleanor, then added quickly, "but I no longer do." Why did she say that? Why? She didn't want Thomas to think she was tied to another man, that's why.

"Oh, I see," he responded, now looking into her eyes. "And do ye still carry affection for this man?"

How could she answer that? She loved Patrick, but she was beginning to feel a strong connection to this young man before her, with his sweet smile and tender eyes. Thomas had stirred something in her that felt electric, as if the short distance between them was humming with energy. It was late September, but the air felt warm and heavy and carried a sweet fragrance to Eleanor as she met his gaze.

She answered deliberately. "Not anymore, Thomas."

———

Within the hour they had arrived at the cathedral. Eleanor gawked at the magnificent building in front of her, rising from the earth majestically like a goliath. Compared to the simplicity of the homes in the village of Graston, this gigantic, rambling cathedral was truly a marvel of engineering.

"'Tis ancient," said Lavinia, now all smiles, who had ridden up beside her. "After the Normans destroyed the original cathedral, it was rebuilt. It took hundreds of years to complete and was finished about fifty years ago. Now it's goin' through another buildin' and fortification."

Fifty years ago. That was about 800 years ago from her time period.

They entered the cathedral directly into the sanctuary where services were held. The stained-glass windows were meticulously crafted, she noted, the floors were paved with marble, and brightly colored paintings decorated the walls. Looking up at the high ceilings she noticed the imposing arches that gave the interior a sense of air and light. They were intricately paneled with gleaming wood. Was the altar the same one on which Thomas Becket was slain by King John's father?

"Better take a seat, Eleanor, dear," said Beja. "You, too, children." Hundreds of people were beginning to be seated, with throngs of more people outside.

"Archbishop Langton is here!" exclaimed an excited Thomas. "He's about to conduct the Mass."

The Adelfrids quickly sat toward the back of the sanctuary as Archbishop Langton approached the front through a door behind the altar. A small group of robed men assembled on either side and in front of the archbishop and began to chant in Latin.

"It's been a long time since the people have been able to worship in public," whispered Thomas, who sat to her right. He motioned to the hundreds of people crammed into the church for the service.

Archbishop Langton approached the lectern. He was tall and lean with an angular face and deep-set eyes. He wore a draped robe of blue and red, and a richly embellished headpiece adorned his head. He had the look of a weary traveler, but one with miles ahead of him before rest would come.

"I speak today of the vices of men," Archbishop Langton began. "They ravage the souls of others, corrupting all uprightness, devastating the laws of nature and producing the seed of all evil among men. They strip a person of his humanity. They whip and seduce their fellow man. They enslave themselves to sin, seduced by the lure of power into slavery. For pride takes God away from man. Envy takes his friends and family from him. The vice of anger takes himself from himself. Greed drives out the beaten one. Gluttony seduces the greedy man. And lust enslaves a man to himself. It is the sin of pride that rises above all others. Through pride, then, the heart is puffed up, but finally, in the end, trampled underfoot and reduced to mud."

Goodness! Eleanor squirmed a bit in her seat. What is he talking about? Could he be referring to the indignities he suffered during the interdict harassment from King John?

The doors of the sanctuary flung open, and King John himself, preceded by a group of armored knights, strode noisily into the cathedral. The King held his head high and walked forward slowly, exhibiting exactly the kind of pride that the archbishop had just preached against. This man was the same one who had thrown a tantrum in the dirt at Dover, foaming at the mouth and uttering hideous curses.

Suddenly, in a display of humility, the King fell on his knees in front of Archbishop Langton and begged his pardon for his sins against the church and the Pope. Langton stepped down from the platform at the front of the church and stood before the kneeling king. He placed his left hand on the King's head, which was elaborately crowned for this show of obeisance, and, raising his right hand toward the sky, said, "I reach up into heaven and exhort Jesus Christ to come down from His throne and place Himself upon our blessed altar as an offering for the sins of monarchs and earthly rulers. His power is greater than any power on earth." He lowered his arm and looked down at the King. "You are forgiven, John, King of England."

King John stood and glared at Archbishop Langton. He was quivering with anger and struggling to get it under control. Finally, he managed to calm himself, smoothing out his face and pasting on a smile for the archbishop and the people in attendance. He bowed his head slightly to the archbishop, then turned around and formed a procession that slowly made its way outside. Archbishop Langton followed, cutting the service short. All the people in the church quickly moved outside to watch what would happen next between king and archbishop.

"Let's go," Thomas said to Eleanor, taking her arm and urging her outside.

"Stay together," chided Beja. "Lavinia, grab the little ones and keep them close."

Outside, the crowd gathered at a distance from Archbishop Langton and King John as they spoke. The King glanced at the crowd and raised a hand of greeting to the people with a haughty look on his face. The men bowed before the King, and the women curtsied, including Eleanor. As she rose, King John's face turned and his eyes riveted on hers. She gasped. Thomas saw the exchange and gripped Eleanor's arm. The King whispered to one of his knights, who quickly made his way to Eleanor and Thomas.

"Thomas the mason," said the knight, "the King would like to speak with you."

Thomas and Eleanor exchanged a glance, and Thomas went forward to speak with the King. Eleanor could see that they were talking about her, because Thomas kept looking back toward Eleanor with a look of concern on his face and motioned toward her several times. After a few minutes, Thomas returned to his family and Eleanor. Unhappiness hung like a mask on his face.

"Miss Eleanor," he began, "I don't know how to say this, but the King has heard of your success as a midwife, and with the Queen due to give birth at any time, he would like you to come to the castle with him right now to assist the Queen when her time comes."

"Great God in heaven," exclaimed Beja. "Please don't let this happen!"

"It's not up to us now, Ma," said Thomas. "She must come with the King; he must be obeyed. But since I'm due back at Windsor soon, I'll accompany her and watch out for her. I'll stay right by her side all the way there," he added quickly.

Eleanor's mind was buzzing, like a pesky mosquito circling a sweaty neck. She panicked. He was a madman, surely, and he wanted her to attend his wife. She was not a real midwife! What if she made a mistake with the King's baby? No, this mustn't happen!

Then she remembered what William the Marshal had said outside the tent all those weeks ago: "We'll have to keep her away from the King, so she comes to no harm."

Chapter Nine

B efore they began their journey, Eleanor was formally introduced to the King. She curtsied and kept her head lowered, avoiding eye contact.

"Where are you from?" he demanded in French. His voice had a nasal, whiny quality to it.

"France," she replied, head still lowered. "I was born in Scotland."

"You're the young woman Sir William rescued from the battlefield, isn't that right?"

"Yes, Sire," she replied, head still down. She spoke with him in her halting French.

"And you've been living with Thomas's family all this time?"

"Yes, Sire."

"Well, they're fine people," he said, "but I'm in need of your services at the castle. Queen Isabella is due to give birth any day, and she lost our last child during the birth at the hands of an imbecile midwife, a thick-handed dog!" He was beginning to sound angry, and his voice rose in pitch. "Thank God it was a girl," he added, causing Eleanor to raise her head in shock. She looked directly into the cold eyes of King John. There was a sternness about his mouth, and the skin around his jaws was slack as it lay in folds on his thick neck.

He shifted and smiled charmingly at her. "Why, you're a beauty, aren't you?"

She didn't answer.

Archbishop Langton had been closely observing the entire

conversation. "Your Majesty," he interjected, and King John whipped his head around to confront Langton.

"What is it, Sir Archbishop?"

"Sire, might I find you another midwife, so that this young woman isn't taken from the home she has become accustomed to and the family she has become a part of? After all, she is not one of your royal servants."

"Mind you don't interfere too much," John spat at Langton. "You've got your church back; you've got your sycophant followers. Rule you the church, and leave me to govern the state and my own affairs."

"Sire," said the archbishop. "You do well to take care how you speak of Christ's Church. Hell yawns for those who refuse to honor God on earth and obey His laws."

A look of terror came over the King's face, and his countenance paled. He backed away from the archbishop as if he might grab his arm and drag him into Hell by himself.

Recovering, with a dramatic gesture King John turned away from the archbishop and mounted his horse for the trip to Windsor. Thomas and Eleanor mounted their horses and, staying close together, began to make the journey with the King and his men. Eleanor glanced back at Beja and the children. The stricken look on Beja's face alarmed Eleanor, and she raised a hand to wave goodbye.

"Thomas," Eleanor whispered to him, leaning over as they rode side by side so they could speak privately, "what shall I do? I'm afraid of the King. He seems intensely focused on me, and I've heard the many stories of his … his behavior with women. And what will Sir William think when he finds out that I'm no longer at your home? Thomas, I'm so afraid."

Thomas's brows knitted together, and his mouth tightened into a hard line as he looked at Eleanor. "Miss Eleanor, I'll get a message to the Marshal. In the meantime, ye must stay clear of the King as best ye can. Ye'll be sleepin' with other servants, so ye shouldn't be alone too much. And if ye find yerself in any distress, or feel ye're in any danger, I'll be somewhere on the grounds, so come and find me. I'll be lookin' for ye every day."

Up ahead, the King turned around in his saddle and observed the two of them, so they quickly separated and trotted behind quietly. When King John turned back around, they put their heads together once more.

"There's a woman at the castle named Agnes," he continued in a whisper. "She supervises the maids. Find her and befriend her. She's an old woman who does many jobs there, and she's also a favorite of the Queen. She'll help ye and watch out for ye. I'll tell her to look out for ye."

After several hours of hard riding, the group arrived at Windsor Castle. "Ye see there, Miss Eleanor," said Thomas, pointing to the wall to the left of the round tower. "That's where I'm makin' some changes, removin' the old wood wall and replacin' it with stone. It seems like a never-endin' job for our crew, but when we're finished, the walls will be a better defense against invaders."

Invaders. She marveled again at the time in which she lived, a time when everyone had to worry about invading armies. She saw the expansive area he was working on and noticed a crew of men moving stone on wagons. "You've done a wonderful job, Thomas," she said, turning to him and smiling.

He smiled back warmly and lightly touched the reins of her horse. "Miss Eleanor," he said, "I … I don't know how to say this, but since I've come to know ye, well I've …" He was cut off by a loud shout from the King to Thomas. Thomas quickly rode ahead to where the King was dismounting.

"Get the girl fed and dressed properly," the King said. "Let her sleep well, then have her brought to the Queen's chambers in the morning."

"Yes, Sire," Thomas said, bowing his head. He rode back to Eleanor looking defeated.

She could sense his unease. What was ahead for her in this castle, with a lecherous and deceitful king lurking around any corner? Thomas settled Eleanor into her room in the castle, shared by several other servant women, all of whom slept on the floor on straw mats. As luck would have it, Agnes was there to greet her.

"Agnes, old friend, please watch over this lass and make sure she's safe," said Thomas. They were all sitting in the kitchen at a large wooden table, much larger than the Adelfrids', eating a bowl of stew with bread and ale. He told Agnes, "The King has a bit of an eye for her, if ye take my meanin'."

"Oh, aye, I do," Agnes answered. "Don't ye worry, young mason," answered Agnes. She was small and wiry, wore a clean dress covered from neck to floor by an apron, and walked slightly hunched over. Most of her gray hair was covered by a scarf that wrapped around her head and created a long loop in the back. "I'll watch her every move, I will!" she said with a laugh. "Ye'll get sick of me pretty fast, missy."

Eleanor thanked her and walked outside the kitchen into a small courtyard with Thomas to say goodbye. "My quarters are at the other end of the castle," said Thomas, "In that corner of the bailey." He pointed beyond where he was working.

"So far away," said Eleanor.

"Miss Eleanor," began Thomas, boldly taking hold of her shoulders and turning her to face him. "I vow to ye I'll protect ye and keep ye safe, if it costs me my life. Ye've become dear to me. I … I … well I love ye, Eleanor," he said, dropping the "miss" from her name. Then he drew her to himself.

Before she had a chance to protest or even process his shocking declaration of love, his lips met hers with a fervent urgency. He kissed her decisively, searching for a response. His lips moved with such passionate insistence that it left her breathless. She felt the gentle brush of his lips against her neck, then back to her mouth with more force. His hands cupped her face, pulling her closer. Finally, she summoned the strength to pull away.

"Thomas, please. Please stop." She was out of breath and could barely look at him.

"Miss Eleanor, forgive me," he said, panting. He had added the respectful "miss" back to his address. "I beg ye, don't hold my brashness against me. I was overcome with my feelin' fer ye."

With both hands against his chest, as if to create distance between them, she looked into his eyes and saw they were moist. "Oh, Thomas, dear Thomas, I'm not angry. But we hardly know each other. You don't love me. You can't possibly love me."

"Beggin' yer pardon, Miss Eleanor, but I do. And it's not just the passion I feel for ye, which, I confess, has overwhelmed me. It's yer sweetness and yer helpful spirit, yer strong mind and beauty, both inside and out. Ye're honest, without the guile and cunnin' of most young lasses. And I trust ye, Miss Eleanor. I think ye're the most wonderful of all God's creations. I … I've never had a sweetheart. I've never …" He trailed off, and Eleanor knew what he was referring to. He had never been intimate with the opposite sex, and neither had she. Yet the kiss she'd just shared with Thomas was more intimate, more fiery, more exuberant and exciting than any kiss she'd ever received from her fiancé, Patrick.

"You know I have great fondness for you, Thomas …"

"I don't want yer fondness, Eleanor!" he declared, almost angrily. "I want yer love. The way I love ye, and I believe ye love me back."

They were both breathing hard, standing a few inches apart, his arms still around her. Eleanor could bear it no longer. Despite her inner turmoil, being torn away first from her life in the 1960s and then from the Adelfrids, then thrust into the path of a lecherous, tyrannical king, Eleanor found herself irresistibly drawn to Thomas. His presence, inches from her, created a magnetic pull she couldn't deny. His burning gaze, his hands around her waist, made her heart race and her breath quicken again. Though her mind was in chaos, her feelings for Thomas surged through her like an unstoppable wave.

"I don't love you," she said, but she leaned forward, wrapped her arms tightly around his neck, pulling him close and pressing her lips to his in another fierce kiss. Their mouths moved together with an intensity that made the world around them fade into insignificance. Time seemed to stretch, until finally, breathless and flushed, they slowly pulled apart, their eyes still locked together as Eleanor moved away back into the castle.

Chapter Ten

Several of the maids, along with old Agnes, dressed Eleanor for her meeting with the Queen. She was given a linen dress, covered with a brightly colored kirtle. With new leather shoes and a simple veil to cover her braided hair, she was ready to meet the Queen.

Eleanor had slept poorly in the room shared by a group of maids. Agnes, who normally slept with the older women in another room, slept close to Eleanor that night, heeding Thomas's instructions to watch out for her. Agnes snored softly as she slept, while Eleanor tossed and turned, the straw from her bed causing her legs and arms to itch.

Eleanor could not believe how her life had changed in one day. First, there was the thrill of that kiss, or more accurately, her many kisses, with Thomas. He loves me! I'm amazed at how quickly my feelings for him have deepened … but is it love? And what about Patrick? He's lost to me. I guess I need to accept that this is my reality, and Patrick is gone forever. It's not a life I want, but after all this time with the Adelfrids, and meeting Thomas, I'm comfortable living in medieval England. There, I've said it.

Correction: I *was* starting to feel comfortable until the King kidnapped me and brought me here. I almost forgot that a few months ago I believed this was all a dream. But those kisses! They were no dream. His lips on mine, his arms wrapped around me. This tyrant, King John, takes me away from my comfortable life, from my growing feelings for Thomas, and now I must play midwife to the Queen of England.

As she curled beneath the covers, Eleanor began to sob, the weight of it all finally crashing down. Her tears soaked the pillow.

Agnes rolled over. "What's got ye worried, lass, with all that twitchin' about and weepin'? Ye'll be treated well here, and perhaps soon ye can get back with yer family in Graston. Don't fret, girl. Agnes will always be here to care for ye."

Eleanor gazed at the wrinkled face of her protector. She smiled at Eleanor, and her eyes were bright. "Thank you, Agnes. I suppose I'm worrying for nothing, but the King …" She lowered her voice. "The King seems to have fixated on me. He stares at me intently, and I have heard that he … that he likes women."

Eleanor was concerned about saying too much. She knew that history would record John as a predatory philanderer with several children born out of wedlock to a parade of mistresses. He would be remembered as the evilest king in English history. And he was right here, in Windsor Castle, somewhere in a room below hers.

Agnes stifled a laugh. "Oh, missy, yes!" Agnes exclaimed beneath her breath. "Why, that's an understatement, to be sure. He loves the women, and fixates on all of 'em, that one does, just like his father, and he takes what he wants. Missy, he can be cruel, that one can. Take care ye keep yerself away from him as best ye can. I know I shouldn't speak thus, but he's a wicked one, that one is."

Eleanor was shocked at how openly she criticized the King, and she became alarmed. Suppose King John desired her. She reminded herself that she was there to assist the Queen, and so she must equip herself for the task ahead. Her time with the Adelfrids had provided some experience, but the babies she helped into the world had been easy ones, except for Heloise's breech birth.

"About a year ago," Agnes continued in a low voice, "The King was havin' a feast with his barons and their wives, and he took a fancy to one of the wives, as is his habit. His barons hate the King, yes they do, and so the baron whose wife he fancied arranged the tryst for the King and his wife, but the baron substituted a common whore for the wife in her chamber to teach the King a lesson. The King bedded the whore and bragged right in front of the same baron, at another dinner, that he'd had her. But the baron only smiled at the King and said, 'Ah yes, My Lord, I heard that ye bedded the filthiest whore in London. My wife was away at Winchester, and we gave the unfortunate strumpet a bed for the night.' The King fumed and pounded his fist on the table, he did, and he stormed out. He hates to be made a fool."

"That's horrible," said Eleanor. "What happened to the baron?"

"Oh lordy, all the barons are in revolt now, missy. They're marchin' against the King with the French. We're at war, Eleanor girl. So, the King, wretched snake that he is, won't be around much anyway. Tend to the Queen, and ye'll be fine. Lassie, the Queen usually does well with her birthin'. She's a young woman, that one is, and had four children with no problems, so don't ye fret. And I'll be around to help ye if ye need me."

In the morning, one of the Queen's ladies came to fetch Eleanor and brought her through a labyrinth of stone hallways, down a narrow flight of steps, and through more rooms until they came to the Queen's suite. When she entered, she gave a low curtsy to the Queen and stood straight to appraise her surroundings. The room was dark and decorated with lush, heavy fabrics and a massive bed in the center of the room with a fur coverlet on top.

Queen Isabella was dazzlingly beautiful, the "Helen of the Middle Ages," as she would be known, with blonde hair and brilliant cornflower-blue eyes. Her figure was slim, except for her enlarged belly, and she was dressed in a beautifully embroidered gown, covered with a light robe fringed with ermine. One of her ladies was dressing her hair and wrapping it in place beneath a veil as she spoke.

"Come in," she said with a smile. "My Lord the King has told me about your experience as a midwife."

"Yes, Your Majesty," said Eleanor.

"Come close," said the Queen. "What's your name?"

"It's Eleanor, My Lady."

"Do you need to examine me?"

Eleanor was a little taken aback. "Um, well yes, My Lady, that would be helpful."

The Queen shooed away her other ladies and opened her gown, which laced in the front. Through the underlying chemise, Eleanor placed her hands on the Queen's belly and probed gently. She wasn't sure what she was supposed to feel, but by looking at her she could tell the baby was still sitting high and had not yet dropped into position.

"My Lady, may I ask, what happened with your last delivery? I understand you lost the baby." The Queen's eyes suddenly became moist, and Eleanor felt pity for her.

"I had a long period of laboring," Isabella said, "but I was able to deliver the baby alive. She died soon after, after many attempts to get her to breath properly. She was born a bluish color, and she never recovered. My Lord the King blamed the midwife, who couldn't get her to breathe, but I'm not sure anyone could have saved my little baby girl."

Eleanor thought about this. "My Lady, when a baby is born blue it means they're not getting enough oxygen," she said.

"Oxa ...?" asked the perplexed Queen.

"Oxygen, it's another word for air. Her lungs, her little chest, could have been too weak, and she may never have been able to survive. Or her little throat could have been blocked with something." The Queen nodded, recovering a little from her sadness. "I'll do my best to help you with this baby's birth," Eleanor said. "By your count, how much longer do you think you have?

"It could be soon," replied the Queen, "a fortnight, maybe more. I am hoping it will not be much longer; I'm tired of being shut up in this dark room." She waved her hand toward the closed drapes. "I have headaches all the time, and I feel weak and tired."

"My Lady," said Eleanor, "in France, where I spent some time ..." Eleanor had to tread carefully. She tried to remember all the lies she'd already told. She must not deviate too much from the truth, or she could get caught in her own web of lies. And her conscience gave her moments of deep shame over the many stories she'd concocted since arriving in this time. But what were her options? If she told the truth, they would lock her up. She prayed God would forgive her. She said, "In France many of the midwives and healers believe that sunshine, fresh air, and some exercise are beneficial to the expecting mother. I recommend that you open the windows if it's not too chilly, and that you allow some sunshine in. If you're comfortable, take some walks outside."

"That would be bold, indeed," said the Queen, a pretty smile touching her lips. "I've always been instructed that I must shut myself up to keep the baby safe."

"My Lady, you won't hurt the baby by walking a bit, as long as you're careful. If you feel tired, stop and sit, or lie down."

The Queen surveyed Eleanor with some skepticism. "You speak queerly," she said bluntly. "They say you're from France."

"Yes, but I also lived in Scotland when I was a little girl, and I've lived in England. My father was a physician, so I've traveled a bit. I still don't speak French well," she added. She had been speaking French with the Queen since she entered the room, but poorly in her own estimation.

Abruptly, the Queen asked, "Do you know how old I am?"

"No, My Lady."

"I'm twenty-six. I've been married to the King for fourteen years. Do you know how old I was when I had my first child?"

"No, My Lady." She was trying to do the math in her head when the Queen spoke up.

"I was thirteen," she said. "Thirteen. A child myself. And since then, I've given the King two sons and two daughters. I was twelve years old when I married the King, and I hadn't yet begun … but the King didn't care to wait."

Eleanor was appalled. Married at twelve, it was shocking, even for the Middle Ages. And the King had forced her to consummate at the age of twelve. What a beast. Clearly, the Queen held the King in some contempt, like almost everyone else in the kingdom.

"My Lady, I hope one day to meet your other children. Are they here at Windsor?"

"The princesses are here; the young princes are at Winchester receiving their training and education. Yes, I'll be sure to have you meet my daughters, Joan and Isabella." Then she said, "That's all, Eleanor," and she turned away from her.

Eleanor left the Queen's chambers and asked one of the guards in the hallway how to find her way to the servants' hall. He pointed the way, and she wound through the hallways. She approached a small landing at the end of one hallway which looked familiar. I think I go left here. But as she turned the corner, she gasped. The King himself was standing in front of her! He grabbed her wrist sharply and pulled her into a private alcove before she knew what was happening.

"Your Majesty!" she shrieked, but he put a rough hand over her mouth to quiet her. He pushed against her, so that anyone passing by would not even know she was there. He spoke to her in a rough whisper.

"Girl, you must not make any noise. I will not harm you, but I command you to be still."

His breath was rancid. It's happening, it's happening, it's happening! Her greatest fear was coming true, the King of England was assaulting her right here in the castle. With his hand held firmly over her mouth and his fleshy torso pinning her against the stone wall, she could not move. She jerked her head to the side quickly to release his hand from her mouth, and gasped, "Sire, please, I beg you, let me go, please Sire …"

He yanked her head forward and clamped his hand against her mouth again, while his other hand groped the length of her skirts. She squirmed and fought as best she could, but he held her too tightly.

"Girl, your protests won't work. I can see the lust in your eyes, and I'm the man to satisfy your cravings. Be still, I say. I will not hurt you, unless you won't stop fighting me, then I may have to use more persuasive measures." He smiled cruelly. His voice was mocking, as if he enjoyed Eleanor's helplessness, like her fear was just a game to him. His dark eyes bored into hers. He pushed against her in a rhythmic motion that made her feel sick to her stomach.

"Miss Eleanor, are ye there, lass?" Agnes called from somewhere at the end of the hallway, moving in their direction. Bless you, Agnes. Please save me!

The King removed his hand from her mouth, but his eyes were burning with anger. He whispered to her, "Next time, girl," and pushed away from her.

Agnes appeared and gave a deep curtsy to the King, struggling a little as she stood. "Your Majesty," she said.

King John grabbed Eleanor by the wrist and pulled her roughly in front of Agnes. "Put her to work, old lady," he said. "I found her dallying around, the lazy wench. I'll have none of that here."

"Yes, Sire," said Agnes, head lowered. "Come girl, let's find ye somethin' to work on whilst ye wait for the Queen's babe to come into the world."

Agnes took Eleanor's arm, and they hurried away as the King glared after them. Once they were in the servants' hall, Eleanor burst into tears.

"Miss Eleanor, don't carry on, I heard ye wailing, and I came a runnin'. I was lurkin' in the hallway, and I knew the King was lurkin' somewhere, too. But I didn't know where. I blame myself that I wasn't standin' outside the Queen's apartment waitin' for ye."

"It's not your fault," Eleanor said between sobs. "Oh Agnes, he vowed to get me next time. What shall I do? He intends to have his way by force. He held me down, he held my mouth, he pushed … Agnes what shall I do?"

"There, there, lass. He's like this with many of the girls. Let's hope a pretty new maid or wife of a baron waves her skirts in front of him soon, and he'll forget all about ye. Though I'll skin alive any maid who dallies with the King, I will." Her voice was angry, and sounded like it was filled with gravel. "In the meantime, let's find ye some work. Can ye help with cleanin' and sewin'? We seem to always be behind on those tasks, and the Queen likes everythin' spotless. What did ye think of her?"

"She's quite beautiful," said Eleanor, still sniffling. "And if I had to guess, I would say she hates the King as much as I do."

Chapter Eleven

L ater that day, while sitting in the kitchen with Agnes and several other maids half-heartedly eating a meal, Eleanor pondered her situation. She needed to feel safe in the castle if she was to continue living and working here. Right now, though, she felt like a hunted animal, with danger all around.

Thomas burst through the doors. He rushed over to Eleanor and knelt on the floor by her chair, taking her hand in his in front of all the other servants.

"Miss Eleanor, I heard what happened. Agnes sent me a message. Are ye alright? Did he harm ye any? Did he … did he …?"

Eleanor, who was still in turmoil from the assault, was so touched by Thomas's concern that tears began to flow again, and she softly placed a hand on his cheek. He covered her hand with his—a careless display of the intimacy that had blossomed between them.

"No Thomas, he did not. But he tried," Eleanor told him. "If Agnes hadn't come when she did, he might have succeeded. He vowed to get me next time, though, and I'm scared."

Thomas stood and addressed Agnes and the other maids. His stance was rigid, his fists balled up tightly, and he quivered with anger. "Ye must all make sure she's never, ever alone anywhere in the castle, do ye hear?" The other maids nodded, wide eyed. "When she goes to see the Queen, there must always be one of ye by her side, or right outside the door. He's got a cravin' for her, there's no denyin', and she must be protected."

"It's my fault," Agnes chimed up woefully, ringing her hands. "I should've been right there outside the Queen's door, waitin' for her."

"No Agnes," said Eleanor. "It's not your fault. You saved me, and God bless you for it, but," she added, "I would feel better if I wasn't alone."

They all gave Thomas their assurances they would never leave her alone, and Agnes wrapped up some meat, bread, and cheese and handed it to Thomas to take with him. "Don't ye worry, young mason," she said, placing the package in his hands. "Here, lad. Eat up. We'll care for the lass." With a twinkle in her eye she added, "I know how important she is to ye, and she's important to us, as well, she is."

Eleanor walked outside with Thomas as he prepared to leave. He looked at her gravely and put his arms around her. "Dear Eleanor," he said, "I cannot bear to think that that beast put his filthy, whorin' hands on ye. If I'd been there, God knows what I'd have done to him. I believe I'd have killed him. Eleanor, I tell ye the truth, I'd kill for ye, I would."

She looked up at him with red eyes, and he drew her into him, wrapping his arms around her in a tender embrace.

———

Day after day, Eleanor performed her duties, always with either Agnes or one of the other maids by her side. She helped with the cleaning and sewing, never-ending chores in the castle, and occasionally assisted the cook in preparing the "trench" bowls—thick slices of bread hollowed out to serve as bowls for pottage and other foods. Both the royals and servants alike ate many of their meals in these trenches and consumed the trench itself at the end of the meal.

Several times over the next week, the Queen summoned Eleanor to attend her. The first time she was accompanied by Agnes, who waited outside the door until she left. The Queen was concerned about pains in her abdomen.

"It appears your baby has dropped," said Eleanor after a brief exam. "The baby is getting into position for the birth. I can assure you that all is well, and it may even speed up your pains if you continue to walk in the gardens."

The next time, a few days later, Eleanor entered the Queen's suite and was shocked to see the King lounging on the bed. "Your Majesty," said Eleanor. She curtsied, ducking her head to hide her alarm.

"Come in, Eleanor," said the Queen. "I have been feeling some pain, but not terribly so, should I take to the bed?"

"My Lady, how frequent are your pains?" asked Eleanor, trying to ignore the King, who grinned at her as he ate figs from a tray, licking his fingers noisily as he eyed her.

"One or two every hour," said the Queen, who also ignored the King.

"My Lady, I advise you to stay in your room. You may walk around the room if you're comfortable, but as soon as your pains become more frequent, please summon me." Eleanor was beginning to worry about the impending birth. Could she pull it off to the satisfaction of both the King and the Queen? If there was anything wrong with the baby, she knew the King's anger would explode on her, especially if it was a boy.

"Thank you, Eleanor," the Queen said, and smiled at her beautifully. "I do feel comfortable that you will be helping me when the time comes."

As Eleanor left the Queen's suite, the King followed her out while the Queen's eyes narrowed with distrust as she watched him from inside her rooms. In the hall, Agnes waited for her.

"What are you doing here?" snapped King John when he saw Agnes.

"Sire," Agnes said with a curtsy. "Young miss is needed in the kitchen, beggin' yer pardon. Come along, missy."

They briskly walked away and turned the corner. "Oh Agnes, thank you," Eleanor said and gave her a quick hug.

"I'll be stickin' to ye like ivy to a tree," Agnes said as they hurried along the stone hallways. "Master mason will have my hide if I don't, that one will."

Two days later, Eleanor learned that the King had left the castle with a large contingent of soldiers and servants to push back the French and quell baronial uprisings throughout the realm. Her anxiety evaporated like mist in the morning sun, and she almost enjoyed her life in the castle. The maids were fun and ceaselessly chatty.

"Eleanor," said Sabine, a dark-eyed chambermaid at the castle, "ye've heard the rumors about King John and his nephew, Arthur, I take it?"

"Yes," said Eleanor, which was the truth, "but I don't remember exactly what happened."

"Oh, miss!" continued Sabine. She was a pretty girl whose name derived from her raven-black hair. She had pulled Eleanor aside after lunch one day. "Arthur, the King's nephew, was thought to be a contender for the throne, so when John took the crown, he had Arthur thrown into prison and nearly starved him to death. I heard the King's men blinded and unmanned him right there in the filthy dungeon, the devils!" she spat out angrily. "It's said that Arthur was the reincarnation of King Arthur himself, that had he taken the throne Merlin would reappear, and England would become like Camelot again."

Eleanor smiled at Sabine's naivety for believing the old Arthurian tales, but she said nothing.

"Then, one night," Sabine resumed as she nibbled on a piece of cheese, "the King crept into the prison, filled with drink and possessed by the father of all lies, Satan himself, and killed Arthur with his own hands, tied a heavy stone to the lad's mutilated body, then tossed him into the river." Sabine's face lit up with excitement as she told the story. "I heard that a fisherman found the corpse danglin' lifeless from his net, and fearin' the wrath of the King, took the poor dead lad himself to Normandy for a proper burial."

Eleanor was stunned to hear this story. She recalled vaguely that John was suspected of killing his nephew Arthur, who had been a rival to the throne at the time, but these details, even if only half true, were horrifying.

"Oh, it gets even worse, Eleanor," Sabine continued with breathless excitement. "Lord William de Braose took charge of young Arthur for a time in prison. His wife, Maud, foolishly riled up the King one day when she accused the King of murderin' his own nephew, which was true, of course—but her words were overheard by the King's men. Well, her husband, the coward, fled England, so John tossed Maud and her son, young William, into prison and starved them to death. I heard they were kept right here at Windsor for a time. It took eleven days for them both to die. Her poor son, who'd done nothin' wrong except fer bein' Maud's boy, was found dead sittin' against the wall. So starved was the mother that she had eaten the flesh off her own son's face before she died, as well."

Eleanor gasped in horror. "Oh yes," added Sabine with a knowing nod of her head. "Starvin' is one the King' favorite forms of execution."

———

Queen Isabella's time had arrived. While the ladies in waiting opened all the drawers in the room, unlocked the chests, and untied all knots on clothing as superstitious symbols of the opening of the womb, Eleanor went about her business briskly and ignored their foolishness. Although a servant, she was in charge of the room as Isabella labored.

"I need some spirits," she told one of the ladies.

"You'll not be drinking now!" the lady replied venomously.

"Not for me to drink, it's for … to clean my hands and to clean the Queen. It's safer for the baby. Bring me clear spirits right away."

"Do it!" the Queen growled between pains.

The lady scurried off, muttering under her breath, as the Queen sat in her bed and moaned softly with each pain. The room was filled with women, and it became humid and stuffy. "Please open the windows a little," said Eleanor. "The Queen needs some fresh air."

A fresh gust of cool air swept through the room as Isabella gave her final push, and the baby arrived, a chubby baby girl, perfectly formed. Eleanor cleaned out the baby's mouth, and she wailed at her rough entry into the world. Eleanor cut the cord, and the ladies whisked the baby away to bathe her.

"It's a girl, My Lady," Eleanor said to the Queen. Her ladies brought the child to her, and her face softened with a sad smile as she gazed at her new daughter.

"Another girl," she said wistfully. "Daughters are dear companions to a mother, but their fathers always want a boy. Especially when the father is a king."

Eleanor looked at the beautiful Isabella and felt sorry for her. She had everything in the world a woman could want—beauty, position, a royal title, wealth, and healthy children. But she seemed more like an unhappy doll, on display and ill-used by a wicked husband whose lusts, it seemed, would never be fully satisfied.

"You've given him two heirs, My Lady," said one of the ladies in waiting. "The King will be pleased."

"Yes, yes," said Isabella with a sigh, waving the ladies away. "Get word to My Lord, the King. And make arrangements for the baptism. Has the wet nurse arrived?"

A large woman approached the Queen and gently took the baby from her. She opened her bodice and began to suckle the newborn.

"Eleanor," said the Queen. "The King and I decided before she was born that if she was a girl we would name her after the King's mother, the great Eleanor of Aquitaine. But it gives me pleasure that she will also bear the name of the midwife who brought her into the world."

Eleanor was profoundly touched. The daughter of King John of England is named, in part, after herself, a woman born on a continent not yet dreamed of 750 years in the future. Another medieval child named after her. The wonder of it staggered her, and she curtsied to the Queen.

Despite the success of the Queen's birth, Eleanor still feared the return of the King. He'll be pleased the Queen is well, though. That's something I don't need to worry about. But, what's in store for me next? I don't feel any safer with the King gone than when he's here—he can show up at any time.

Chapter Twelve

Eleanor was sitting in the kitchen, mending some clothing, when Thomas came in. "There's a fair within walkin' distance, one of the biggest of the year, and I'd like ye to visit with me," he said. "All the maids will be goin', and all the other servants, staggered for the next few days. Let's ask Agnes if ye can take the day, shall we?"

"That sounds like fun, Thomas," said Eleanor. "I'd love to go, if Agnes can spare me." Agnes gave her blessing, and after checking on the Queen and the baby, Eleanor prepared to depart and experience the Middle Ages' version of fun, with Thomas as her guide. Life in medieval England was filled with hard work and threats all around her, but Thomas and her friends at the castle were a bright spot, and she intended to enjoy the day.

It was about an hour's walk to the village festival, which celebrated the Feast of St. Matthew. They heard and smelled the fair long before they arrived. The smell of food cooking, animals, and the throng of people were powerful but welcome. As they progressed along the road more and more people joined their caravan, people of all kinds. Wealthy noblemen and women arrived on richly bedecked horses and in ornate carriages. Knights arrived on their chargers, pushing aside the peasants and lower classes as they entered the fair, as if they were the star attractions. But mostly, Eleanor saw throngs of everyday people making their way on foot into the fairgrounds, many with wagons loaded with goods and food for trade, with children struggling to keep up. All of them wore faces filled with anticipation.

The first thing she noticed was the complete lack of similarity to the dozens of fairs she had attended during her modern life, including the last one in Bouvines, France, where she had passed out and awakened in this time. Those fairs had been modern interpretations of medieval festivals, with attendees wearing jeans and carrying transistor radios, modern food, and cars parked in nearby lots visible to everyone. And no one arrived on horseback.

The people around her, most from the peasant class, were simply dressed in rough fabrics that were wrapped and belted together for maximum coverage and minimum attractiveness. The merchant class and nobility had more flexibility and options in their clothing. She saw more colors and embellishments among these people, but the common thread was the mingling and enjoyment they all exhibited at the festival.

She and Thomas made their way through the many exhibits, stalls, and entertainment. Thomas took her hand in his to keep her close by, and the feel of his skin on hers, that small touch, sent an electric thrill through Eleanor. To their right, as soon as they entered, was a pair of dancing bears, jumping up and down on their hind legs, ribbons attached to their collars and ears, while their masters strummed tunes on lutes and small harps.

"Try this," said Thomas, handing her a trench, the ubiquitous bowl made of bread, filled with a type of fish stew. She smelled it warily. Convinced it was safe, she ate.

"Delicious!" she said. Thomas smiled at her, and they shared the rest of the bowl.

Presently, they heard a commotion and turned to see a group of knights entering the fairgrounds. She recognized the magnificent white steed of William the Marshal. He slowly made his way through the fairgrounds with Alfred close behind him. Throngs of people gathered around the Marshall, bowing as he made his way. He greeted them all warmly. "Look!" she exclaimed, tugging on Thomas's arm. "It's the Marshal."

Thomas and Eleanor made their way through the crowd to where William was stabling his horse. When he saw them, a huge grin broke out on his face, and he slapped Thomas heartily on the back, causing him to stumble. Then he saw Eleanor.

"And who's this ye have with ye? Why, it's the French lassie! Look here, Alfred."

Alfred gave Thomas a hearty greeting and bowed his head slightly to Eleanor. "Hello, young miss. I hear'd ye've gone to Windsor. Is this knave watchin' over ye, I hope?"

William approached her and laid a hand on her shoulder. "I've been unable to check in on ye at the Adelfrids, girl. I learned that the King had taken ye to his castle, and I heard ye did a fine job deliverin' the Queen's babe. Has the King ... has he stepped out of line with ye?"

A look passed between Thomas and Eleanor.

The Marshal's face darkened, but he said nothing.

They found a private spot away from the throngs of people to sit and talk. Thomas and William were locked in conversation, while Alfred brought a mug of ale to Eleanor. The other knights had scattered and were enjoying the fair.

"How have you been, Alfred?" she asked.

"Well, miss" he began, "The King has signed a treaty with King Philip of France, finally puttin' an end to the hostilities. As the Marshal of England, Sir William was there at the signin' with King John. I tell ye, Miss Eleanor," he said, leaning toward her and lowering his voice, "the King was in fits over havin' to sign the treaty. And ye've seen him when he's not happy; he loses his temper somethin' fierce—but he waits till after it's over, then he pitches a grand one, that he does."

"Yes, I've seen it," she agreed, remembering the first time she saw him when they landed at Dover.

"Now all the English territories across the Channel are gone," he continued, shaking his head. "After centuries of English rule. It's hard to believe it, but it's true. Yet, it's my thinkin' that it's not over with the French, and Sir William agrees. The barons are in revolt against the King over his loss of French lands and his high taxes on the people, not to mention his taxes on the barons themselves. It's rumored that many of these barons have joined forces with Philip's son, Louis, and may be plannin' an invasion."

"Oh no!" Eleanor exclaimed, deeply concerned about the country that was now her home, but also her own safety as an employee of the despot king, whom everyone seemed to hate. This tyrant King was also dangerously unstable.

The men were soon locked in conversation, so Eleanor decided to explore the festival on her own. "I'm going to walk a bit," she told Thomas. She stopped at several stalls where goods, food, and trinkets were being sold. Merchants from all over Europe were selling exotic spices, fancy rugs, and fabrics. To her right was a group of people dressed in biblical garb re-enacting the story of Jonah and the whale. The whale was a large leather tarp with eyes and mouth painted on. As Jonah's fellow seamen threw him into the water, the whale's mouth opened, and Jonah disappeared behind the tarp. One of the actors continued narrating the story, and the whale opened its mouth again and Jonah spilled out onto the ground. The crowd clapped and cheered, with Eleanor joining in.

Continuing, she watched a juggler, noting that behind him was a stage where a magician was performing a magic act. He had a large box on the stage with a curtain drawn around it. Eleanor's body went rigid, her breath catching in her throat. She recognized the scene. And the magician. About fifty yards away was the same magician who had hurled her back to medieval England after she went inside the same curtained box.

And as she stared, unable to move, Simon the Seer stood straight, seeming to sense her presence, and slowly turned around to face her.

Chapter Thirteen

"**E**leanor, what's wrong! Yer shakin' like a leaf in the wind." It was Thomas who spoke. He had come up behind her and put his hand on her arm. He looked worried. Without turning to him, she said, "I need to talk with that magician. I met him … I've met him before." She wanted to tell Thomas the truth, to blurt it all out, but she also knew he would never believe it, never believe she was from another time.

"I'll go with ye," Thomas said. "Ye look frightened, Eleanor, and I don't want to leave ye alone."

"No, Thomas," she said. "I'll be alright. Stay here. I'll be back soon." She walked toward Simon, who had stepped down off his stage and was moving toward her. Thomas, in the background, edged closer to the pair but kept some distance. Now they were face to face. Yes, this is the same man, the same eyes, the same long black beard. She remembered how his black eyes had spread across his face until it seemed the whole world was covered in black. She was terrified and began to tremble.

As if sensing her fear, a slight smile appeared on his face. But his eyes weren't smiling. "I was hoping to see you at one of these fairs," he said. "I know how you like fairs. And magic shows."

Eleanor could not speak.

"Surely, you've been looking for me, Eleanor," he continued. "After all, I'm your only way back to the future."

That jolted her out of her silence. "What are you doing here? How did you get to this time? The same way I did? What do you want from me?"

"So many questions," Simon responded. That smile. He reached out an arm toward her, and she shrunk back. Immediately, Thomas was beside her, and he put an arm around her.

"Who are ye?" demanded Thomas.

Simon, composed and calm, the opposite of Eleanor, looked squarely at Thomas, and his smile disappeared. "Ah, I see you've found a protector. Pity."

"I want to …" began Eleanor, but she was unable to finish.

"You want to go home," Simon completed.

"Who are you?" she demanded. "Why did you send me here? How is it possible that you're even here when I saw you at the fair in Bouvines in the future?"

"How am *I* here?" he asked with a laugh. "How are *you* here? That's really the question, isn't it?"

"Yes," she finally answered him, "I want to go home."

Yes, she wanted to go home where there was no more danger, no more killing, no more deranged King John to threaten her, where Patrick waited for her, and there was no more Simon the Seer. But there was also no more Thomas. She tossed that thought aside, unwilling to dwell on it.

Simon spoke. "Did you get them?" he asked.

She didn't understand. "Get what?"

He stared at her, hard, appraising. What did he want from her? She could not figure it out. If there was something she needed to do to get back home, she would do it.

"What do you want?" she finally asked, matching him stare for stare. "What do you need from me so that you'll send me home?"

He frowned for a moment, like he was confused by what she was asking. He became composed.

"Not yet," he finally answered. "It's not yet time. But keep safe, Eleanor. Until we meet again."

"Whoever ye are?" cut in Thomas—he had pushed is way between them—"leave this lass alone. Don't ye come near her, or ye'll have to answer to me. Do ye understand?"

Simon smiled again, but only with his mouth. His eyes never smiled. Looking back and forth between Eleanor and Thomas, he bowed low and backed away.

What should I do? Desperation gripped her, and she couldn't move. He's my only path back to the future, I can't let him get away. But he *was* getting away, moving back to his magician's platform and the crowd that had gathered to watch his tricks. His tricks, his tricks, tricks that had launched her back in time, yet he was in this time, too. I wish I never had to see him again—but I need him to get back to my time.

"Who is that man?" demanded Thomas. He looked concerned and a little angry. His hands formed tight fists, the movement sharp, like he was drawing a weapon.

"Thomas, let's sit down somewhere, and I'll tell you how I know him. Maybe it's time you know the whole story."

Time. Time is the key to my story. Time used to stretch out before her and behind her in a line she moved along like a piece on a gameboard, like the game of Monopoly, sometimes taking a detour, but always moving forward toward the goal. Now time was moving in a circle, languorous and shadowy, with no beginning or end, incomprehensible, without a future on the horizon, a circle she wanted to complete, but in which she was trapped.

They walked to a quiet spot on the edge of the fairgounds and sat beneath a tree. They had food with them, and as they ate, Eleanor kept an eye out for Simon the Seer. She did not *want* to see him, but she also did not want him to get away. As she told Thomas her story, it became clearer in her mind that she needed to talk with Simon again and ask him to send her back to her own time. She simply couldn't stay here. What place did she really have in medieval England, in the year 1214? She may never marry or have children or have a meaningful life in a time when women were prey for unscrupulous men.

Seeing Simon was the final piece of evidence that her mind needed to believe she had actually traveled back in time and that Simon had sent her here—*now*—for a reason. She had to know what the reason was. She turned to Thomas and began her story with the blunt truth.

"I'm from the future, Thomas, from a place called America that hasn't been discovered yet in this time. It's across the ocean. In the future, explorers will sail there and discover the land I come from. That's why I sound different. That's why I looked different when the Marshal found me. I was in France, in Bouvines, when I woke up in this time. But when I left the year was ... the year was 1964."

Thomas was stroking her hand as she spoke, but when she said 1964, he stopped and looked at her with a puzzled expression. He didn't speak.

She continued: "It was that magician who sent me from 1964 to this year, 1214. I was visiting a festival in Bouvines at the time, where people came dressed up in old-fashioned clothes and pretended to be from this time period. They were pretending to be at a fair like this one. But Thomas, it was all make-believe, because in the future we don't dress like this, we don't have jousts, we don't get around on horseback. We have cars and buses and airplanes …"

She was getting way ahead of herself, and Thomas was staring at her uncomprehending. "At the fair in 1964, the same magician who's here today put me in one of his magic shows, and I disappeared. It was supposed to be a magic trick, pretend. But I woke up on the battlefield in Bouvines when the battle—the real Battle of Bouvines—was ending. There were a lot of dead and dying men lying around. And that's where the Marshal found me. I don't know why I'm here or how the magician was able to send me here, but here I am, and he holds the key to my return. My return to my time."

Thomas surprised her by asking, "What's a car?"

She couldn't help smiling, and then she laughed. "Oh Thomas," she said, "I don't know what to do. But I should go back and talk to the magician."

She stood, and Thomas stood with her. "I'll go with ye, Eleanor. I don't understand much of what ye said, but I believe ye're sincere. And I believe ye're scared. I don't want ye to try to go anywhere that takes ye away from me, but if ye must get back to yer family, I understand. I want ye to be happy, Eleanor."

Eleanor's troubled heart calmed at his words. Her worried face softened. "Oh Thomas, how could I ever leave you?" And she put her arms around him. They made their way back into the fairgrounds and headed for the magician's tent. "I think it was here," she said, standing in an empty spot.

"It was," Thomas said. "He's pulled up stakes and fled. Look there." He pointed to a stake lying on the ground, where the tent had been held down. Eleanor was almost relieved. But Simon had said, "Till we meet again."

"Now what?" asked Eleanor, more of herself than Thomas. Instead of getting some answers, all she had were more questions.

Thomas grinned and took her hand in his. "Now, dear, sweet, beautiful Eleanor, ye stay here with me."

Chapter Fourteen

E leanor sat with Agnes by the window of one of the upper rooms of the castle. She had asked her if she could go home, go back to the Adelfrids, now that the Queen's baby had been born and both were doing well, but Agnes could not allow her to go without the King's approval.

The first snow of the season was under way, and Eleanor and Agnes watched large, wet flakes fall from the window. King John had not been seen for several weeks. He was dealing with the baronial uprising and a rebellion in Ireland. From the gossip she overheard, she learned the King wasn't dealing well with any of these crises in the realm. He only seemed to make more enemies. She knew that England would prevail, but a violent period of history was beginning, and she had no choice but to live through it. Perhaps she wouldn't survive. There would be a lot of death and destruction; what a sobering thought. She didn't know where the King was right now or when he would return, but the castle was a much happier place without him.

Thomas had been called away to Dover castle, about a day's journey, to supervise the construction of towers on the castle walls. He had come to see Eleanor the morning of his departure.

"Eleanor, I don't know how long I'll be gone, but I'll do my best to get back to ye soon." They stood outside the kitchen doors, their usual meeting place. "Be wary, keep yer eyes open at all times. Don't go anywhere alone. Agnes will be lookin' after ye, but keep yer wits about ye, and stay safe. I don't know where the King is now, but I'm to meet his aides in Dover for instructions. And whatever ye do, stay away from the magician if he shows up. Please, Eleanor, don't be takin' off with him any time soon."

She gave her promise. "Thomas, you know how fond I am of you. I won't disappear without letting you know. I promise you."

"How *do* ye feel about me, Eleanor?" His eyes crinkled at the corners as he put her on the spot.

She looked down, a little embarrassed. What could she say to him? In her heart, she knew she loved him—in her way—in the only way possible given the trauma and upheaval of her life in this time. Love seemed an impossibility in this unreal reality she was living through, but it was slowly happening to her. She wanted to be with him, and she thought about him endlessly. She pictured him standing above her with his wry smile, his gentle kiss, his firm kiss, his strong arms wrapped around her waist. His kindness, gentleness, protectiveness. He totally and utterly accepted her for who she was, strange as she was to everyone else in this time. She used to think about Patrick that way, but poor Patrick had been out of her mind for months, or lingered there only around the edges as a dim reminder of what didn't exist anymore.

"I'm fond of you, Thomas, you know that." She was still looking down.

"Only fond? Is that all, Eleanor?" He spoke with a mischievous tone, but there was no mistaking the seriousness beneath his words.

She looked up at him. "I … I like you very much. Alright, maybe I do love you a little bit, Thomas, but only sometimes," she added. "Is that what you want me to say?"

He laughed and grabbed her, lifting her in the air and whirling her around. "Yes, yes, that's exactly what I want you to say! That'll do for now, my sweet, beautiful Eleanor!"

She laughed, too. "Put me down, put me down, you fool! Go on, then. Go build your silly castle." He grabbed her roughly, kissed her thoroughly, and went on his way with a wave and a smile on his face.

<hr>

Several days later, the King returned and held a huge feast in the banquet hall. It was attended by several hundred lords, ladies, and courtiers, including many ill-tempered barons. Eleanor and Sabine, along with a few other maids, stood half-hidden inside the doorways and assisted the servers. They carried food up from the kitchen and handed it off to the servers, who in turn handed them the half-eaten food from the previous courses to take away. It worked something like a bucket brigade.

Every kind of meat imaginable was served—hare, stag, chicken, heron, wild boar, pigeon, and too many fish to identify. Some of them were baked into gigantic pies covered in egg yolk and jelly. Sugar plums dusted with gold, pies delicately painted with silver flakes, it was a stunning spectacle. And the wine and ale flowed freely.

Eleanor was pleased to see Isabella sitting beside the King. She had been churched and was deemed ready to resume her royal life again. She was the most beautiful woman Eleanor had ever seen, young and slim once again, with pale, translucent skin and pink lips. She wore a green-velvet gown; a dainty gold crown rested on her head and glittered with tiny jewels. Queen Isabella looked magnificent, like a fairytale Queen, but there was always a look beneath her smile that hinted of sadness.

Eleanor observed King John carefully. He became absorbed in conversation with one of his barons and banged on the table angrily. The conversation in the hall quieted and all eyes turned to the King. He backed away from the baron and slapped the back of another man, shaking off his anger and charming his way through a new conversation.

What is in your heart? Eleanor pondered this question. I see the exterior man, a stout, angry ruler who has lost half his kingdom to the French—land held by England since the Norman invasion nearly a century and a half before—a man who seems to care little for the loss or the consequences for his people. But are you really the evil ruler that historians have imprinted on the pages of history? Do you ever have remorse for your actions? Is there a conscience in there?

She shook off her thoughts. Her vague memory of John's fate was that he comes to a bad end. But how or when, she could not recall. Her eye caught the tall figure of William the Marshal, sitting in the far corner of the banquet hall. Beside him was a beautiful, dark-haired woman. His wife, no doubt, the Countess of Pembroke.

"Look sharp, lassie, and stop yer dreamin'," said one of the servers, handing her an armful of platters and dishes that needed to be carried below. Sabine and another maid carried them to the kitchen, while

Eleanor remained at the edge of the hall watching with fascination.

"Look," Sabine whispered to Eleanor when she returned, pointing to the man with whom John had argued minutes before. "It's Baron Robert Fitzwalter. I'm surprised he's showin' his face here after what the King did to his daughter."

"What?" asked Eleanor with some trepidation.

"Oh, it's a terrible tale," she began excitedly, once again preparing to horrify Eleanor with a tale of the King's wickedness. "Sir Fitzwalter's daughter, Matilda, was a beauty. And ye know how the King likes beautiful young ladies. Well, the King made advances, and she rejected him flat out, she did. I heard she slapped his face, which of course was not what ye do to the King of England, especially this king, who's got too much pride and anger for his own good. He was furious with her. He locked her in the tower, he did, and sent her messages. He said all she had to do to free herself was give in to his desires. She held firm, because Matilda was a good and pure young miss, raised in a noble house. But it was her undoin'. Soon the King tired of waitin' for her to give him what he wanted. He sent her an egg, a cooked egg, beautiful and good for eatin'. It looked like a gesture of kindness from the King after weeks of bein' held hostage. But it weren't kind at all. The beautiful lady Matilda ate the lovely egg, clasped her breast, and died. Yes, Miss Eleanor, he poisoned her. Then he sends her poor dead corpse home for burial. Or so the story goes. Poisonin' is one of the King's specialties, it is."

Eleanor was aghast. Could this story of the King's savagery be true? "How can the baron show his face here?" she asked Sabine.

"The King denied he had any involvement, of course. He told Fitzwalter he'd put Matilda in the tower to protect her, since Fitzwalter hisself was bein' held hostage in France at the time. But it's said ..." she drew closer to Eleanor and whispered, "it's said that it was King John who persuaded the King of France to capture Fitzwalter and put him in jail over no charges whatsoever. It was purely for the ransom. King John then pays the baron's ransom as compensation for poisonin' his daughter. So now, Fitzwalter is said to be formin' a revolt against the King with the other barons. Which is why I'm surprised to see him here; it may be dangerous for him. Oh, yes indeed, Miss Eleanor, our King's a devil, he is. Pardon my sayin' it." Sabine crossed herself.

Eleanor stored this information away, wondering if it could be true.

She glanced at the King. He was smiling and boisterous, holding tight the Queen's hand while he laughed and chatted with his lords and ladies. He gave the command for the dancing to begin. Tables were pulled away, and a group of musicians began to play. The King and Queen danced with the others, holding hands while they gaily sang and twirled in circles. The Queen, elegant and diaphanous in her stunning gown, moved with grace, while the King, squat and clumsy, danced with joyful abandon around his beautiful Queen.

As the banquet was winding down and people were beginning to disperse, she noticed the King conferring with some of his guards at the far end of the banquet hall. At the other end she saw Sir Fitzwalter form his own cadre of barons and prepare to leave. Was something about to happen?

It happened moments later, outside at the gate to the castle. Eleanor and the other maids heard the commotion and rushed to one of the upper balconies to watch the skirmish. The King's men were drawing the large iron-and-wood gate shut as Fitzwalter and his men were attempting to leave. Several of the men made it through the gate and quickly grabbed longbows hidden outside. They shot two of the King's men who were closing the heavy gates, while above them the King's guards fired down on them.

Eleanor recoiled with a jolt when she saw the two men pierced with arrows. She spotted a tall man swinging a sword high above his head. It was Sir William the Marshal. He battled magnificently, but Fitzwalter and most of his men made it through the gate. At least one of Fitzwalter's men was hit with an arrow from a tower above. Fitzwalter and his remaining men leaped onto their waiting horses and rode off, with the King's men, and William the Marshal, in hot pursuit.

As Eleanor watched the drama unfold, she thought of the old movies she loved to watch about battling knights and castle sieges. The reality was quite different. The sword battle at the gate went on for at least fifteen minutes. Two castle guards and one of Fitzwalter's men were killed. The sword thrusts and arrows finding their marks were grotesque. The victims writhed in pain on the ground, leaking blood as their lives drained away. She could barely make herself watch, but she desperately wanted to know what was going to happen. Several of the men still alive on the ground were killed with quick thrusts of a sword into their chests. Eleanor winced and felt her stomach turn. She had no idea what would happen with the men being pursued, but she understood one thing: The baron's war had begun.

Chapter Fifteen

The castle was a hotbed of danger and intrigue.

Later that night, as the maids were finishing up their work cleaning the banquet hall, Eleanor overheard several barons speaking in low tones. The King had scurried out of the hall at the first sign of violence, and now he was locked away with his advisers.

"Did you see the King run away at the first sign of trouble?" said one of the barons.

"I've never seen him move so fast!" said another.

These were the loyal barons?

They snickered. One of them tittered, "They don't call him John Softsword for nothing." Their whispers became too faint overhear.

The violent scene at the entrance to the castle had so disturbed Eleanor that she slept fitfully. She dreamed she was fighting alongside William the Marshal. There she was, wielding a weighty sword with ease, parrying blows from numerous attackers. She and Sir William fought and fought but could not make any headway. The men came out of the darkness, faceless and fearsome, attacking with brutal force. She and the Marshal struck them down, but more kept coming, a steady, never-ending stream.

She turned her back for a moment to glance at Sir William, and a sword was thrust into her side. She felt nothing. No pain. She fell to the ground on her back and watched as her attacker pulled the blade out and wiped her blood off on his tunic. And still she felt nothing. Blood oozed from her wound and she cried. Everything went dim and she thought, *I'm dying.* She heard a buzzing noise, the same noise she'd heard months ago when she'd woken up on the battlefield at Bouvines. And when she opened her eyes, she was there again, in Bouvines, lying next to the same dying man she'd first seen on the battlefield. He moaned and cupped his hands over his wound, as he'd done before, the large gash in his side leaking blood. But now she was lying next to him with the same wound, bleeding, dying, on the Bouvines battlefield.

In the distance she heard a pounding beat, hoofbeats, and William the Marshal, clad in his battle armor, rode up to her. He had been fighting beside her a moment ago. Now he looked down at her bleeding body, and she looked up at him unable to speak, confused, pleading for help with her eyes.

"Missy," he said. "Get yerself up. Time to get up."

"I can't," she finally moaned. "I'm hurt. Look at me."

"Get up, ye daft girl," he commanded. "Yer havin' a dream. I need to speak with ye."

Eleanor opened her eyes and saw the face of Sir William, leaning down and shaking her by the shoulders. She had been sleeping in her cramped room with several other maids. It was still dark outside. The other maids huddled under their blankets, peeping over the tops, watching the Marshal shake her awake.

"What's wrong?" Eleanor asked.

"Get up and come with me. I need a word with ye." She wrapped a shawl around her nightclothes and walked outside the maids' room into an alcove with the Marshal. Alfred, as usual, hovered nearby. "I'm leavin' with the King soon," began the Marshal. "As you witnessed last night, there is trouble in the realm, and we're formin' an army to quell the barons' revolt."

"What happened last night after you chased Fitzwalter and his men?" she asked.

"We caught up with several of them and dispatched them. But Fitzwalter himself got away. He's formin' an army, too, and there's talk that the French may attack. We must prepare."

He frowned, a worried look creasing his face. The Marshall had been a faithful servant of every king he had served, beginning as a young knight under King Henry II, John's father. Eleanor could see that his loyalty to King John was being tested, but he did not waver. John was the most hated King in England's short history, with a record of cruelty and abuse of his people that was unequalled. But Sir William, once promised, never went back on his oath of fealty. She wondered why he was telling her all this.

"Lassie, I want to make sure ye're cared for," he said. "I know ye want to get back with the Adelfrids, but it's not safe right now to travel through the countryside. I ask ye to stay here until things quiet. Where's Thomas?"

"He left several days ago for Dover. He's working on the castle there."

"I'll get word to him to get back as soon as he can to look after ye."

"Won't the King be angry if you take him away from his work?"

"I have my ways and my methods," said Sir William with a confident grin. "So never ye mind. The King is too preoccupied anyway to care about the blasted castle at Dover, at least not now."

<hr>

She waited a week, but still Thomas had not returned. She checked on the Queen and her baby one morning. At Agnes' command, Sabine accompanied her and waited outside the Queen's apartment. Eleanor curtsied and approached Isabella, who was, as usual, in the company of several ladies. Her long blonde hair was not yet hidden beneath her veil, and it hung down her back in a cascade of shimmering gold.

She had adorned herself with some of her jewelry, including a silver circlet on her head decorated with sapphires, a pearl necklace, and a large, ornately decorated ring with a massive ruby in the center. She and her ladies sat at a small table in the adjoining sitting room playing cards. Baby Eleanor was in the Queen's arms, and the wet nurse sat in the corner, waiting for the next feeding.

"How do you feel, My Lady?" asked Eleanor.

"Restless," the Queen responded abruptly, staring at her baby girl and stroking her delicate little face. "I'm anxious to get out of the castle and go somewhere, anywhere, but My Lord the King tells me it's too dangerous. I expect him back any time now. We'll have word soon on what's happening with the barons."

Eleanor panicked when she heard that King John may be coming back soon, but she checked herself. "Where would you go, My Lady?" Eleanor gently took the baby from her, laid her on the bed and examined little Eleanor. She had no modern instruments to use, so she relied on her intuition. The baby was gaining weight, her color was rosy, her breathing was clear, and her beautiful rosebud mouth gurgled and cooed as she looked at her namesake with bright shining eyes.

"We usually go on procession at this time of year," the Queen said. "The household moves south to Dover. Most years we have more dances, more plays, more feasts. But the King wants us all to remain here at Windsor while he deals with the rebellious barons."

"Perhaps, if you're up to it, you could go for a ride on the grounds close to the castle," suggested Eleanor. "As long as you have no pain, it's perfectly safe and may be good for your spirits."

"It's chilly outside," said the Queen petulantly, gazing out the window. Then she brightened. "Let's do it. Let's go for a ride. You come with me and my ladies."

Eleanor was taken aback. "Me? But My Lady, I'm only a maid."

"Oh pish," the Queen blurted. "I notice you're acquainted with the Marshal of England. So that makes you more than a maid, and you're more than a midwife. There's most certainly more to you, Eleanor," she added, appraising Eleanor like a chess player surveying the board. "We'll go this afternoon."

She turned her back on Eleanor as a sign of dismissal, and Eleanor curtsied and left the Queen's quarters. When the door was closed behind her, she glanced around but did not see Sabine. Panic gripped her. The castle was quiet.

"Sabine," she whispered. "Sabine, are you there?"

Eleanor slowly made her way back downstairs to the kitchen when she heard a muffled noise in an alcove to her left. It was the same alcove the King had dragged her into weeks ago when he'd assaulted her. As she slowly, with trepidation, approached the darkened space, she heard heavy breathing and muffled grunts. She knew it was the King, returned home as the Queen had predicted, and he had a woman pinned against the wall the same way he had pinned Eleanor. She squinted into the darkness and realized in horror that it was Sabine. King John had his entire body pushed up against the maid, with one hand over her mouth and his other hand groping her body. The King whispered to Sabine in honeyed tones as she tried to squirm away, but he had her against the hard stone wall.

Eleanor backed away, but Sabine managed to wrench her face away from the King's hand, and she turned toward Eleanor, her eyes wide with terror. *Help me!* Sabine mouthed. King John grabbed her by her hair roughly, and Sabine shrieked. The King looked over at Eleanor, and a slow, wicked smile spread across his face.

"Please, My Lord, no!" Sabine begged, her mouth free. "I'm a maiden, I beg of ye, please let me go." Roughly, he pushed Sabine away, the entire time keeping his eyes on Eleanor. Eleanor reached out to Sabine and grabbed her hand as the hysterical maid stumbled toward her and flung both her arms around Eleanor's neck. They fled, leaving the King in an angry, heaving state.

That's enough. I won't take any more of this. I have to escape. Thomas is not here, and there is no one here who can protect me from this madman. I must protect myself. I must get away. I must get away. And as she and Agnes comforted Sabine and soothed her tears, Eleanor began to hatch a plan.

Chapter Sixteen

A t the stables, Eleanor mounted a small, smooth-riding horse that she hoped would know what to do. She had a plan—to get away from the castle and the King—and she hoped this horse would become her accomplice.

She was still a timid rider but was becoming more comfortable since horses were one of the few modes of transportation. Queen Isabella mounted her horse with practiced ease. She was dressed in a long black-velvet gown covered by a long coat. A fur wrap was attached around her shoulders, and she wore a high hat with a feather. She wore red-leather boots that laced to her ankles.

They trotted around the grounds for about thirty minutes, the ladies chatting and gossiping with their Queen. "And what does Hugh say?" teased one of the ladies to Isabella.

"Quiet!" snapped Isabella. "I know nothing of him. He's in the past. Though his son seems a fine prospect for little Joan. My Lord the King may arrange this once the hostilities have ceased."

They began to ride more briskly, and Eleanor found herself enjoying the ride. Several guards accompanied the ladies, but they were paying no attention to Eleanor, and instead rode close to the other women, flirting and joking with them.

They had wandered into the royal forest that surrounded the castle grounds. Presently, they came to a small opening in the woods with a stream along the edge, and they dismounted to allow the horses to drink. Again, Eleanor stayed behind, but the Queen called to her. She had a lovely flush on her face, and Eleanor could tell she was enjoying herself.

"Eleanor, what a wonderful idea this was." she said. "I feel alive again. I do love riding, and I feel a vigor from the exertion."

"I'm glad, My Lady. Exercise is good for you."

"Exer ... what was that word?"

"I mean, exertion, My Lady. It can be good for you, especially after a birth. It helps you get back to your old self."

"Forget what you overheard earlier," the Queen said, changing the subject abruptly.

"My Lady?"

"About Hugh."

"I know of no one named Hugh."

"I was betrothed to him when My Lord the King requested my hand. It was many years ago."

"Oh," said Eleanor. "I did not know."

"The Pope gave me a dispensation to dissolve the betrothal, then I was free to marry the King. But that was a long time ago. Hugh de Lusignan married someone else after I came to England, his wife died, and now he has a son who is the right age for my little Joan. That's all we were discussing."

"Yes, My Lady."

Isabella looked at Eleanor and held her gaze. "Do you have a young man, Eleanor?"

Eleanor hesitated. She instantly thought of Thomas, but then the sweet face of Patrick, who had been her fiancé only months ago, took shape in her mind. "I ... yes, I do. We've barely met, but we like each other's company." She was thinking, of course, of Thomas.

"Who is he?" she probed.

"He's Thomas Adelfrid, the mason."

The Queen's eyes widened. "Ah, yes, young Thomas. I know who you speak of. He's a handsome one, isn't he? And strong. And good with his hands."

Eleanor blushed and lowered her eyes. Eleanor said, "He's kind."

Isabella smiled at Eleanor. "That's so important, kindness. I'm glad for you, Eleanor. I should tell you that the King wants another child right away, another male heir, so there's a chance I may be with child soon and needing your help." Her voice had taken on a hard edge.

Eleanor's heart sank. She had hoped she would be going home

soon to the Adelfrids. Her escape plan became more urgent. After they had watered the horses, they mounted and prepared to head back to the castle. They were on the edge of the royal forest, but the guards were urging the ladies not to go any further. Eleanor glanced around and patted the satchel that was tied around her waist, beneath several layers of clothing. It contained food she hoped would sustain her on her trip back to Graston and the Adelfrids. She had to get away, she kept telling herself. She couldn't bear to stay in the castle where King John could prey on her and the other maids whenever he desired.

She thought of Sabine, and she felt a pang of guilt at the thought of leaving her to the predations of the King. But she had to escape.

Thomas, where are you? I need your help! As the party proceeded away from the dense woods, she slowed and widened the distance between herself and the other ladies and guards. After a few minutes, when she saw they weren't looking back, she knew this was the moment. Now or never. It would be now.

She galloped into the woods, and within minutes she had vanished in the dense forest.

Chapter Seventeen

The only thought in Eleanor's mind was to escape the King. He's a monster. And if Thomas isn't around to protect me, I must get away. Forget about my promise to the Marshal that I would stay at the castle. I have to escape. But this time, she was escaping to the Adelfrids; she had no plans to try to get back to France.

She estimated it would take about eight hours on horseback to get to the Adelfrids, traveling directly east from Windsor. Since the sun would be setting in a few hours, she knew she would be spending the night in the woods. It reminded her of her ill-fated attempt to escape after William the Marshal rescued her from the battlefield. That horrifying event was seared into her memory. In her mind, she could still see Archie's head flying through the air and landing with a thud on the ground, the dead man's eyes wide open, as if he was shocked that he had just lost his body, rolling a few times and settling in the dirt as blood seeped out. Did his lips move, only for a second? It was ghastly, but she would rather face ruffians and rapists in the woods than King John in the castle.

She met no one at all as she rode through the woods, trotting briskly and sometimes galloping when the terrain allowed. I'm heading home, to the Adelfrids, my adopted family, where I first met Thomas. The thought of him made her angry. Where was he? He promised to protect me, and he's let me down.

She rode away from the sun as it was setting. She could barely make out her surroundings, so she moved further into the thick woods and found a spot to rest. She tied up her horse, gave him some of her food, and huddled against a tree. It was bitterly cold, but she had layered her clothing and tucked in extra hose and a wool scarf to wrap around her head.

She shivered. Wrapping her scarf around more tightly she began to make out the sound of voices deeper in the woods. They were men's voices, laughing and chatting among themselves. Thieves, rapists, and criminals, most likely. She remembered Archie, his severed head flying through the air. I must not let them find me. She got up and untied her horse and slowly led it away from the noise.

Suddenly she heard branches snapping around her, and out of nowhere several men emerged holding swords above their heads. She froze and put her hands up in a modern gesture of surrender that only made sense if you were being held up at gunpoint. But she didn't know what else to do.

"Stop, please," she begged. "Don't harm me, please."

She appraised the men and decided they were not rapists and criminals but looked like soldiers. A large white charger emerged from the woods with Sir William sitting atop, sword in hand. He took one look at Eleanor and cursed at her.

"By God's bones, woman!" he began. "Ye dull-headed ornery fool. Ye liver-eatin' fopdoodle. Ye promised me yesterday that ye'd not leave the castle, that ye'd stay put for the sake of yer safety, and here ye are, stuck in the woods on a freezin' night, with nothin' but this piddlin' palfrey …" He was yelling at her as he dismounted.

Fopdoodle? Eleanor sank to her knees, tears stinging her eyes. When, when would she ever be safe? When would life here, *now*, offer less anxiety, less backbreaking work, less danger, less uncertainty?

"Stop yer blubberin', ye daft woman. Don't ye know ye've been rescued? Yer safe with me, but ye took another risk that could've ended in yer harm. Stop yer cryin' and stand up." His angry tone softened slightly.

She stood as he dismounted. "Sir Marshal," she began. "May I speak with you alone, please sir. I can explain." She wiped her tears and nose.

He walked her roughly into the woods, pulling her by her arm, then turning her around to face him abruptly. "Well lass? What could ye possibly say to soothe my temper? I'm feelin' mighty angry right now, so ye better conjure a good tale."

Eleanor was taken aback. She had no intention of conjuring

anything. He needed to know how intolerable her situation was. So, she told him everything, leaving out no detail, even the foul breath that issued from the King's mouth as he made lewd utterances and threats of violence, spittle always clinging to the edges of his beard, his rough, groping hands, like an animal, pushing, clawing, hurting her, grinding his lust into her skirts, his smirking stare when he encountered her in the Queen's chambers, and finally his promise that he would get her alone again. And then she told the Marshal about his attack on Sabine.

"It's no conjured up tale, sir," she said. "Please believe me; every word is true."

Sir William released his grip on Eleanor's arm. He looked alarmed, but not completely surprised. His mouth tensed, and he began to grind his teeth.

"Damn the brute!" he finally said. "He's been a monster since childhood, that one has!" The Marshal was looking off into the distance, as if remembering something. "He used to pull the wings and legs off insects, his nanny told us. Then he'd kill and dismember little animals to see how they worked inside, was his excuse, but he liked the killin'. When he was old enough to bed a woman, he bedded every woman he could, put babies in 'em, and left 'em. And he's been known to force hisself on women before, I'm sorry to say."

The Marshal shook off his thoughts and turned to Eleanor. "Take no heed of what I'm sayin', missy. I shouldn't talk against the King; it's not right."

"Sir William, I would not speak to anyone of it. Haven't I already spoken ill of him? But what am I to do? He's after all the young maids in the castle, not only me, and who knows where else, but he'll soon manage to get me alone, and I'm terrified that he'll succeed in …"

"Where's young Thomas?" the Marshall demanded, a little angry. "He should be lookin' after ye."

"He was supposed to return from Dover Castle but hasn't yet. Even if he's with me at Windsor, he can't follow me every minute in the castle. He's got his own work to do. Can't you help me get back to the Adelfrids? I feel safe there, outside of the King's grasp. Sir Marshal, I wasn't running away to France, I was running back to the Adelfrids."

"Let me think on it, girl," he answered. "I may have to speak with the King hisself about his behavior. It will be an unpleasant talk, but I may need to do it."

"Won't that make him even angrier? He might take it out on me." Then she had an idea. "I know … why not ask Archbishop Langton to speak with the King? The King may be more afraid to cross the Archbishop, knowing the consequences."

Sir William looked at her with some admiration. "That's a fine idea, lass. Let me think on it. In the meantime, we need to get ye back to the castle. Only the King or Queen can release ye, but the King has the final word. It will take time to get word to Langton, but it's a good idea, Eleanor."

She thrilled to hear this magnificent man, the famed Sir William the Marshal of England, the greatest knight of all time, call her by her first name instead of "girl" or "missy," or worse, a "dull-headed ornery fool" and "liver-eatin' fopdoodle."

"We'll take ye back to Windsor with us and tell the Queen that yer horse got turned around, and ye got yerself lost in the woods. As long as ye're back soon, ye'll not be punished for tryin' to escape. Do ye understand?"

She nodded.

"Be aware, Eleanor, that runnin' away from yer duties at the castle, without bein' properly dismissed, is grounds for … well, it would be a serious offense. Do ye understand? Good." To his trusty squire Alfred, he called, "To Windsor, man. Tell the others we'll be back by nightfall."

As they approached the castle, the sun was beginning to dawn. Suddenly Alfred, who had ridden ahead, yelled back to Sir William that strangers were approaching.

"'Twas wrong, Sir William. No strangers they, 'tis young Thomas and his aide."

Eleanor perked up. Thomas was finally back! But she decided to play it cool. She was annoyed that he hadn't come back sooner, that she had to make a dash for freedom by herself. She noticed Sir William staring at her from the corner of his eye with an assessing look.

"Go if ye want," he said. "Go see Thomas."

"No sir," she replied. "I'll wait till he comes here to meet us."

The Marshal smiled tolerantly.

Thomas, off in the distance, recognized Eleanor and galloped toward her.

Her heart jack-hammered in her chest with each pounding of the hoofs, and without realizing it, she had slid off her horse as Thomas leaped from his, and they ran toward each other.

"Eleanor, my darlin'," he began, sweeping her up in his arms. "I was mad with worry when I heard ye'd gone missin'. Oh, my sweet Eleanor, it's glad I am that ye're found. Are ye hurt? Did ye suffer any calamity? My dearest Eleanor, please don't ever worry me like that again. I cannot bear it."

Eleanor clung to him and sobbed against his neck.

"It's glad I am that ye waited so patiently for the lad to come to ye, Eleanor." It was the sarcastic voice of Sir William, who smirked at the pair as they embraced.

"Thomas, Thomas, I'm alright. I got separated from the Queen and her ladies; then I got lost in the woods and it became dark. The Marshal and his men were nearby and found me, thank God."

"Sir William," Thomas said, turning toward the Marshal, who had dismounted. Thomas sank to his knees as a sign of respect and fealty. "I thank ye exceedingly and sincerely for rescuing Miss Eleanor. I am indebted to ye, Sir William."

"Rise up," said William. "'Twas nothing, but this lass must be more careful. She could have been harmed alone in the woods. Ye will be more careful, eh lassie?"

"Yes," said Eleanor. "I promise." She exchanged a sober look with the Marshal.

"Be sure ye keep yer promise, missy."

"Yes, Sir William. I will. I promise." And she meant it this time. In her teeming mind, Eleanor knew she had to figure out a way to protect herself if she was going to stay at the castle indefinitely. She would not continue to live in fear of the tyrant King.

Perhaps he should begin to fear her.

Chapter Eighteen

"**W**hat kept you so long, Thomas?"

Eleanor and Thomas were sitting in the kitchen later that day after Eleanor had presented herself to Queen Isabella. Earlier, the Queen had been frantic when she noticed Eleanor's disappearance but was relieved to learn she had been found unharmed.

"Eleanor, I was greatly distressed when I looked around and did not see you," the Queen said earlier in the day when Eleanor checked on her. "What in heaven's name happened to you? How did you get lost in the woods?"

Isabella, as usual, was dazzling in a velvet gown with jewels sparkling from her neck and fingers.

Eleanor had her answer planned. "My Lady, I dallied too long by the stream. I thought I would cut through the woods to catch up. I got turned around, and soon darkness came. I decided to stop wandering, and I sat on the ground to wait for morning."

"You must never do that again," chided the Queen. She had completely bought Eleanor's story. "The woods are not safe at night for a young woman alone, even the royal forest." She leaned closer to Eleanor. "There are villains everywhere."

Eleanor looked at her wide-eyed. The only true villain here in the castle is her husband. The King of England, John Plantagenet. Also known as John Lackland, and more often these days, John Softsword.

A few hours later, Eleanor sat in the kitchen eating some lunch. Agnes was distraught and was tending to her like a mother hen. "Eleanor, child, we were beside ourselves, we were," Agnes lamented, handing her a trencher of rabbit stew and a mug of ale. As Agnes fussed over her, Thomas patted her arm soothingly.

"I'm fine," Eleanor said between mouthfuls. "Please don't fret, no harm came to me, and I learned my lesson about wandering off in the woods. I'm glad to be back." She hoped she was convincing. She thought it unwise to tell anyone, even Thomas, that she had tried to escape.

Sabine sat by her side and stared at her, goggle-eyed and speechless. "I'd have been beside myself with terror," she said to Eleanor. "Yer mighty brave, bein' alone in the woods like that."

Eleanor said, "How are you, Sabine? Has anything … is everything alright?"

"Yes, Eleanor," Sabine answered. "Everything is fine. Agnes goes with me everywhere now. I won't give him another chance, I won't."

"Say, what's that?" exclaimed Thomas. "What is she talkin' about? What happened, Sabine?"

Eleanor broke in. "What kept you so long, Thomas?"

"Gad!" he exclaimed. "There was much more work to do at Dover than I thought. The King was there for a few days with his soldiers, and he wanted me to get work completed on the towers before I left. I still haven't finished all the work, but I got them faced with stone well enough. I wanted to get back to ye, Eleanor, because I promised ye I'd protect ye."

Eleanor's heart melted, and she smiled at him. And as though no one else existed in the bustling kitchen, he leaned over and kissed her gently on the cheek, took her hand and kissed it, too.

"The King assaulted me!" Sabine exclaimed, breaking into the tender moment.

"What?" Thomas leaped to his feet. "What did he do? Did he … did he …?"

"She's alright, Thomas," said Eleanor. "Now sit down and lower your voice." She told him what happened. "I got her away and took her straight to Agnes."

Thomas was standing up. His jaw clenched, and his fists became tight balls.

"Thomas," said Eleanor, "there's nothing you can do, so calm yourself."

"Yes, lad," piped in Agnes. "Calm yerself, or ye'll get into some mischief. Listen to Miss Eleanor."

He took a deep breath and sat.

"We can't do anything to prevent the urges of the King," said Eleanor, "but if you could stop in more often it would make us feel safer. And I've asked the Marshal to speak with the archbishop about the King's assaults on the maids of the castle. Who knows who else he's been attacking."

"Ye've done what?"

"The Marshal liked the idea," she continued. "Who else can we go to?"

Thomas stroked his beard, deep in thought. "Eleanor, it's a good idea," he finally said. "And I promise ye, I'll stop in as often as I can. If I could, I'd live right here in this part of the castle with ye." He turned to Agnes, Sabine, and the other maids. "Ye must continue to look out for one another. Ye must stay together. Use any wiles ye have to prevent the King from havin' his way with ye, from even touchin' ye. It's not proper, even if he is the King!"

—❖—

A few weeks later, with the winter wind blowing in great gusts outside the castle and the fires blazing inside, Archbishop Stephen Langton and a large entourage, including Sir William the Marshal, rode up to the castle and requested a meeting with King John. He could not refuse an audience with Langton, although he was clearly not happy at the surprise visit.

Eleanor and several of the maids hovered in the hallway outside the meeting room. The King had not harassed them in recent weeks, mostly because he was rarely at Windsor. But Eleanor learned that several other maids, as well as the wives of some noblemen, had also been accosted by the King. Eleanor was by no means special in that department; King John had an eye for nearly every young woman whose path he crossed. The King and his advisers had entered the private room before the archbishop, the King swearing and uttering curses against Langton for all to hear.

"This papist best not poke his long nose into affairs of the realm today, for I've given all I can. I bowed to the rascal once, and by God's teeth, I will not grovel to him again. Never!" He banged his fist, or something that sounded hard, on the table as he shouted. "This heavy-handed propagandist of Rome reminds me of the words of my father when Thomas Becket strove to usurp his crown, 'Who will rid me of this troublesome priest,' my father said. Well, who will rid me of this troublesome archbishop?"

There were gasps in the room. Those words were infamous, words that had rocked the Middle Ages, this age she was now living in. King John's father, Henry II, spoke them more than forty years earlier, prompting four of his knights to savagely murder Archbishop Becket at Canterbury Cathedral. King Henry was blamed for uttering the proclamation that spurred his knights on to murder, and the cathedral became a shrine almost immediately to the memory of Becket.

"Majesty," said one adviser, "I pray you use caution in your words. No one must construe your words as a call to violence against Archbishop Langton."

"Of course not!" protested John. "I mean no violence toward Langton. I exhort every man in this room that I mean no violence to the Archbishop. I wish only he would not pester me with inconsequential church matters when I've so much on my mind."

"We don't know why he's requesting an audience, Majesty, and we must not make rash statements," said another adviser.

Before the King could respond, the Archbishop, with Sir William and the other men, approached the meeting room and were ushered in. Sir William, who saw Eleanor peeping around a corner, gave her a wink. The maids walked around the outside of the meeting room and stood in another hallway where they could hear nearly every word with their ears pressed to the wooden walls.

"God grant you peace and prosperity," said the Archbishop to the King. Eleanor imagined he held out his hand for the King to kiss his ring. That will make the King even more furious, she thought. "I pray the Queen, the young prince, and your other children are well."

King John grunted. "Sit down, sit down."

They heard drinks being served around the table, and the Archbishop began to speak. "No thank you," he began, probably waving away an offered glass. "Your Highness, let's begin with the 20,000 pounds the realm …" he paused, seeming to choose his words carefully, "appropriated from the revenues of sees and abbeys during the interdict. This money was supposed to be returned upon the lifting of the interdict."

"Yes?" said the King.

"We've received only 3,000 of that back," Langton said. "You agreed that the monks would be recompensed. They're struggling to meet necessities right now because they have no funds. They can't help those in need, their pantries are bare, their hospitals have no provisions, their orphanages have more children than they can feed, their homes for the aged are bereft of supplies. And travelers, when they cannot find a room elsewhere, are sadly turned away from the monasteries for lack of food, heat, and adequate shelter. The monks are not even able to keep themselves in food and clothing."

"Wine and women, don't you mean?" responded the King sardonically.

"Your Highness," answered the Archbishop, "I strongly reject your insinuation."

"Everyone knows," continued the King, his voice smooth now, his anger under control, "that the monks long ago developed worldly habits. The little they give back to the poor is not even worth 3,000. Why should the crown reimburse them any more when they don't use the money wisely? They've amassed a fortune for themselves and for Rome, but where is the advantage to England?"

"Remember, Your Highness, England is a vassal of Rome," responded Langton calmly. "You pledged your loyalty and fealty. When Rome is advantaged, as you put it, so, too, are the good people of England."

"You will not tell us how to govern this realm," John said, his voice rising slightly in pitch.

"But we will tell you how to govern the religious life of your people. This is the duty of the Church … Your Majesty."

Langton and the King were silent. Eleanor pictured them staring at each other with simmering dislike.

"So be it!" exploded John. "You shall have another 10,000 by the end of this month."

"You owe the church 17,000," said the Archbishop with quiet authority.

"Ten!"

"Seventeen. But you may pay us 10,000 now, and the remaining seven in three months' time. Sire, I do not revel in having to request payment that is due. My role as archbishop is quite varied, and part of my duty is to ensure payments are received when due. I must also oversee all the operations of the abbeys ..."

"You're doing a poor job of it!" snapped the King.

"I've only now recently returned to England, Majesty, and I assure you we are addressing any improprieties that have been called to our attention. The priests and monks are vital for the villages and wider regions to operate within the Church. They must be funded and protected from pillaging and plundering by ... well, let's just say by some enthusiastic soldiers of the realm during the interdict."

"Your abbeys," the King spat out, "should be earning their own money, not relying on the people to supply it, or the pontiff to send money. They should certainly not rely on me to send it."

"We agree. We are working to ensure more self-sufficiency," Langton said. "But I must remind you that the 20,000 was taken from the abbeys. It is not yours, Sire. It must be returned."

Eleanor recalled reading that Archbishop Langton was the one who divided the books of the Bible into chapters and verses. Was he at work on that now? And it was Langton—*is* Langton, she reminded herself—who orchestrates the writing and signing of the Magna Carta, an event she knew was coming soon. And here she stood, ear pressed to the wall, mere yards from a man whose name would be etched into history, celebrated for his myriad accomplishments and contributions to the Christian faith.

"I'm glad you're so busy, Lord Archbishop," said the King dismissively. "But so am I. Have we finished? Or is there something else you wish to discuss?"

"Yes, there is something else. It has come to my ear that you have dallied with some wives of your nobles. And some of the servants who work here at the castle are fearful of your ... your attentions, shall I say?"

There it was. The gauntlet had been thrown down.

"There have been reports that some of the young women have

felt pressure from you of a carnal nature when meeting you alone in the castle. I say this with all respect, Sire, but with an admonition that you must not compromise the wives of your nobles, nor the young maidens who work for—"

The Archbishop was cut off by King John, who let out a loud yell. "What is this accusation!" he began. "By God's teeth, I never laid a hand on any of the wenches!"

Eleanor, and the other maids with their ears pressed to the wall, leaped back as something hit the wall from the other side. Oh no. Was he going to throw another tantrum? She waited. They all waited, not daring to even breathe, but heard nothing for seconds. Then, in a low growling voice, the King spoke.

"Never … how dare they … so, this is what you think of me? That I would attack a woman against her—"

The Archbishop stood. The maids could hear him push his chair back. "You should not use that language or tone with me, Your Majesty," Langton said in a loud, commanding voice. "What's more, Sir, I hear rumors. I hear rumors of the daughters of nobles, such as the poor young daughter of Baron Fitzwalter, who died in your tower. You are King of this island, but I am archbishop and represent Pope Innocent. And I can assure you that being King of a vassal state does not give you the right to harm or oppress anyone unjustly, whether it be the noble ladies, the noble daughters, or the lowliest of servants in your employ." He let that comment sink in for a moment. "The law of God supersedes the laws of this realm and your own lusts. You are not, I remind you, above the moral law of the universe."

"How dare you!" John erupted. A fist pounded on the table.

"I'm not finished!" thundered Langton in reply. The Archbishop had final lost his temper. "I also remind you of your marriage vows, taken before God. If I hear another report of any noble lady or servant girl coming under any lascivious pressure from you, it will be reported to the Pope, and you will receive the due consequences. Rome does, I regret to say, turn a blind eye to the dalliances of vassal princes, but when you dally with the married noble ladies or young virgin maids, and when one of them dies under mysterious circumstances, that's another thing altogether. I hope I'm clear on this issue, Your Majesty. You may employ or discharge any servant you want for any reason you want. That is your right as King. But you must not impose your wanton desires on them against their will. This is a grievous sin, forbidden by Scripture, and I pray God will help you control your lusts."

Then Langton added, "Your sins will send you to hell, Sire, lest your repent and turn from them."

There was dead silence. It was well known that the King had a dread of going to hell, though he lived the life of a devil deserving of it. The door opened, the maids scattered, and the meeting ended abruptly.

Chapter Nineteen

T homas gave Eleanor a long cape made of fox fur with a hood to keep her warm as she rushed in and out of the castle. He had made it for her himself, he told her with pride. Winter was ravaging Windsor Castle, with fierce winds and snowdrifts so deep they made stepping outside nearly impossible. Eleanor was happy for any moment she had with him, no matter where they were or who was watching.

She thought rarely of Patrick these days, but when she did, it was a pleasant reminiscence of a bygone time. Sometimes she wondered what he was doing. Had he started to date someone else? Did he mourn for her? She didn't miss him anymore, not really, but she still had a deep fondness for him. Patrick was a kind, steady, and gentle man. Similar, she realized, to Thomas, yet two very different men in many ways. Thomas, so impulsive, so shy at times, so bold and daring when needed, quick to anger but quick to cool down. He, too, was kind and gentle by nature. At these times, her thoughts threatened to overwhelm her, so she relished the hard work that kept her daydreaming at bay.

In mid-December, the Queen told Eleanor she was pregnant again. "I believe I'll give birth late next summer," she said.

"How are you feeling, My Lady?"

"I feel well. I usually have no ill effects when I'm with child, until the end, of course. I have asked the King to give you permission to go home for Christmas. The King is greatly diverted by the mutinous behavior of his barons and will not be holding the usual celebrations and merriment this year at Windsor. Therefore, he does not have need for every maid to be at the castle. So, Eleanor, you may go home for a time, and I will send word to you when I need you back."

Eleanor's spirits soared. She was going home, back to the Adelfrids!

Downstairs, Eleanor threw on her fur cloak and ran across the castle grounds to find Thomas. He was working inside to shore up the stone along the south end of the castle.

"Thomas!" she said, panting from her run through the snow. "I have great news. The Queen and the King himself have given me permission to go back home, to your parents. The Queen is with child, so I'll need to come back when she needs me, but for now I'm free to go! Thomas, I'm free! I can go home. We can go home."

He caught her up in his arms and whirled her around. "Eleanor, my dearest, what grand news that is! I can leave at any time, since all work closes for the Christmas feasts and festivals. I've only stayed nearby to keep my eye on ye and to be near ye. Won't Ma be happy to see us both!" He whirled her around again and pecked her on her lips when he finally let her down. "Be ready to leave first thing in the mornin'."

They rode all day and arrived at the Adelfrids as the sun was setting. It was cold riding, and her face burned when they would occasionally urge their horses to gallop, but her new fur cloak kept the rest of her warm. Beja and Richard ran outside as they approached their home, arms wide as they pulled both Thomas and Eleanor down from their horses and engulfed them in big hugs.

"Ye didn't let me know ye were comin'!" exclaimed Beja to Thomas. "I would've prepared my best meal and tidied myself up a bit." She smoothed her loose hair back after finally letting go of Thomas.

"Ma, Pa, it's good to be home," Thomas said. "We didn't know we'd be comin'. The Queen gave Eleanor leave to come home for the holidays, though she'll be returnin' later, now that the Queen is with child again."

"Oh! Another babe," Beja exclaimed.

"Hope it's a boy," Richard added. "Another prince would be welcome."

Inside, Eleanor smelled kindling wood, a burning fireplace, baked bread, stewed meat, sweet cakes, and ale, all rolled into one irresistible odor. It smelled so familiar and friendly that she almost got dizzy taking it all in. It smelled like her family. Sitting at the table, the maid Mary rushed around serving everyone with a big smile on her face. All the children had congregated around Thomas and Eleanor. Lavinia hugged her enthusiastically, almost causing Eleanor to stumble backward. She grabbed a seat next to Eleanor and excitedly peppered her with questions.

"What is the Queen like? I hear she's the most beautiful woman in all the land. What about her gowns? And her jewels? What color is her hair, and her eyes? Does she dance beautifully? Tell me about the other maids at the castle."

"Lavinia!" snapped Beja. "Give her a moment to chew her food and settle in, will ye? We'll all hear about the Queen soon enough."

Eleanor could sense that Beja was as eager to hear the details of her stay as Lavinia. "Well," began Eleanor, washing some meat down with ale, "the Queen is exquisitely lovely. I've never seen hair so beautiful. It's a golden color, and when it's let down, it shines and curls down her back like golden ribbons. Her eyes are bright blue, and when she wears her blue-velvet gown, they sparkle like sapphires. The Queen is a doting mother. This new baby, little Eleanor—"

"They named the baby after you, Eleanor?" said Lavinia with a clap of her hands.

"No, after the king's mother, Eleanor of Aquitaine. But the Queen told me she was happy it was my name, too."

"Oh!" they all said in unison. "What a wonderful tribute from the beautiful Queen," added Beja. "Ye must forgive Lavinia. She's a romantic fool now that she's got herself a sweetheart."

"Oh?" said Eleanor, turning to Lavinia. "Who is this lucky man?"

"Never mind about that," she answered, her face turning red, "It's only Dicun, from the next village over. I've known him forever. Tell me about her gowns!"

They were interrupted by a loud knock at the door. Mary rushed to open it, and a large man stood in the doorway, his clothing rough and unkempt. He wore a look of concern on his face.

"Miss Beja," he began, "I apologize for the interruption, it's so sorry I am to break into yer meal time."

"It's no bother," said Beja, "what's the problem, Jacob? Ye look mighty worried."

"It's my wife, Prissy, she's deliverin' now, but she's strugglin' somethin' fierce. We thought we could do it ourselves, to save the money, ye understand, but she's in terrible pain, and I heard the young miss here had come back." He motioned to Eleanor. "I hoped maybe she could come out and lend a hand, her being a perfessional and all."

"Of course I will," Eleanor responded, standing up quickly.

When the baby was born healthy, Jacob said, "Bless ye, Miss Eleanor." He handed her a loaf of bread and a piece of cloth with eggs wrapped inside.

As they prepared to mount their horses and leave, Beja, who had accompanied Eleanor, along with Lavinia, turned to her and gave her another big hug. "Looks like yer back in the saddle, missy, so to speak."

Eleanor smiled at her warmly. "I'm so glad to be home."

Chapter Twenty

"**S**o, what is this with you two?"

Beja and Richard, who was always the quiet one but had a stern look on his face, sat at the table a few days later with Thomas and Eleanor. The children and Mary had been sent to their rooms, Lavinia reluctantly. "I'm a grown woman," she had protested. "I should know what's going on."

"Off with ye!" ordered Beja.

"Go, girl," said Richard, giving her a kiss on her cheek. "Ye know I'll fill ye in later." And he winked at her.

Thomas and Eleanor looked sheepish and glanced nervously at each other.

"Don't deny it," Beja continued. "I see the looks that pass back and forth. I see the little touches, which I disapprove of heartily, Thomas. And ye, little missy, I hold ye to account. Ye must remain pure at all times, mind ye. No pattycakes, I tell ye. I'll not tolerate it."

Eleanor began to open her mouth to object, but Thomas quickly spoke up.

"We're in love, Ma, Pa. We love each other deeply. I feel abundant love for Miss Eleanor, the dearest and sweetest lass I've ever known. She's smart and helpful, she's hard working and inventive and caring. She's beautiful, too, and I want her to be my wife."

They all looked at Thomas in shock, including a stunned Eleanor. Her jaw dropped and she gazed at Thomas in wonder. Could this really be happening? She'd been in this country, in this time period, six months, and this man wanted to marry her. How could she possibly marry him? She was from another time. She still had a fiancé. She expected to get back to her home, her time, at some point, didn't she? But did she really have a fiancé anymore? She admitted to herself that her feelings for Patrick had dimmed, like the memory of him. She could barely see his face in her mind. He had black hair, dark eyes, he was handsome, she remembered, but the details were fuzzy. Thomas's face, on the other hand, was always vivid in her mind. His large, round eyes gazed at her like she had just floated down from the heavens to stand before him. His thick brows that came together when he was concerned or angry. His wavy brown hair and full beard that scratched when he kissed her. He had a wide mouth and a smile that completely altered the landscape of his rugged face. And when he laughed, he became childlike.

I'll always admire Patrick, but I love Thomas. Do I really believe I'll ever make it back home? The magician. He's the key, but will I ever see him again? And if I do, will I still want him to send me back to the future? There are so many questions and concerns swirling around in my mind, and now Thomas had plopped down another one for me to ponder: marriage.

What would it be like, being married to Thomas? It would be wonderful. He loves me, and I love him. We could live together in our own home. While he works as a stone mason I can help the local women as a midwife, and we can come home to each other at the end of every day. Maybe we can have children.

She was so deep in thought that she didn't notice Thomas, Beja, and Richard all staring at her, waiting for a response.

"I … I … I do have deep feelings for Thomas."

Thomas breathed a sigh of relief and smiled at her. He took her hands in his.

"No pattycakes in this house!" Beja said with a firm voice. He quickly removed his hand from hers.

"Marriage?" continued Eleanor, finding her voice and turning to face Thomas. "We've never talked about that, Thomas. So much of this is new to me, and I've only been here since July. I'll be called back to the castle soon."

"I'll be goin' back, too," he said excitedly. "We can be together at Windsor. We'll find a small cottage, or I'll build us a new one, whatever ye want, Eleanor."

Beja stood. "That's enough talk of marriage right now. Clearly, ye've taken the lass by surprise. And ye've not received our blessin' yet, either. Quiet about it fer now, and maybe we'll discuss it again."

———◆———

Later, Thomas sat alone with Eleanor, holding her forbidden hand. "I'm sorry, Eleanor, I didn't mean to embarrass ye or shock ye with my declaration. It seemed to flow from my heart to my lips and out it came."

How could she be angry with this sweet, heroic man? She adored him. She grabbed his other hand. "Thomas, I'm not angry. I was surprised. We don't know each other well. And you remember what I told you, about being from a different … a different time? You remember the magician? None of that has changed. I really don't belong here, Thomas, although I love you dearly. I don't belong here."

She could tell that her words had wounded him. He looked down at his hands that covered hers. "If ye love me, Eleanor, that's the biggest hurdle we've conquered," he said. "I understand all ye've said about going back to yer time and yer people, and I believe ye, dearest. But ye're here now, and if ye don't get back I ask ye to think about blessin' me with yer hand. I want ye to be certain, though, so I'll not press ye more." He sat up straight and squared his shoulders. She saw something change in him. "But remember, I love ye greater than my own life, Eleanor."

Chapter Twenty-One

After the Christmas celebrations had concluded, the food was all consumed, and the gifts were given, Eleanor began to relax at the Adelfrids and resume a life of some normalcy. The cloud of danger she lived under at the castle seemed to have vanished like morning mist under the rising sun.

As a gift, the Adelfrids had given her a bundle of fabric, dyed a beautiful blue. She knew how rare it was, since most people wore undyed linen or wool clothing. She would stitch this into a beautiful dress.

Lavinia approached her shyly and handed her a gift, wrapped in clean cloth and tied with a string. Inside was a jar filled with pure alcohol, clear as glass. "Goodness, Lavinia! How did you ever get this distilled to such a clear color? This will be such a help during birthing." Eleanor had accepted her new role as the region's premiere midwife, even took pride in it, but every birth made her nervous. She might be the best midwife in medieval England, but she would be considered a bumbling fraud in her own time.

"Ma, Pa and myself worked on it and refined it till it sparkles like water," she said with a big smile.

"It's a perfect gift, Lavinia, thank you!" And she gave Lavinia a hug, which gave the young woman great pleasure.

Lavinia showed Eleanor her gift from her beau, Dicun. It looked like a fur muff. "Look, Eleanor, Dicun made it hisself, from red fox fur, the rare kind. Feel how soft."

"It's beautiful, Lavinia. He must be very sweet on you."

"Oh, yes," she answered, "Very. He wants to marry me, but Ma and Pa won't hear of it, not yet."

"Do you want to marry him?"

"I reckon so; he's a good man." She looked Eleanor straight in the eyes and laughed. "Yes, he's a wonderful man, Eleanor, and so handsome!" They both held hands and laughed together.

———

There were constant rumors of baronial tensions and skirmishes with King John and his army. Eleanor knew the tension would come to a head this new year, 1215, but once again she could not remember when the barons' war with the crown would begin in earnest. And Eleanor had not yet heard from the Queen at the beginning of March. She dreaded being called back to the castle, especially when the nobility was nearing a boiling point.

One reason for the hostility was taxation, causing perpetual public unrest throughout history. King John had levied yet another tax on the barons to fund his army and continuous warring with France, the peace treaty having been broken almost before the ink was dry. Moreover, his vast expansion of the realm's forest holdings left the common man with no lawful ground to hunt, driving many to poaching out of sheer necessity. The punishment for poaching was severe, but only if the poachers, often working in organized rings, were caught. Fines, public confinement in the stocks, imprisonment, and even the severing of hands were common punishments.

In mid-March, just as she was returning from a birth several miles away with Lavinia as her assistant and Richard as an escort, she noticed the white steed of William the Marshal being led into the barn. She raced inside, eager to see Sir William and speak with him about the court news.

"Well missy," he said, turning to her as he sat at the table with a large flask of ale. He was leaning back on his chair and his long legs were stretched out in front of him. "And how are ye farin'? I heard ye'd left Windsor, and I wanted to check on ye, and of course bring ye all the news."

She made a hasty curtsy to the Marshal. "I'm well," she began. "I'm glad to be home with the Adelfrids. I expect I'll be called back soon by the Queen, though. How is she? Have you seen her?"

"She does well, missy. Same lovely Queen as ever. Says little, but ye know there's a lot behind those dancin' blue eyes and those rosy closed lips. Sometimes I get the feelin' she's bidin' her time. For what, I don't know, but she's a deep well, that one is."

"What's the latest with the King?" asked Richard. "We'd heard he marched off with half his army to engage the French."

Sir William accepted a large plate of food and devoured it hungrily. The ever-present squire Alfred, sitting by the fire, was already asking for seconds. "May I have another fig tart, Mary? They're delicious." And he gave her an impertinent wink, which made the maid smile and duck her head in embarrassment.

"There'll be no flirtin' in the kitchen," Beja said firmly. "Mary, we'll let ye know when we need ye." Mary scurried away, but Eleanor knew she would be listening beyond the doorway.

"The big problem facin' the King," said Sir William between bites, "is not the French, not yet, at least, but the barons. They're formin' their own army to force the King to make concessions. I learned the other day that Archbishop Langton met with the barons a fortnight ago and presented to them the coronation charter issued by Henry Beauclerc, son of the Conqueror and the second of our Norman kings. The charter is more than a century old, but it carried the force of law in the realm when it was issued. In that parchment," he continued, leaning forward and peering at each listener intently as he spoke, "Henry Beauclerc promised to rule justly. He gave the Church greater financial freedom, and he allowed the people, mostly the barons, ye understand, to keep their family inheritances, and a lot of other liberalities that benefited all the people of the realm."

He paused for a moment and surveyed his audience. They were all waiting for his next words. "Well then," he continued after a long draught of his ale, "I'm not knowin' if Henry Beauclerc kept many of these promises, but the charter itself was an official proclamation. So, Langton read the entire charter of Henry to the barons, who'd assembled at Canterbury Cathedral, then he outright condemned the King for not adherin' to any of them and for over-taxin' the good people of England, for bein' rumored to have murdered his nephew Arthur with his own hands, though I doubt the King would have the courage to do it hisself.

Beggin' yer pardon for the criticism of His Majesty, but I feel we're all good enough friends I can speak plainly. And with a loud acclamation, the barons agreed that the coronation charter of Henry Beauclerc must be reissued, that the King must be forced to accept it, and that the common folk should be protected from tyranny. And the barons one and all swore an oath and bound themselves to each other to conquer or die defendin' the liberties sworn by Henry Beauclerc, first King Henry of England."

"My goodness!" exclaimed Beja.

Eleanor, more than any of those seated around the table, even the Marshal, knew how momentous the moment was. Soon King John would be forced to sign the Magna Carta, the Great Charter, which would serve as an inspiration for the Declaration of Independence and the U.S. Constitution. But blood would be shed along the way.

"Sounds like war," said Richard, who never minced words.

"Aye," said the Marshal. "And ye know I'll be in the thick of it. I've sworn my oath to the King, and I'll keep it, but it remains to be seen how he'll respond to the barons' uprisin'. I can promise ye this, he won't take it lyin' down."

"We'll be prayin' for ye, Sir William," said Beja, and the entire family nodded. The mood was somber in the room as they sat at the table. Sir William turned to Eleanor and said, "I've got some news for ye, lass, and it's not happy news. I saw Thomas at Windsor, and he asked me to get word to ye, and to break it to ye gently. I'll tell ye straight out, which is the best way, to my thinkin'.

The maid Sabine is dead."

Chapter Twenty-Two

Dead. It's not possible. The peace and happiness she'd known over the last several weeks at the Adelfrids vanished in an instant.

"I heard the tale from Thomas, mind ye, who heard it from the old gal Agnes," said Sir William. "Thomas said that as the young maid was dwindlin' away, approachin' her end, she warned Agnes to check the eggs."

Eleanor gasped. The eggs. The nobleman's daughter in the tower. A poisoned egg. Was it payback for the rebuke the King had received from Archbishop Langton about dallying with the maids? Or, worse still, could it be a message to her that her complaint to the archbishop would not go unpunished. This is my fault. If I hadn't asked the Marshal to have the archbishop speak to the King, Sabine would be alive. Poor Sabine, whose life had barely begun, dying a pitiful death because the vile and spiteful King John couldn't get his way.

"Now, girl, don't let yer imagination run wild," said Sir William. He was eyeing her carefully. "I've got more news for ye, and it's not as ill as what I've just related, but it won't be welcome news." Eleanor looked up at the Marshal and braced herself. "Ye're wanted back at the castle. The Queen still has time before her birthin', but she's feelin' poorly and would like ye to be close by. I'm to escort ye. First thing in the morning, missy."

Eleanor squared her shoulders and nodded her head, resigned to the abrupt change in her circumstances. How many times must her life come crashing in around her? Don't be dramatic, she scolded herself.

You must beat the King at his game. You can't hide from him forever. You have an advantage, Ellie; you know what's going to happen. You know he signs the Magna Carta. He is forced to sign it soon, but I can't recall the circumstances. What happens next? Does life get any better in medieval England when the tyrant John is gone? If I'm destined to live out my remaining days here, it would be nice to remember what happens, but it's all a fog.

In her room, she knelt on the floor by her bed, head bowed, and prayed out loud.

"Lord God," she began, *"in the many months I've been here, in this time, in this place, I've barely uttered Your name or asked You for Your help. I've leaned on my own understanding, or lack of it, to get by, and look where it's gotten me. Pursued by a tyrannical madman bent on harming me and everyone around him. With a young man in love with me, and me with him, but nowhere to take it, no future in sight for us. You hold my future in Your hands, Lord, and I ask You to preserve me, and give me protection over my circumstances. If I'm to wind up in the clutches of King John, please Father, protect my life and give me the wisdom, the right words, and the right frame of mind. Help me, oh Lord, to remember 'thy will be done.' You've placed me here for a reason, so I ask for Your forgiveness that I've complained so often about my life. You've placed me among some good people—the Marshal, the Adelfrids, Thomas, Agnes and the other maids, even the Queen—who have been a shield for me. Help me, oh Lord, in the days ahead to discern right from wrong, to be slow to speak and quick to listen, to curb my temper, to always do what's right in your eyes, even when it feels like I'm walking into danger. Thank you, Lord, for the grace, and love, and generosity you've shown me among these people, my new family. I pray in the name of your Son, Jesus Christ, amen."*

Eleanor rose up with tears in her eyes, ashamed of herself for not trusting God before now and vowing to put herself fully in His hands. And then, unbidden, the Spirit spoke to her in a still small voice and a memory emerged in her mind—and a plan began to form.

Chapter Twenty-Three

At first light, Eleanor reluctantly mounted her palfrey with her small parcel of belongings and began her journey back to Windsor Castle with the Marshal and Alfred, his ever-present righthand man. Joining them along the way was a contingent of twelve more knights, all armed and ready for battle if necessary. As Sir William explained, it was his duty to defend the King, but the barons and the people they represented had a right to be fed up. King John had pushed nearly every last person in England to the breaking point.

It was frigid cold, and even the fur cape Thomas had given her wasn't enough to keep Eleanor comfortably warm as they traveled. As the sun was setting, they arrived at Windsor. The Marshal saw her to the kitchen entrance safely and gave her a final word of advice.

"Don't show fear around the King," he said. "He hates it, and he'll take advantage of it. Ye must show him the respect he's due, but don't cringe or cower around him. Have a word with Agnes and make sure she protects ye and all the young maids whilst ye're movin' about the castle. He must not be allowed to be alone with any of ye, or he'll do his worst."

"Sir William, do you think it would help if I spoke with the Queen about it?"

"No, lass, don't step out of line and even think of it. She's the Queen, remember, proud, beautiful and determined to prosper herself above all. She's got a kind heart toward those she loves, especially her children, but make no mistake, she's not yer friend, nor yer ally. Above all, she loves the power that comes with bein' Queen, so always keep that in mind. That's a woman with deep passions lyin' beneath the surface."

This assessment from the Marshal was discouraging. She had thought the Queen would be more sympathetic to her plight. After all, she had on a few occasions let her guard down and expressed contempt for her husband. But Eleanor took the Marshal's words to heart and was pondering them as she sought out Agnes. The old servant came running toward her as soon as she entered the kitchen, where some maids and castle guards sat around the table eating their late-day meal. In the few months Eleanor had been gone, Agnes appeared older, her stooped frame was thinner, and the hair that poked out from under her cap whiter and more gnarled.

"Eleanor, dear lass!" she exclaimed as she ran as fast as she could hobble across the stone floor to greet her. She flung her arms around Eleanor's neck and instantly began to sob. "Sabine, poor Sabine. I reckon ye've heard. A sweet girl, no guile in her, dead, oh missy, what're we all to do now? It's a time of great sorrow, 'tis. Great sorrow."

Eleanor pulled Agnes into a private corner where they could sit and talk. She wiped away Agnes's tears with the kerchief tied around her neck and patted her hand. "Stop crying, Agnes, please, and tell me what happened. I must know. Don't leave out anything."

Agnes looked up at her with red, raccooned eyes, her nose running. She wiped it on Eleanor's kerchief, and shook her head. "It was most foul, Eleanor dear," she began. "Sabine had become a little lost without ye, seeing as how she loved to gossip more than anything else in life, and without yerself to listen, no one else would give her any mind, havin' heard all her tales before. So, she went about her chores in a slowish way, she did, but she always finished her work well. It's my own fault! I wasn't watchin' her proper!" And Agnes began to blubber all over again.

"No," said Eleanor sternly. "You must not blame yourself, Agnes; you only did her good. Continue, please."

She continued to snuffle and blow her nose as the story unfolded. "Well, we, I mean myself and some of the other maids, accompanied her and each other as best as we could as we went about our chores, but with the King gone so much, we let our guards down, I admit it, young miss. I wasn't watchin' as careful as I should. One day, she comes back with a big smile on her face, and she takes me aside and shows me something she had wrapped up in her apron. 'Look, Agnes, look what I've got here, a golden egg!' When she unwrapped it from its paper, I saw that gold it surely was, painted gold, I reckoned. 'Where'd ye get it?' I asked. 'From one of the guards,' she said, but I learned later that weren't true. 'Oh,' says I, 'Is it meant to be eaten?' And she says, 'yes, I'm told it's got more flavor than other eggs.' So, right there in front of me, she ate it in two bites. I thought it rude of her not to offer me a nibble, but now it's glad I am she didn't." Agnes began crying again. "I didn't mean that, Eleanor," she rasped. "Gladly I'd trade my tired old life for her young one."

Eleanor patted her hand again and urged her to continue.

"Well, the next day, she took ill. She sent word that she couldn't get out of bed fer all the sickness she was havin', first her stomach, then the flux, then the stomach again. I checked on her, and she looked right sick, pale and dark around the eyes. I told her to stay in bed, and I would check on her later. I sent a girl up with some tea and sweet bread, but she never touched it.

"Later I visited her room and sat beside her, tryin' to cheer her up. That's when I began to wonder if the egg had been tainted in some way, not poisoned, mind ye, but maybe bad with decay. I mentioned the egg to her, could it have made her sick, I asked. She burst into cryin', though no tears came out. She was dryin' up from no food or drink. That's when she told me it weren't no guard what gave her the egg, 'twas the King hisself. We hadn't known he'd come back, but come back he had, and he'd lain in wait for poor Sabine. 'He was kind,' she told me. 'Never laid a hand on me, only said he were sorry he'd been too forward with me and he gave me the egg as a sort of peace offerin', then he patted my arm and bade me off,' said she.

"She never spoke a word again. The next day, she laid in bed, her eyes sinkin' into her face, starin' into nothin', not eatin', not drinkin'. Then another day, and then another, and by that time she was shrinkin' up to a mere wisp, only vaguely resemblin' a livin' girl. It took five days for her to die. So we buried her." Then Agnes added, "Her family never claimed her."

Agnes bowed her head as she relived the horrifying scene, sobbing again noisily.

"Agnes," Eleanor broke in, wiping away her own tears, "don't worry. I've given this a lot of thought, and I realize there's no way to avoid the King in his own castle. But I have a plan that I hope will convince the

King to leave us alone. Let me think on it some more. But don't fret so, and please don't ever blame yourself for Sabine's death. It was that devil who killed her."

Chapter Twenty-Four

Eleanor met with Queen Isabella the next day and found her in good health, though thin and pale. Eleanor advised her to eat a bland diet to soothe her stomach, and she left the Queen's chambers. Would the King be waiting for her? She almost looked forward to it.

Agnes waited outside and began to escort her back to the kitchen where chores for the evening meal were getting under way. As they turned a corner, there was the King, but he was not alone; he was walking with several of his military advisers, their heads low and deep in conversation. When he saw the maids, he waved his advisers on and addressed the women.

"Please accept my condolences on the loss of one of the maids," he said with feigned humility and compassion. "When news reached me, I was shocked that one so young and robust could succumb so quickly."

Agnes squeezed Eleanor's hand, digging her nails into her flesh.

"You must all take better care of yourselves." The King began to grin wickedly and turned to walk away.

"Your Majesty," said Eleanor to the departing King.

He turned abruptly at the impertinence of having his back addressed by a maid. His eyes narrowed.

"Sire," she began boldly, dipping into a deep curtsey, head lowered, "the Lord has placed something on my heart to tell you." She hurried on, before he could stop her. "There will be an earthquake in a fortnight in the low country, close to Dover. It should be of no concern to you here at Windsor, but take care if you are traveling in that area. It will cause damage and will be felt as far as Canterbury."

This was the memory that God had given, the memory of having read about this earthquake which created widespread damage in the winter of 1215 to the poorly constructed homes in the area and some damage to Canterbury Cathedral.

The King's face changed dramatically, and Eleanor saw a look of fear pass over it. Then he composed himself.

"God spoke to you?" He face had gone pale. "He spoke to *you*?"

"Yes, Sire, the God of the universe. The God of Heaven and hell."

The King gasped. That got him.

Agnes, behind Eleanor, tugged at her skirts and whispered, "Lass, we need to go. What are ye doin'? What are ye sayin'? Quick, girl, let's be off."

John took a few tentative steps toward Eleanor, and she noticed a tremor in his hand as he raised a finger toward her. "What do you mean saying this to me? You dare threaten the King?"

"No, Sire, I assure you, it's no threat. I mean only to alert you, Sire," Eleanor responded, her eyes lowered. "Sometimes the Lord speaks to me by placing a future event in my head. This time I felt you should know, since you've been traveling so much of late." Eleanor knew that God Himself had delivered a means of protection from the King: her memories. She would not lie, but not volunteer any information that John didn't need to know.

"The Lord Himself speaks to you?" he asked again.

"He does, sometimes, but not in a clear voice exactly, it's more like an idea that will come to me."

"And He wanted you to warn me about this earthquake? He told you that?"

"Sire, alert you, but certainly not a warning from me. God showed me this event so that you could be prepared." True enough, she thought. "I am in no way a prophetess of God. I am not a fortune teller, which God detests. Yet sometimes God tells me what will occur. This earthquake will surely happen because God is never wrong. It will cause no damage here at Windsor, but be aware that you should avoid the low country around Dover at that time."

The King backed away from her, clearly afraid. "We shall see if your vision comes to pass, girl," he said. "If it doesn't, your life will be forfeit, for it will be a sign that you are a witch in league with the Devil."

Then King John of England, the most powerful man in the realm, scurried from her like a rat fleeing a sinking ship, vanishing into the castle's dark recesses.

Chapter Twenty-Five

As Eleanor and Agnes quickly made their way below to the kitchen, Agnes chided her for her boldness. "Girl, what were ye thinkin' speakin' to the King hisself in such a bold manner? Did ye mean what ye said about the earthquake? How could ye know such a thing?" Agnes was eyeing her with some wariness.

"I meant every word," Eleanor responded. "God truly put that earthquake in my mind to warn the King about the danger. I believe He wants to use these memories, I mean these ideas," she quickly corrected herself, "to protect me and all the maids from the King's advances, from his wrath. Look what happened to poor Sabine. I spent a lot of time wondering how to come back here and feel safe; I prayed and prayed about it when I was at the Adelfrids, and this was God's answer to me. I know He will give me other … other ideas to share with the King so we can all feel safe."

Agnes tut-tutted and nearly sprinted her old body to the lower level, dragging Eleanor with her. As they approached the entrance to the large kitchen with its numerous fireplaces and large center table, she heard a familiar voice and an unfamiliar one.

"Sounds like the new girl," said Agnes. "We've hired on a new maid to replace poor Sabine." Whenever Sabine's name was mentioned, it was usually preceded by the descriptive "poor."

The "new girl" was giggling when Eleanor walked into the room. With brown hair tucked beneath a cap, a few shiny ringlets escaping below its edges, the new girl, whose name was, she learned later, Estrilda, gazed up at Thomas with a broad dimpled smile, pillowy lips, and uttered peals of laughter at everything Thomas said. She lightly touched Thomas's hand as he rested it on the table beside her.

"Oh aye, Thomas!" she giggled. "Ye're so right about that. Thomas, ye're like a magician, keepin' me laughin' so!" And there ensued more tittering from Estrilda.

Eleanor was overcome with immediate dislike for the new girl. But why should she feel jealous? Hadn't she told Thomas she could not marry him, could not commit to him, that she was planning to return home to her time? You have no right to your feelings, she admonished herself, but her feelings were still there, threatening to boil over if she didn't get them under control.

"Eleanor!" exclaimed Thomas when he saw her enter the kitchen. He dashed over to her, abandoning Estrilda. "How are ye, Miss Eleanor? I promised to check in on all of ye when I could, so here I am."

"Fine, Thomas. Everything is fine. I've just checked on the Queen, and she's doing well."

"Young mason," chimed in Agnes, "she did more than check on the Queen. This missy had a little talk, shall we call it, with the King hisself."

"What?" said Thomas. He looked alarmed and tugged Eleanor away from the others, so they could talk. "Tell me, Eleanor, what happened? Did he … did he do anythin'? Say anythin'?"

"Thomas, I assure you, everything is alright. I, well it's hard to describe what we discussed, but I told him that there would be an earthquake in a fortnight around Dover and told him that God gave me the vision to alert him to the danger. And it's true, God did give me this as a memory, because don't forget, Thomas, I know what's going to happen in this time we're living in."

Thomas's mouth fell open. "You gave the King a warnin'?"

"An alert," she said, growing weary of explaining the difference. "And he was genuinely afraid. I'm certain the earthquake will occur, just as I remember it does, and there will be a lot of damage in that area, so you, too, should be careful if you're traveling around Dover, and your family, too. It will happen in about fourteen days."

Exactly fourteen days later, a strong earthquake with an epicenter in the Dover Straits hit in the afternoon. History would record it as having a 6.0 magnitude, enough to cause widespread damage in southeastern England, the low countries, and interrupting a synod convened at Canterbury Cathedral. The quake would much later be referred to as the Earthquake Synod. Once word reached Windsor Castle, Agnes and the other maids rushed to congratulate Eleanor.

"Missy, ye said it would happen and bless me if it didn't happen!" said Agnes. "Ye've got the gift, ye have!"

"I'm not a prophetess, Agnes. Please don't spread that around."

"Eleanor," chimed in Estrilda, as they all sat around the large servants' table, "I'm agog! Ye predicted an earthquake, and it came to pass! Ye can say ye're not a prophet, but ye're great at predictin' things!" Estrilda was beginning to grow on Eleanor, she had to begrudgingly admit it. She was a pretty, innocent, kind-hearted, and vivacious young woman who enjoyed life. There was nothing wrong with that.

Soon Thomas burst into the kitchen where all the staff was congregating and talking about Eleanor's bold prediction that had come to pass. He slowly walked over to Eleanor and said, "I should not have doubted ye, Miss Eleanor. When it comes to things that will happen, ye speak the truth."

———

Later the same day, Eleanor made her way to the Queen's chamber. She went alone, refusing to allow Agnes or any of the maids to accompany her. She knew the likelihood was high that at any moment she could be confronted by the King. When she entered the Queen's rooms, there was John, standing by the window with Isabella as they looked out over the gardens below. Her youngest child, little Eleanor, was toddling on the floor, attended by her nursemaid. Eleanor gave a low curtsy, and the Queen retreated to a small room off the main chamber to be examined.

"How are you feeling, My Lady? Any sickness lately?"

"No," she answered with a smile on her pretty face. "I'm so glad that's behind me. I feel much better." She had a rosy glow on her face and seemed happy. "See how I grow!" she added, gazing down at her growing belly which she cradled protectively in her arms. "I believe this one will be another prince."

Eleanor smiled at Isabella. "I hope so," she said.

When the two moved back into the main chamber, the King was gone, and Eleanor knew he would be waiting for her outside, lurking in one of the hallways. Her chest tightened and her heart drummed against her chest. She braced herself for whatever he had in store for her. She moved through the labyrinth of dark, windowless halls that weaved through the castle until, suddenly, the King emerged from a shadow. She curtsied again and lowered her head, waiting for him to speak.

"You were right about the earthquake," he began.

"Yes, Sire." She continued to gaze at the stone floor.

"How did you know? I must understand." His voice was calm, relaxed even, as he spoke to her.

She raised her head, looked directly at him and spoke. "Your Majesty, as I told you, the Lord speaks to me sometimes with a vision of what's to come. Sometimes these ideas are vague, but they are always true. That's how I know they're from God. I worship only Him. So, if I see a future event, I know it has been planted in my mind by God Himself."

He stared at her, not with a look of anger or malice, but with genuine surprise and, could it be, admiration? "What's next?" he asked. "What else do you see?"

She was prepared for this question. Since she had already proven herself, she knew he would want predictions to prepare for threats to his realm. History would conclude that King John never took good advice and walked squarely toward his own doom, but she would still give him bits of information to prove she could predict a future event. Every event she was now remembering was something she had read about the reign of King John.

She paused for a moment, as if deep in thought, and said, "What has come into my mind is that you will be asked by the Pope to mend fences with the Church and the barons by going on a crusade to the Holy Land."

His eyes widened, and he began to protest.

But she went on. "I don't know if you'll actually go on this crusade, Sire, but you will agree to go, and there will be peace between you and the barons for a time. But only a short time."

She had no clear memory of whether the King goes on the crusade, but her guess was that he doesn't go; John despised the Church and didn't care at all about advancing Christianity in the Muslim-controlled regions.

He looked at her thoughtfully. "When will this happen?"

"I'm not sure," she answered. "Perhaps in a few weeks, maybe sooner. You will receive a message from Pope Innocent about this, but I'm not clear when it will come."

Instead of striding away from her arrogantly, King John shocked her thoroughly by thanking her in a gentle voice and quietly walking away.

Chapter Twenty-Six

As February ended and March began, the grumblings of the barons reached a fever pitch. "These mutterings of discontent are too volatile, much too volatile." The voice was that of one of the King's advisers, a powerful and loyal baron. He was speaking with another of the King's men, who Eleanor did not recognize as she overheard their conversation in one corner of the great dining hall.

Eleanor and several of the other maids were helping to pass the dishes to the servers at the banquet, a small dinner party attended by the King and Queen, with several of their young children bouncing around their mother, and a few other lords and ladies of note. In their midst was the Marshal of England, Sir William. As one of the most notable and important advisers in all of England, the Marshal was keeping close to his King as tensions mounted.

"Yes, Sir Gerald, I agree," said the baron's companion. Their voices were lowered, unaware that behind them, separated by a large, heavy tapestry, were several servants, including Eleanor, listening to their every word.

"What would the King do if he knew that even now Fitzwalter was in France meeting with Prince Louis to gain the support of the French for their rebellion?" asked Sir Gerald. "That treacherous snake!"

"Should you alert the King?" his companion asked. "After all, if he finds out that you didn't tell him, well …"

"I believe he must know, or at least suspect," said Sir Gerald. "John is still seething over the loss at Bouvines. Talk is that Louis is already building an army to invade our realm." The baron paused and added, "Yes, I believe I must talk with him now and make sure he knows about Fitzwalter."

Peeking around the tapestry, Eleanor saw Sir Gerald approach the King, who stood and moved off to the side to speak with him. In moments, John's face darkened, and Eleanor feared he was heading for another tantrum. But the King composed himself and quickly left the banquet hall with the Marshal and Sir Gerald, leaving alone the Queen who, though visibly pregnant, was soon laughing and joking, surrounded by admiring courtiers.

Again, Eleanor's memory began to sharpen as she witnessed the unfolding drama. Prince Louis would be the greatest threat that King John would face. He would be supported by the barons and be declared King of England, but she was fuzzy about the timeframe. It was coming soon, though. Very soon.

Is time continuing to move forward along a similar path in my own time, the 1960s? Are there two parallel timeframes moving at the same speed? Will they diverge again, as they did when she woke up on the battlefield in France? Her mind could not process the myriad paradoxes her situation presented. She had no choice but to live in the present, or rather the medieval present, and try to forget about the time when she disappeared from the life she's always known, the life she'd grown up in, and the people she'd come to love.

As Eleanor and the maids were carrying discarded food and dinnerware back to the kitchen, a palace guard stepped in front of her, blocking her path. "The King commands yer presence in his privy chamber," he said. "This way girl." He addressed her in a perfunctory manner, as if he could not believe the King of England would ever need to speak with a common maid, even if she was the Queen's midwife. "Let's go, girl, quick now."

Eleanor followed the guard up into the wing of the castle that housed King John's private quarters. When she entered the room, there sat King John, Sir William with a scowl on his face, Sir Gerald, and another man whose back was to her. As the man turned around to face her, she gasped. It was Simon the Seer, the magician who had tossed her into the Middle Ages. He was not dressed in his magician's cloak or theatrical cap, but wore a dark velvet robe trimmed in fur, belted at the waist. He looked like a prosperous nobleman of the era. Simon smiled at her as she recoiled from him, backing away. She collected herself and curtsied to the King.

"Do you know this man?" asked the King.

"Yes, we met at … at the fair last year."

"This is Simon Faramond, a seer. And you, also a seer, I thought you two should meet." The King paused and glared at her. "Because you see different things."

"Sire," answered Eleanor, head bowed, "I am not a seer or a prophet. I only receive thoughts, ideas, from God that always prove true." She glanced at Simon from the corner of her eyes. "I claim no special gift, except those ideas of the future given to me by God." They were nothing but memories of her college studies, she reminded herself, but she could not say that to the King.

Sir William said nothing but surveyed both Eleanor and Simon with deep concentration.

Simon spoke up. "I do claim a special gift, Your Highness. I can predict the future and tell you what events will transpire."

"Devilish dealings!" spat out Sir Gerald, who angrily leapt to his feet. "Diviners and soothsayers have no role in your realm, Sire."

"I received confirmation this evening," said the King, ignoring Gerald, that the nobility of England is meeting even now with our enemies in France to plan an invasion. You," he added, pointing at Eleanor, "told me I would be asked to go on crusade, and it was as you said. Yesterday I received a parchment from Pope Innocent asking me to take the oath. You have twice been correct about what will occur, so I ask both you and Simon, what will transpire with the French? Will Fitzwalter be successful in his meetings with Prince Louis?"

Simon spoke first. "Sire, you will surely triumph over Fitzwalter, who will come back to England tail between legs to beg for mercy. But you must show him none for his treasonous behavior. And you shall surely beat back the French when they make a pitiful display of war against you."

The King and all eyes turned to Eleanor. Please Lord, she prayed silently, give me the right words. "Your Majesty, that is not true," she began, directing her opening comments toward Simon. "Sir Fitzwalter does, indeed, align himself with the French. He is still smarting from the death of his daughter, with rumors of …" She paused, knowing she could not accuse the King of killing Fitzwalter's daughter with a poisoned egg.

King John tensed and bristled,

But she continued. "Yes, Sire, he will align with Prince Louis, and they will eventually march against England. There will be war and many deaths, and your reign will be severely threatened. But you have opportunities before you to appease the nobility before these dire events occur. And if you seize these opportunities, you will prevent much bloodshed and suffering among the people." She knew the signing of the Magna Carta was imminent, the greatest opportunity the King faced to appease the barons and the people of England. Eleanor could not fathom why Simon was giving the King obvious false advice. If he was from the future, he knew it was false. What could his reasoning be? To gain more favor with the King? To discredit her?

"Sire, you will be pressured to sign a document easing restrictions on the people and the barons," said Eleanor. "That agreement, once signed and honored, will ease tensions with the barons."

"Trickster!" blurted Simon, pointing a finger at Eleanor.

She turned to him, her eyes blazing. "You're the trickster, Simon. I don't know why you're giving the King false hope that there won't be war with the French, but there will certainly be war. You, of all people, know this to be true. Stop tickling the King's ears with things he wants to hear, and tell him the truth."

Simon was furious. He appeared to be prepared to lunge at her, when Sir William stood, his large muscular frame dwarfing everyone else in the room. "Watch yerself, magician!" he warned. "Don't take another step toward the girl or 'twill be yer last."

The King told Simon to leave the room. When he had stormed out, John spoke. "I prefer Simon's prediction, but yours has the ring of truth. I will never allow Fitzwalter to bring me to my knees, nor allow the French to wage war against us. This will not happen!" He pounded his chubby fist on the table and dismissed her. She left, fearful that she would run into Simon in the castle, but she made it to the kitchen without incident.

Later that day, she learned that Simon had fled Windsor after the King declared him guilty of sorcery. Where is he now? Will he show up again? He wanted something from her, but what?

Chapter Twenty-Seven

I n early May, the rebel barons seized the city of London in a bloodless coup. Most of the city's inhabitants were in church at the time and were blindsided by the attack. Led by Robert Fitzwalter, the band of barons called themselves the "Army of God." Fitzwalter promptly issued orders to attack, ransack, and burn the houses of the Jews in London to seize their wealth to fund the rebellion against King John. Hence, what would be known as the First Barons' War had begun, with the Jews of London the first target of violence. Fitzwalter and his army also took Lincoln and Exeter, but an attack on the Tower of London, which was well fortified by the King's men, was unsuccessful, and that indomitable fortress stood.

The King was nowhere to be found, having decamped with his entourage at the first sign of trouble, taking the always vigilant Sir William the Marshal with him. The Queen was still within the castle walls, vulnerable and expecting her child without her husband's protection.

"My Lady, perhaps you should keep to your rooms with plenty of guards outside to ensure your safety," Eleanor advised her one day as she visited the Queen for her regular checkup. She found Isabella nervously pacing her rooms, looking out the window expectantly for news to arrive of the uprising in nearby London.

"I intend to," she said. "I'll not take any risk with this child. What have you heard, Eleanor? Do you learn any more among the servants than we ladies are being told?"

"My Lady, I only know that the barons have taken London. I also heard that they attacked, ransacked, and burned down the homes of the Jews to help fund their rebellion. I don't know if there are any deaths."

The Queen shrugged and waved her hand in the air. "I believe I shall give birth in autumn," she said.

"Yes, My Lady, probably around September."

"I understand you have made some predictions for the King, and they've proven true," she said.

"Yes, My Lady, a few times."

"How do you know these things? Is it necromancy?"

Eleanor was shocked at the suggestion. "No, certainly not the dark arts. I … I get ideas about what will occur from God Almighty, but by no means do I know everything, My Lady. I did not foresee this attack against London."

"What do you see in my future, Eleanor?"

Eleanor remained silent, again taken aback by the Queen's question. She knew this beautiful young woman would be widowed in the months ahead, but her future was not clear to Eleanor. God was withholding these memories from her on purpose, so she answered honestly. "I know little, My Lady, only that you will have a healthy child. I don't even know if it will be a prince or princess. God does not show me everything."

Isabella gave her a penetrating look, possibly trying to decide if she was telling her the truth. "Thank you, Eleanor, you may go."

⬩

When she entered the kitchens below, Eleanor found Thomas waiting to speak with her. Hovering near Thomas, as usual, was Estrilda. All three of them were warily observed by Agnes. "May I speak with ye, Eleanor?" Thomas asked, walking toward her—with Estrilda padding behind him like a faithful dog. "Estrilda, lass, could ye give us a moment to speak in private?" Thomas said gently.

Estrilda put her head down and moved away. She was so besotted with Thomas that she would take any crumbs he would throw her way. Eleanor feared what Thomas would tell her. Was he going to marry Estrilda? Had he finally given up on Eleanor after her bitter rejection of his marriage proposal? If that was his message, she didn't want to hear it.

"Eleanor," he began once they had both moved into the larder, that most private spot in the busy public kitchen. "Ma has asked me to come and talk with ye. Lavinia's to be wed. Ma would like ye to come for the weddin' and …"

"Oh, that's happy news, Thomas!" She stopped and surveyed his face. Something was wrong. His brow had creased, angry. "What is it, Thomas? What's wrong?"

"She's to have a babe," he spat out. "I could wring Dicun's neck, I could! He dared to take advantage of my own sister, right under our noses!" He was seething with anger.

"Oh!" said Eleanor, digesting the information. "Thomas, calm yourself. If she marries, it will all be well."

"My own sister!" he exclaimed again. He banged a fist on the wall of the larder, causing Eleanor to jump. "Behavin' like a common trollop, I tell ye, our Pa is beside hisself, and so is Ma, though she's more of a practical nature than is Pa. Lavinia simply won't discuss it, and Dicun, that knave, denies it. I tell ye, he denies that he ever laid a hand on her. And her with her belly already swellin'!"

Eleanor took his hands in hers to try to calm him. "When is the wedding? I can talk to the Queen and see if I can be gone for about a week."

"The weddin' is in three days, Eleanor, so we'd need to leave tomorrow mornin' at dawn."

"Thomas, if Dicun says he didn't touch her, is he still willing to marry her? Knowing she may have been with another man?"

Thomas dropped his head into his hands and moaned. "Yes, he says he loves her and wants to be her husband. He'll marry her and claim the babe as his own."

"Good. I'll talk to the Queen straightaway and be ready to go first thing in the morning."

———

After receiving the Queen's blessing to leave, "but only for one week, Eleanor, for I will be needing you soon," they left at dawn. The weather was frosty in the morning but warmed up by midday, and they stripped off their cloaks as they rode. With tensions high across the realm, they rode hard, keeping a wary eye out for bandits and mercenaries. A strained silence existed between them. Eleanor told Thomas about seeing the magician, Simon, at the castle.

"What could the King be thinkin', Eleanor? The man's a soothsayer and a devil."

"He was gone by that evening after making false predictions for the King. Don't forget, I know what's going to happen, and he wanted to tell the King only what the King wanted to hear. But now I'm worried about when I'll see him again."

"I thought that's what ye wanted, Eleanor," said Thomas, "to find the man again, so he can take ye back to yer time." He spoke quietly, but there was a rawness beneath the calm—like a wound not quite scabbed over.

"Thomas, I don't really know what I want. I often think I could stay here and be happy, but I'm not from here, from this time, and if I'm ever to get back home, I suppose the only one who can get me there is Simon." Seated next to Thomas on a fallen tree, nibbling on some dried meat and cheese, she could contain her curiosity no longer. "Thomas, I notice that you and Estrilda have been keeping a lot of company," she began.

He turned to look at her, expressionless. "Yes, Eleanor, a little, not a lot. She's a nice young lass, and she's got no family to speak of. She's a little … well, she's a little silly at times, but still a nice girl. And she likes me and wants to be with me." His last words were thick with disappointment and bitterness.

"Oh," said Eleanor, who hadn't expected Thomas to wax poetic about the virtues of the chronically giggling Estrilda. "I'm happy for you, Thomas. I hope you'll …"

"Eleanor, please don't say more." Thomas looked pained, and he stood. "My feelin's for ye have not changed. But ye've made it clear to me that ye're lookin' to leave, that ye've got no interest in marryin' me or settlin' here. There's no wrong in my spending some time with Estrilda, a lass who enjoys my company. So I'll not bother ye any further."

"Thomas, I'm so …"

"No more talk," said Thomas. "Let's mount. We'd best be gettin' on before the sun sets."

With his words, her heart broke, like shattered glass.

Chapter Twenty-Eight

They arrived in Graston as dark was falling. Beja greeted them at the front door, and Eleanor fell into her arms, exhausted and happy to be home with her adopted family.

"Eleanor, dear, it's so good to have ye back," said Beja. "It's glad I am that ye're here for the weddin', but it's not the happy time we hoped it would be."

"Where is Lavinia now?"

"She's tendin' to the critters outside. She won't talk to anyone about it. Her Pa is beside hisself, angry and fumin' about who it might be, but she won't talk."

"Thomas, too. He's spitting mad but seems to blame Dicun for her pregnancy."

"Oh, I'm sure it weren't Dicun. He's a good lad, and I believe him. And besides, Lavinia says it weren't him," Beja said.

"You should let Thomas know. I'm afraid he'll do something rash next time he sees Dicun."

Lavinia came in with her arms full of firewood, which she laid down on the hearth. When she saw Eleanor, the dour look on her face vanished, and she ran to embrace her. "Eleanor, I'm so glad to see ye!" she exclaimed, hugging her around the neck. Emotion swelled in Lavinia's eyes and tears rolled down her cheeks.

"I'm glad to see you, too," Eleanor said.

Lavinia sniffled, cleaned her hands, and removed her apron, exposing a swelling abdomen. Stiffening her spine, she joined the others for the evening meal in the kitchen.

Eleanor decided to make some small talk to lighten the mood. "I saw the Marshal recently at the castle," she said.

"How is Sir William doing?" asked Beja.

"He is well but seems worried about the rebellion among the barons and the lawlessness in the countryside," she said. Lavinia shot her a look of concern, her eyes wide, then looked away, as if trying to disguise her distress. Why would this news be of undue concern to her? Lavinia is safe here at the home of her parents. "And the Queen is doing well with her pregnancy," Eleanor added, but regretted bringing it up immediately when she again saw Lavinia's discomfort.

Richard banged his fist on the table and stood, towering over Lavinia. "You will name yer seducer, girl, or I'll bring Dicun in here right now and flay him alive."

Lavinia fled the room in tears, followed by Beja, then Eleanor. All of them made their way to the upper room, where Lavinia slept. She threw herself onto her straw bed and curled up, facing away from the door, sobbing. Beja and Eleanor entered.

"Lavinia …" began Beja.

"Don't, Ma! I cannot bear to hear Pa scold me like that, but I cannot say more!"

"Mistress Beja," said Eleanor. "Let me sit with Lavinia for a few minutes."

"I won't talk to ye, either!" Lavinia wailed.

"You don't have to talk," said Eleanor. "Would you like me to examine you? To make sure everything is alright with the baby?"

Beja left the room, shaking her head, and Lavinia sat up, sniffling. "There's not much to examine yet, it's early days. But go ahead."

Eleanor laid her hands on Lavinia's belly and felt for a baby, but Lavinia was right; there was little to assess. "There's nothing amiss that I can tell," she said. "How are you feeling? Any sickness?"

"A little, but it's startin' to pass."

"When do you think … when do you think you became pregnant, Lavinia?"

"'Twas four months ago," she answered, looking away from Eleanor, a little unhappy.

"Lavinia, you don't seem happy about having a baby. I know the circumstances are less than ideal, but you're getting married in a couple of days, and everything will work out."

Lavinia glared at her, and Eleanor was shocked at the hostility in her look. "Pa despises me and the whole town is talkin', Eleanor."

"But you'll have a husband and a little baby soon, and you'll be able to settle down and put this behind you."

"It'll never be behind me. Never. I don't want this baby, but I've got no choice, have I?"

"Lavinia, why don't you want this baby? Is it …" She didn't know what question she meant to ask. Is it Dicun's? If not, whose is it? Those were the questions on the tip of her tongue. "Lavinia, what can I do? Is there any way I can help you through this?"

She wiped her nose on her sleeve. "Try to convince Ma and Pa that Dicun never laid a hand on me. It's the God's truth, Eleanor. He's a good man and would not take advantage. Pa must not question Dicun about this, because he doesn't know who it is, either. And he's willin' to marry me, to give the baby a proper father."

"What about the real father? Wouldn't he agree to marry you?"

Her face hardened. "That isn't possible."

"Is he already married?" Lavinia looked down at her hands in her lap. "Oh," said Eleanor. "I understand."

"No, Eleanor, ye don't." Lavinia laid back on the bed and turned away, refusing to talk anymore.

⁂

Two days later, early in the morning, Eleanor and Mary tended to Lavinia as she prepared for her wedding, while Beja buzzed in and out of the room. Lavinia's dress was a bright green and yellow, blue being the color of purity and therefore not quite appropriate. Mary created a circlet of wildflowers for her hair, while Eleanor tucked parts of the dress in, and let out other parts to accommodate her growth. She was still hardly showing, but her mid-section was expanding. Using large stitches, Eleanor worked on the wedding dress as Mary kept up a stream of chatter.

"Lord, Miss Eleanor, it's been a panic around here. Well, you didn't know the Hildeths, but the mother, Mistress Oriana, had her ninth babe a fortnight ago and struggled mightily. We all said we wished Miss Eleanor was here to make the goin' easier. But after nearly twenty hours, with Miss Beja and Lavinia helpin', she gave birth to a baby boy, her second after seven girl babes, can ye imagine? And what with the unrest all over the parish, well the Carey barn was burnt down by ruffians, loyal to Baron de Malet, and Baron de Malet stomped around the countryside demandin' more taxes, because all the barons are takin' up arms, then …"

As Mary continued her narrative, Eleanor noticed that Lavinia's entire body had tense, her back straight as a board. While pinning her sleeve, Eleanor felt Lavinia's entire arm go stiff, then her body began to shake. Her eyes were wide, and she stared straight ahead. Her hands were balled into fists. Eleanor understood.

"Mary," said Eleanor, "would you give us a few moments alone?"

When they were alone, Eleanor led Lavinia to the edge of the bed to sit down. She was still shaking but allowed herself to be seated. Eleanor sat beside her. "Lavinia," she began, "was it the baron?"

Lavinia began to cry, burying her face in her hands. "Yes! Yes, 'twas!"

"What happened? Can you tell me?" Lavinia continued to sob. "It's alright. I won't tell anyone, Lavinia. Tell me what happened. Don't cry. You're safe; he can't hurt you."

"Can't hurt me? Do ye see my condition here, Eleanor? I'm carryin' the baron's babe!"

"I understand, but he can't hurt you anymore. You have a good man who wants to marry you, and you'll have a baby soon to love."

"I don't know. I don't know," she muttered, her face still in her hands.

"Tell me. Tell me what happened."

Finally, Lavinia looked up at Eleanor, tears streaming down her face, and said, "Lord de Malet raped me."

Chapter Twenty-Nine

"I took the carriage out that mornin', as I always do, to check on all the tenants. It usually takes me all day to complete this chore, but it's somethin' I enjoy," Lavinia said. She was sitting on the bed, wringing hands, but she was composed and had stopped crying. "I like to make sure they've got all they need to carry out their duties. I love lookin' in on the wives and the little children. I bring sugar treats for them and little cakes for the mums, to let them know our family cares for them and doesn't only use them for their labor, ye understand? And I do care for these families. We've got the best tenants of anyone in the region.

"But, as ye know, the baron, Hugh de Malet, is the true owner of our land, even though it were Adelfrid land goin' back to the Conquest. Now we're just caretakers, so to speak, with the barons controllin' everything. Course, they expect us to do all the work and make sure the tenants do their share, and they reap a tidy profit from our labors and caretakin'. No matter, that's what I was doin' early in the year days after yer visit at Christmas. I was ridin' around, wrapped in a big fur to keep the chill off, visitin' the tenants and doin' my job, as Ma and Pa expect of me.

"I had just finished visitin' the Maynard clan. They have seven children and the mother expectin' her eighth. I left them with some extra cakes and loaves of bread, knowin' it would come in handy, but none of our tenants ever struggle fer food, we make sure of it. The mother, her name is Goodeth, mentioned right casual that the baron and his men had been seen on the property, but she'd had no encounter with them.

I should've taken her comment to heart, I should've, but at the time it meant nothin' to me.

"I continued to the next tenant home. It was about a ten-minute ride, so I wrapped myself up well against the cold. As I was passin' the Maynard's barn, which can barely be seen, mind ye, from the family's home, Baron de Malet came out from behind the barn on his large horse. He was all decked out in his baronial finery, fur around his neck and on his head—no rabbit or squirrel, mind ye—wearin' a long velvet overcoat and shiny boots. A few of his men came out, too, and sat on their horses behind him. I was a little spooked, to be honest. They all took me by surprise emergin' from behind the barn for no good reason, but I pulled up and greeted the baron, givin' a little bob of my head to be polite. 'Good day, Lord de Malet,' I said. 'I was makin' the rounds of the tenants, leavin' the Maynards, I was.' I knew, of course, that the barons throughout England were in revolt, but I'll tell ye truthfully, Eleanor, I did not know it was a declaration of war, so to speak. Nor did I know how lawless the barons were becomin'. I know the King's men have always been rough with the local peasantry, but that's been the way since I've been a wee girl, no matter who sits on the throne.

"Feelin' a little uncomfortable, I tapped my horse and began to move on, givin' a polite wave as I did. But the baron pushed forward, nearly in front of me, causing my horse to rear up a bit. I reined her in and looked at the baron, and he looked at me, and said, 'I hear yer gettin' married, young Lavinia.'

"Course, he uses his high-soundin' language, I guess to impress me and let me know he's so far above me. That's how he's always been, but I've had little dealin's with him over the years.

"'Yes, Sir de Malet,' I said. He says, 'Ye've certainly grown up to be a lovely woman.'

"'Thank ye,' I said, growin' more uneasy.

"'I must say,' he says, turnin' to his men behind him, 'I do hate to think of this pretty young woman bein' deflowered by one of the dirty local peasants.'

"I could not believe he said such a thing, especially about my Dicun. Dicun is no dirty peasant, but of the merchant class, like us, and he's a kind, decent man. I became outright scared at that comment and tried to back up my horse, so I could get away, knowin', of course, that if I tried, they could easily stop me.

"Then he says, 'Or have ye already been deflowered, Lavinia?' At that I jumped out of the carriage and began to run back to the Maynards, but they easily caught up with me. His men jumped off their horses and grabbed me, one of them coverin' my mouth so I couldn't scream.

"'Bring her into the barn,' said the baron. Now he was barkin' orders and actin' like a tyrant. He had a look on his face that terrified me, Eleanor. I thought he might kill me. Still, I fought and kicked, but the men overpowered me with no effort. They carried me into the barn, me wrigglin' and tryin' to yell, and they stuffed a dirty rag in my mouth and threw me on the floor.

"The baron said, 'I claim my right of prima nocta.'

"I could not believe my ears, Eleanor. Prima nocta is some kind of ancient myth, givin' the lord the right to bed the bride-to-be who lives on his land. It hasn't been done in centuries, if ever. That's when I knew he was goin' to have his way with me. And … and he stripped off his coat and his furs, and he reached inside his hose, not even botherin' to pull it down, then he pushed up my skirt, and … and …"

Eleanor pulled Lavinia close to her, and they both cried. "Lavinia, what about the other men? Did they …?"

"No," she said, wiping her face on a towel, careful not to stain her wedding dress with tears. "No, they all ran off right after that. I think they heard someone comin' or thought they did. The baron warned me not to tell anyone what had happened—what he did to me—or he would kill me. He said it that plainly. And I tell ye, Eleanor, he can do it, too. That's why I've told no one, only you because ye've guessed it. If I tell Pa or Thomas they'll do somethin' rash. Ye must not tell anyone. I raced home after that, and a few weeks later I learned I was carryin' his babe. I don't want that scoundrel's child, Eleanor. I want a baby with Dicun, not the child of a baron who would defy all the laws of God and the realm only to have a few minutes with a girl he hardly knows."

"What did you tell Dicun?"

"I told him I'd been violated, but by a passin' stranger who I'd never seen before and who got away. I said I would understand if he wanted to break off the marriage. I assumed he would, then I'd have to tell Ma and Pa, and maybe go into a nunnery to have the babe. I don't know what they would have done with me. But Dicun, bless him, put his arms around me and said he loved me and would never allow me to go into a nunnery or be shunned by the townsfolk, so he agreed to go ahead and marry me and claim the child as his own. He reminds me of Joseph, the father of our Lord, who married Mary knowin' she was carryin' a child, and not fully understandin' how it happened. He's a good man, my Dicun is."

"Lavinia, it will all work out. Don't cry."

Lavinia turned to Eleanor with wet, red eyes and nodded dully. But Eleanor knew she wasn't sure at all that anything would work out.

Chapter Thirty

A subdued Dicun and Lavinia were married around midday, with the unsuspecting priest in attendance blessing the marriage. There was a sumptuous meal served afterward, but the Adelfrids were as restrained as the young married couple.

After the ceremony, Dicun and Lavinia quickly departed. Though Lavinia's dream had been to live in her own cottage on the Adelfrid land, this was no longer an option for her. She would not live on land owned by the baron, who could come upon her at will. She and Dicun had set up housekeeping nearby, and Lavinia would care for her husband and child in their own small cottage a few miles away.

Eleanor was saddened to think that no longer would the lively Lavinia rise with the sun and begin her chores for the Adelfrid family with a smile on her face. And no longer would the tenants wait expectantly for the cheerful weekly visit from Lavinia. In the face of such injustice, Eleanor knew the baron should not be allowed to get away with his crime, but how could he be held to account? She had no answer.

In the following days, Beja peppered Eleanor with questions about Lavinia. "Did ye learn anything?" she had asked. "Was it Dicun? She denies it, but her Pa is convinced he's a scoundrel. What man, he says, would marry a girl in such a condition, knowin' she's strayed?"

"She says the baby is not Dicun's," was Eleanor's reply, determined to keep not only Lavinia's secret, but keep Lavinia's life intact by not betraying it. "I believe her, Beja. She has the utmost respect for Dicun for going through with the wedding, knowing the baby is not his. He's a good man, and I believe they'll be happy."

"I cannot understand our sweet girl allowin' herself to be seduced. We raised her to be strong and keep herself pure. Her father is not takin' it well."

"Beja, please reassure him, if it can be called reassuring, that Dicun is not the father. He loves Lavinia so much he's willing to raise another man's baby. That makes him one in a million."

"Yes," said Beja, "he is a good man. Hard working and he clearly loves our girl. I could not be happy seeing her with anyone else."

Soon it was time for Eleanor to return to the castle. She and Thomas began the trip back to Windsor the next morning. Beja had loaded them with food for the journey. "Dear, I hope ye can come back when it's time for our Lavinia to give birth. We'll all feel more comfortable if ye're assistin' her."

"The Queen will have had her baby by then, so I'll do my best, Beja. Good-bye, take care, and be careful with all the unrest. It may be best for several of you to travel the property together, instead of only one." Beja eyed her carefully at that comment, but only nodded and said nothing.

———

After they departed, Thomas asked, "What was that all about, tellin' Ma to travel the property in pairs? Our land has always been safe. There's not a tenant on it who would create a problem."

"Yes," said Eleanor. "You're right, but I've been hearing about trouble in surrounding areas, and there's a lot of agitation, Thomas. I want to see your family stay safe in times of trouble. And more trouble is ahead, that much I know."

Thomas looked at her with alarm. "What do ye know, Eleanor?"

"I know that the King will soon be forced to sign a charter giving away some of his authority and granting it to the barons, and even some rights to the common people. There will be war across the land, and we're already seeing the unrest. I meant to ask you, Thomas, speaking of the barons, I heard Hugh de Malet was in the area and wondered if he spoke with your father while he was here … about all the unrest."

"Not that I'm aware of it, Eleanor. I didn't know he was in Graston." Thomas was thoughtful, and they rode for a while without talking. When they stopped at midday to eat, Thomas brought up the subject of Lavinia. "Were it Dicun? I know ye spoke with her a good bit, and I need to know."

"No, I believe her that it wasn't Dicun. I believe she loves him even more for agreeing to raise someone else's baby."

"Then who? Who would take advantage of her? And how could she give herself to another man when she's preparin' to wed ..." He stopped and stared at Eleanor, deep in thought. "Lawlessness in the area, ye said. Ye heard about it? Was Lavinia preyed upon?" He stopped again, and Eleanor could tell that he was connecting all the dots in his head. "So, ye heard Hugh de Malet was in Graston, but Pa never saw him. And ye heard about bands of ruffians, did ye? And ye warnin' Ma not to let anyone go out alone, did ye?"

"Thomas, I ..."

"Tell me, tell me now, Eleanor. Was it one of the baron's men?"

"I ... Thomas, no, it ..."

"Or was it the baron hisself? Don't lie to me, Eleanor; I'll not take it well if ye do."

"Oh, Thomas," she muttered, shaking her head. "Poor Lavinia. She was attacked by the baron. His men were there, too, but they all ran off when they thought they heard someone. He threatened to kill her and ruin your family if she revealed it to anyone. She's a brave girl, Thomas. She was raped by Baron de Malet."

Thomas jumped to his feet and pulled her up. "Let's go, Eleanor. We've got several more hours and we need to make good time." He quickly helped her onto her horse and leaped onto his with ease. They traveled at a rapid trot, barely speaking. The muscles on the back of Thomas's neck were taut with tension, and his shoulders were rigid as he rode. What had she done? What would he do now that he knew the truth? Had she endangered the entire Adelfrid clan, including Lavinia?

Eleanor and Thomas arrived at Windsor Castle before dark, tired from their ride and hungry. Thomas did not stay to eat but departed quickly. "I must go, Eleanor," he said. "Be careful. There are liars, thieves, and blackguards everywhere these days—yes, even in the castle. I don't know where the King is at present, but if he's not here, he'll be back. So, guard yerself. As ye know, havin' predicted it already, times will only get harder and more dangerous. Promise me ye'll take care and not roam the castle alone. Take the advice ye gave my Ma and always have someone else with ye."

"I promise," she said. His warnings seemed especially ominous considering he was armed with new information. She knew that the usually sweet-natured, gentle Thomas had a temper. Combined with his love for his family and devotion to them, she feared he would take the law, such as it was, into his own hands.

Two weeks later, as June got under way and Windsor was green and lush, Eleanor learned from Agnes that the baron of Graston, Hugh de Malet, had been murdered, pierced through the heart and robbed by a gang of thieves.

Chapter Thirty-One

The following week, the King arrived back at Windsor. He entered the outer courtyard unexpectedly, accompanied by a colorful entourage comprised of knights, seasoned mercenaries, common laborers, and a peculiar assortment of tagalongs who faithfully trailed the monarch wherever his whims led. Whispers circulated that King John, whenever away from the castle, always carried with him the entirety of his earthly possessions, a bounty that included the full assemblage of the crown jewels, along with silver and gold goblets and tableware. Queen Isabella, who was granted a mere handful of jewels for her daily rituals, saw most of her adornments swiftly gathered up as the King embarked on his journeys. Arriving directly behind the King were Sir William the Marshal and the Archbishop of Canterbury, Stephen Langton. The castle was abuzz with rumors about the meaning of the gathering, but everyone assumed it was to discuss how to handle the rebellious barons.

"Eleanor, dearie," said Agnes, who hobbled up to Eleanor while she sat with the other maids. "May I have a word with ye?" Eleanor followed her to the outside courtyard.

"Is something wrong, Agnes?" she asked.

"Not wrong, exactly. There's someone who wants to talk with ye, and he's waitin' for ye in the storage closet down the alley there." She pointed to an alcove with a door at the end that shielded a small room for storing outdoor items.

"Who?" she asked with some trepidation.

"Ye'll see," said Agnes, "but keep yer voices down, and be discreet. And don't spend too long out here or ye'll be missed." Agnes scurried away as Eleanor slowly walked toward the door. As she approached it, she noticed a crack in the wood, about eye height, with a gray eye peering out at her.

"Thomas!" she exclaimed. The door opened quickly, and Thomas shot an arm out and pulled her inside.

"Quiet, please Eleanor," he said, gently covering her mouth. Except for the small stream of light coming in through the crack, the closet was completely dark.

"Thomas," she began, "what happened? What did you do to the baron?"

"It had to be done, Eleanor. He defiled my sister and had it comin'. There wouldn't be any justice for Lavinia if we'd gone to the sheriff; they're all in the pockets of the barons. God Hisself demanded justice. But I regret that I've now got to hide."

"Does anyone else know? Why must you hide, Thomas?"

"One of the baron's whorin' companions saw me and was able to run off before I could catch him. The other ran away first thing and never saw me. Already, this knave has mentioned my name to the King, though as ye know, the King has no love for the rebellious barons. But I don't dare show my face, Eleanor, not now, so I'm on the run."

"Where are you staying?"

"Don't worry about that. There's plenty of folk livin' in the woods secretly who are helpin' me hide and takin' care of other folk like me. I'm doin' fine, Eleanor, but I'm sorry to be away from the castle where I can keep my eyes on ye.

"Look," he said, pointing to a corner of the closet. She strained her eyes to see what he was pointing to, and a small sliver of light from the hole in the door illuminated the initials he'd carved—E and T. She smiled at him, wondering how long those initials would endure before time wore them away.

"I'll be alright, Thomas. Please take care of yourself." And then she touched his face in the dark, turning her own face up toward his. That invisible electric charge, that thread that bound them and locked them together, intensified, and when her hand found his lips he kissed her fingers. She pressed her mouth against his, and he responded quickly, his mouth hard on hers. He grabbed her face, knocking off her cap and groping roughly in her hair. He did not stop for an instant kissing her lips, her chin and neck, both breathing hard in the blackness of the closet.

Breathlessly, Eleanor finally spoke. "Thomas, you mustn't stay too long or you'll put yourself in danger."

He groaned in frustration, still holding her tight. He relaxed slightly and rested his head on her shoulder, breathing hard with one hand still entangled in her hair. Finally, their breathing slowed, and Eleanor laid her head on his chest, both of them still locked together, arms wrapped around each other.

"Thomas, I'm sorry I was cold to you before. I've missed you, and I've been blind with jealousy over your … friendship with Estrilda."

He laughed. "Ye've got to be daft, woman! There's no way to compare a silly, whinnyin' creature like Estrilda with a thoroughbred like yerself."

That elicited a laugh from Eleanor. "Thank you for saying that, Thomas, although I've grown fond of that silly girl."

"She's a good girl, at that," he agreed, "if ye like silly children." They both laughed again, then he added, "Eleanor, I'll be watchin' out for ye as best as I can. If ye need to get word to me, ye can leave me a sign. Leave me a sign—here, this cap of mine." He handed her his hat, a felted wool cap with a short brim, similar to the modern newsboy cap. "Place it at the edge of the woods, by the well on the far side. When my companion at the castle spots it and gives it to me, I'll know ye need to speak with me. I'll wait for ye here, in this closet, or wherever my companion tells ye I'll be."

"Thomas, does your family know about the baron?"

"No, I kept it from all of them. I didn't want to put them in danger, but I fear they may be questioned by the sheriff. Never ye fear, I'm watchin' out for them, as well. These are treacherous times, Eleanor, so ye must be on yer guard. War will be breakin' out with even more fierceness between the King and the barons. 'Tis no wonder the barons are in an uproar. But it's the common folk who suffer, 'tis a pity."

"Yes, Thomas, war will be breaking out, and the French will be drawn into it. But England survives, have no doubt about that. The question is, will we survive? And what will King John do next?"

Chapter Thirty-Two

The signing of the Magna Carta was imminent. Archbishop Langton had refused to hand over his home, Rochester Castle, to the King because the demand was made "without judgement," as Langton said. Eleanor learned from court gossip that the King was so infuriated that the archbishop would not give him the castle that he called Langton a "notorious and barefaced traitor," only one of the disputes that prompted the meeting now in session in a private room in Windsor Castle. The issue of the baronial revolt was the main topic on the table.

To the delight of the maids, the King requested drinks and food be delivered to the gathering, giving the staff the same opportunity as before to eavesdrop. Eleanor and a few other maids, joined by a curious Agnes this time, pressed their ears against a drafty outer wall to listen to the deliberations.

"With all due respect, Sire, I do not believe that the Lord God intended the world to be ruled by kings," Langton began. Eleanor heard an audible gasp from the men inside, but ominously there was no outburst from King John. "Kings throughout history are predisposed to rule oppressively and with disregard for the law," he continued. "Are subjects obliged to obey a king who makes unjust decisions? Your demand for my castle is an example. If a king condemns a man to death, to cite another example, but the prisoner has not been convicted by a court of the realm, is the executioner obliged to carry out the sentence? I assure you, Highness, that I am no subversive, and I respect the political nature of your rule and the rule of all monarchs. The Scriptures say, 'Let every person be subject to the governing authorities. There is no authority except from God.' Yet, the Lord is displeased when there is no justice. Your onerous disregard for upholding English law and baronial rights, not to mention the rights of the Church, and your oppressive taxation of the people and other offenses of your reign, have brought us to this point. If you do not agree to abide by the charter of your predecessor, Henry Beauclerc, son of the Conqueror, as the barons demand, there will be war. It is inevitable. Already the French are amassed on the other side of the Channel, ready to join with the barons. The charter, though more than a hundred years old, still carries the force of law, Sire. It promises that the kings of England will rule justly, allowing barons to retain their properties, refrain from onerous taxation, and other assurances to grant liberties to the people. We all urge you to sign this renewed charter as a peaceful solution to the uprisings throughout the realm and the threat of French invasion."

There was a long pause while the King's men whispered among themselves. Finally, the King spoke in a measured voice. "What say you, Sir Marshal?"

Eleanor heard a chair pull out from the table as the Marshal stood to address the group. "Sire, this realm is at a breakin' point. Aside from the barons, who believe their rights have been usurped, the common folk fear the oppression of the King's men, the tax collectors, and the harsh sentences carried out to impose dread upon the people. Poor, starvin' peasants who dare to snare a rabbit in the King's forest have their hands cut off by your men, so that they have no chance of supportin' their already famished families. Wanton ruffians, includin' the King's men and even the barons, are rapin' and pillagin' across the land without restraint, without even the fear of God to hold them in check. The common folk have no recourse but to try to fend for themselves against a lawless realm, and when they do, they're punished severely, sometimes killed, boiled alive, flayed alive, for standin' up for their wives and children. Then there's the French. It's said that Fitzwalter has already offered the crown of our England to Prince Louis if he launches an invasion. Signin' this Great Charter will be the peace offerin' with the barons that will stop Louis from advancin', because, I assure you, Your Majesty, the French have the might, the will, and the wealth to take our England back and turn us all French. It must not happen!"

The Marshal's voice was booming and quivering with righteous anger toward the end of his speech. There was silence. The maids heard him sit down and pull in his chair, then more sympathetic mutterings were heard. The women scurried back to the kitchen with old Agnes waddling behind as fast as she could.

⎯⎯◆⎯⎯

Several days later, on the 15th of June, 1215, the King's men assembled at a field called Runnymede which lay along the Thames River in London, about an hour's ride from Windsor Castle, for the signing of the Magna Carta. At the last minute, Eleanor and a few other servants were told to accompany the royal entourage. "You will attend me at Runnymede and advise me of any ill omens of the day," the King wrote to Eleanor in a brief note stamped with the King's seal. The kitchen staff was stunned to see a royal courier deliver the scroll to a common maid in the kitchen, and all of them wanted to know what it said.

"The King wants me to attend the signing ceremony," was all she said. "I suppose he needs an extra maid." She did not add that at the bottom of the note he had written, "Am I in danger?" How could Eleanor answer this? Of course he was in danger, because, although he would sign the Magna Carta, he would still go to war against the French and continue to devastate the country. All of John's failures would be brought about by one man: John.

The King rode a large black horse within a tight grouping of guards at the head of the assemblage, a grouping that included Sir William the Marshal. They rode briskly for about twenty minutes, and presently she saw one of the King's men ride back to the servants and urge her to ride forward to speak with the King. "Get goin', girl," said the officer. "God only knows why he wants to speak with a wastrel like you, but get up there and talk with yer King."

My king, she thought. Was that really true? When she'd left the future, Lyndon Baines Johnson was president, John Kennedy having been assassinated the year before. Here she was ruled by a maniacal dictator, not a president. She spurred on her horse and rode ahead, meeting the King off to the side where they spoke.

"Sire," she said, with a slight bow of her head.

"What say you? What is to occur, and what are the dangers?"

"Sire," began Eleanor, "there are no dangers that I foresee. This charter will be a great benefit to the people of England and will help soothe the barons. I see no risk or dangers whatsoever." She knew, of course, that he would refuse to adhere to the charter, but the peaceful, sunny day at Runnymede held no threats to the King.

"You rightly predicted that I would be pressured to sign this charter. Alright girl, stay close, and alert me if you get a warning in your heart that anyone present, especially the barons, wishes to do me ill."

"Yes, Sire. If I sense any danger, I will alert you." She saw the Marshal throw her a skeptical look, and they rode on.

For hours under a hot summer sun at Runnymede, the King, Archbishop Langton, and the barons discussed, rewrote, and negotiated the document. The King had a tent set up in the field, while Eleanor and the other servants brought him and the other men refreshments. He looked bored and sat quietly sipping a tankard of spiced wine while the men scurried over to him with a suggestion, then scurried away again to the scribes. Archbishop Langton caught sight of Eleanor and discreetly made his way to the cluster of servants.

"Take this," he said, pressing a small book into her hands. It was a book of Psalms, initialed on an inside page with a verse from Psalm 71 written in the archbishop's own hand. "Deliver me, O my God, out of the hand of the wicked, out of the hand of the unrighteous and cruel man."

"For your comfort, my dear," Langton said, closing his hand around hers on the book. "Stand fast in the Lord and He will protect you." He moved away and joined the others.

After nearly a day of deliberation, the charter was ready to be signed. The scribes worked furiously to make copies. King John put up no resistance, a sure sign, she knew, that he intended to ignore it almost before the ink was dry. Eleanor surveyed the scene around her, the King putting his seal to the document, the Marshal, archbishop, and barons assembled as witnesses, the city of London with its teeming inhabitants as a backdrop, and she breathed deeply. She was witness to a momentous event in history. Moreso, she had, somehow, become an unwitting adviser to King John of England—his air of boredom no more than a practiced performance.

The ride back to Windsor was uneventful. Eleanor could not see the King at the head of the train but knew, without doubt, that he was seething. Hot, tired, and hungry, the entourage arrived back at Windsor, and the King quickly disappeared. Not thirty minutes later, one of the castle guards, a friendly man named Bartholomew who enjoyed the kitchen company—more frequently because of the presence of an always smiling and bubbly Estrilda—arrived out of breath, eager to share some castle gossip.

"Ye won't believe what's happened above in the King's chambers," he began, panting from racing down the stairs. "Gather round, gals, the King's men must not hear me tell it." They huddled together quickly, Eleanor among the most eager to hear what had happened and Agnes pushing her way through by bending over and shuffling through the gaggle, emerging nearly upright in front of Bartholmew.

"Well," he continued. "The King straightaway strode into his chamber, alone, mind ye, and closed the door and locked it from the inside. I stood guard outside, as I always do, and suddenly I heard a noise like a growlin' beast. I peered through the keyhole, as no one else was guardin' the door, and what do you guess I saw? The King, rolling on the floor, kickin' his feet, foamin' at the mouth, I tell ye, spittle flyin', bleatin' curses at all the barons, namin' them one by one and callin' down hell and damnation on each man."

"Goodness!" said Agnes. "Is the King alright? Did he harm hisself?"

"No," said Bartholomew. "After a time, he calmed a bit, and he lay on the floor breathin' heavy. He finally stood, a frightful mess with his crown on the floor and his hair standin' straight up, his tunic awry. He walked toward the door, so I leaped up and stood at attention. He opened the door, his face red as fire, and he said, 'Call Pandulf. Quick man, find him and send him to me.' I ran to get the papal legate, that oily scoundrel, and urged him to attend the King. Pandulf entered the King's chamber, then they shut the door again and locked it, and that's the last thing I heard. I was relieved by another guard and so … well, here I am tattlin' the whole disturbin' tale to all of ye."

The King's mask had dropped. Eleanor was worried about what would happen next. It didn't take her long to find out. The next day, she was again told she would be accompanying the King and his entourage to Rochester Castle, the Archbishop's home in England.

She wondered if Stephen Langton would be one of the war's first casualties.

Chapter Thirty-Three

The next morning, Eleanor left Thomas's cap at the edge of the woods by the well. She needed to speak with him quickly, before she left with the King's caravan. While waiting for him she went to see the Queen.

Queen Isabella, wearing a light linen gown with extra pleating around the waist for her expanding size, removed her veil and fanned herself. One of her ladies scurried over to assist her, but Isabella shooed her away. "I can do this myself, Matilda, please go away," the Queen said irritably. Matilda left in a hurry, and when she had gone, the Queen addressed Eleanor. "I'm not concerned, Eleanor. But perhaps you should be."

"My Lady?"

"You'll be traveling with my husband. He'll expect something from you."

Eleanor froze.

"Not that," the Queen continued with irritation and a wave of her hand. "He'll expect you to predict his future," she continued, "and it better be good. He's already angry that you didn't warn him of the dangers of signing the Great Charter."

"But, My Lady, there were no dangers. Nothing ill occurred."

"Oh yes, it certainly did. He signed, and now he regrets it. That is the ill that occurred. His regret."

Eleanor was speechless for a moment, then she said, "I'm sorry, My Lady. I could not foresee that His Majesty would have such regret. What

I could see was that he would be in no danger if he signed. My sense was that signing would prevent the barons from declaring all-out war, and so far they appear to have been appeased."

"But don't you realize, Eleanor," said the Queen, drawing close, inches from her face, "that the King will never, ever give up his authority to the barons, to the clergy, or, God forbid, to the common people. That will never happen. My husband's authority comes from the Almighty, and it cannot be diluted by a piece of parchment."

Eleanor could only apologize for her lack of foresight, and she quietly left the Queen's chambers. When she had packed a satchel, filled with food and drink by a fretful Agnes, she stepped outside to see if Thomas was waiting for her. At the end of the alley, she saw a finger waving from the slit in the door. She ran and once again he pulled her inside.

"What's happening?" he asked. "What is the urgency?"

"I'm leaving within the hour to accompany the King to Rochester. He signed a charter of liberties yesterday, but now he wants revenge. And first on his list is the Archbishop at his castle in Rochester."

"Eleanor, ye must be careful," said Thomas with a furrowed brow. "The King, I hear, is out for blood, and he's not safe to be around. If the Marshal is nearby, stay close to him. And I promise ye, I'll follow the King's caravan discreetly in the woods to keep my eye on ye. But take no chances, and say nothin' to get the King's blood boilin'. Promise me."

Eleanor became more worried with every word he uttered. "I'll try, Thomas, but the King wants me to predict success for him, and that's not going to happen. At least, not in every instance. I'm not even sure what happens next because my memory of these events has become shadowy. The King will know if I lie to him, and that may be worse than giving him the truth, which is almost all bad news."

"Use care. Be cautious with all yer words, and maybe he'll be pacified."

The King, pacified? Not likely. He wanted everything to go his way or heads would roll. Perhaps even hers.

"I must go," she said before darting out of the storage room with a quick kiss, then dashing inside to finish packing up.

—◆—

The King assembled a full royal baggage train, which included a portable chapel for worship and a portable treasury to carry the royal jewels, including hundreds of thousands of silver coins packed in large barrels. The crown jewels of the realm went everywhere with King John, and they were guarded by armed soldiers. The horses pulling the heavily laden carts strained under the weight as they moved over the unpaved roads, creating a baggage train that grew to nearly two miles in length, by Eleanor's estimation, as it snaked eastward. Eleanor and the other servants, including Estrilda, who buzzed with anticipation at the adventure ahead, were scattered in clusters along the train to serve the hundreds of people traveling with the caravan. From Windsor, it took more than eight hours by horse to travel to Rochester. There was still light, but the sun was beginning to cast shadows across the landscape as they pitched their tents a distance from the castle.

Word reached Eleanor that Archbishop Langton had fled England when he learned the King was marching toward his castle at Rochester. He may have already crossed the English Channel into France and safety.

"I heard the papal legate, that Pandulf fellow, has sent a dispatch to the Pope hisself from the King, asking that the Great Charter be annulled on grounds that it was illegal for the barons to force the King to sign a charter against his will," said Bartholomew, who was also attending the King in the caravan. "We'll see if the Pope agrees. He's no fan of the barons, despite all his bickerin' with the King, and he'll want to protect his rights as overlord of England." Bartholomew leaned down to whisper to Eleanor. "By the by, Eleanor, ye've got a visitor in the woods to yer back, yer friend, so to speak, watchin' out fer ye. He's the one who's had me watchin' fer the cap to be placed by the well."

"Thomas!" she exclaimed.

"Shhh, girl, quiet!" Bartholomew chided. "He's an outlaw, at least for the present. The sheriff has been questioning everyone about the death of that baron fella, Hugh de Malet, so it's not safe fer anyone to know he's about, ye understand?"

"Yes, I'm sorry," she said under her breath, but thrilled to hear that Thomas had been able to follow her in the woods throughout the day.

The castle loomed in the distance, a towering stone structure that was heavily guarded and occupied, she was told, by hundreds of knights prepared to fight to defend the archbishop's property. Inside, the castle constable had switched his allegiance away from the crown and had allowed rebels to enter to defend the castle against the King.

After setting up tents for the night, the King rode through the camp declaring, "At dawn we siege the castle!" He looked every inch a King in that moment, sitting almost tall in his saddle, covered in chainmail armor and wearing a gold crown atop his helmeted head. He carried a sword in one hand that he raised aloft, completing the picture of a warrior king preparing for battle.

When darkness had nearly enveloped the camp, save for a sliver of moon, Eleanor snuck away to the edge of the woods where she had bedded down with the other maids and tried to locate Thomas. In a few minutes, she heard him whispering to her from the forest.

"Eleanor, psst, come a little closer where I can speak with ye for a moment."

She slowly crawled away from the camp and soon saw his outline in the woods. "Don't get caught, Thomas," she said. "Please stay hidden. So, Bartholomew is your friend at the castle? I wish I had known. He's a good man."

"Aye, he is a good man. But I don't want to put him in danger, so don't call for me too often. Only when ye need me. Just know that I'll be watchin'."

His shadow grew larger, and she felt a soft touch on her hand as he reached out for her and pulled her to him. "Someday," he said, kissing her gently, "I pray I can grab ye and kiss ye for hours without stopping. I'll leave ye weak and helpless and beggin' fer me to stop."

She wanted to beg him now to never stop. As he spoke, he kissed her, his hands wrapping around her waist. She responded with equal ardor and wrapped her arms around his neck, kissing him back.

"Oh, Eleanor," he said in a husky voice. "My dearest Eleanor. How will I ever make it through the night after yer kissin'?" She could not respond. Reluctantly, they parted, and he backed away, disappearing into the darkness, leaving her alone in the woods.

Chapter Thirty-Four

The siege of Rochester Castle began at dawn when one of the King's men walked out to the castle and demanded, in a loud cry, that the rebels surrender the castle to King John of England. The response was an arrow from a crossbow, shot from the top wall into the shoulder of the hapless mouthpiece for the King. He fell to the ground moaning, while three other men raced forward to drag him away. One of them, too, was hit with an arrow from the wall, but this one landed well, in the neck, and he fell immediately.

Watching from a distance while helping to care for all the fighting men, Eleanor was horrified at the scene. It reminded her of movies she'd seen growing up, *The Adventures of Robin Hood, Ivanhoe*, in brilliant Technicolor, when men in brightly colored doublets and hose battled their enemies to the death, bloodlessly falling to the ground and stirring no more. The reality was different. This scene was set in dark, muted colors, with men moaning pitifully, the one with the shoulder wound shrieking in pain, while the man with the neck wound panted and gurgled before laying still. There were no bright colors, only the dark red of the blood that stained the ground as they were dragged away.

The King's forces bombarded the castle with stones hurled from a trebuchet. This relentless battering went on for the better part of the week, as stone by stone the outer wall was damaged. On the fourth day, as the battering continued, Eleanor was called away from her duties and told the King wanted to speak with her. She had expected it; her memories of reading about this event had sharpened.

"What say you?" he demanded after shooing away his counselors until they were alone together. "What do you foresee?"

"Sire," she began, trying to choose her words carefully. "I believe you will be victorious in taking the castle. But I don't have a strong feeling about how long it will take or what kind of casualties there may be."

"That's good," he responded, "because I intend to take this castle and hold the rebels to account for their treachery." He paused, then added, "If the archbishop, that dog, were here I would make sure he never left alive. I received word this morning that the Pope has agreed to annul the charter I was forced to sign at Runnymede. See, he is on my side and against that of the traitor Langton. The Pope declared the charter null and void of all validity forever. Forever, woman. Why did you not see this?"

"Your Majesty, I simply cannot see everything. The Lord lets me remember … know what He wants me to know." The King fell into a state of contemplation and waved her off. She returned to the camp and her duties, filled with dread over what would occur next.

She had a long wait. The battering of the castle lasted for weeks. At the beginning of the third week the outer walls were finally breached, and the rebels retreated to the safety of the stone keep in the center of the castle. Wiley as ever, the King ordered a tunnel dug beneath the castle. As the King's men were digging the tunnel, some of the inhabitants emerged. A handful of emaciated men, starved to near death, called out for mercy before stumbling through the metal gate of the keep. The first to arrive could barely walk. He shuffled haltingly as though every bone in his body ached with the effort. His cheekbones protruded in his face, the flesh around his eyes was sunken and purple. As he emerged beyond the castle, the King's men raced forward, grabbed him and dragged him away. He was followed by another half-dozen men in the same pitiful condition.

The prisoners were forced to lie on the ground on their stomachs with their hands outstretched. The King's decree hung in the air, and to Eleanor's horror, an executioner's axe descended with brutal efficiency, severing hands with a series of merciless strokes. So weak were the men with starvation that they barely cried out, yet it was the subsequent amputation of their feeble feet that unleashed a haunting chorus of wails, resonating through the expanse of the forest. They lay on the ground bleeding, and finally their bodies lay still.

"Let that be a lesson," boomed the King, aiming his fierce anger at the remaining inhabitants of the castle. "England is not ruled by the whims and greed of its barons but by the authority of the monarchy, granted by the Almighty. All those who surrender will be allowed to live. If you do not surrender by nightfall, you will perish."

Eleanor backed away from the gruesome scene with revulsion. She would never erase the bloody images from her mind, not as long as she lived. Soon she was in the woods, looking for Thomas. When she was deep within its dark recesses, where she could no longer hear the camp activity, she heard Thomas whisper to her. "Eleanor, over here," he called softly. They came together, and he drew her to him. "I heard what has happened," he said. "The King is a brutal man, never carin' who suffers as long as he gets his way. 'Twill be over soon, though, as the poor devils inside can't last much longer."

"It was dreadful, Thomas. The men had already surrendered. He is an evil beast!"

"Ye'd best go back, Eleanor, I hear some men enterin' the wood." Then he smirked at her. "There's no time for ye to grab me and paw at me, kissin' me to near death against my will, whilst ye admire my handsome face and form."

"Oh!" she exclaimed in mock exasperation. "You'll get no more kisses from me ever!"

He looked at her and with a smile said, "We'll see about that now, won't we? Go now, quick. I'll be nearby, always."

———

The next day the tunnel was completed. An order was given by the King to "send to us with all speed by day and night forty of the fattest pigs of the sort least good for eating to bring fire beneath the tower." When the herd of pigs arrived, they were driven into the tunnel beneath the castle, slaughtered pitifully by the King's men, and set on fire. Soon the camp heard the wails of the people inside, starving people driven mad by the aroma of cooked pig. Within hours the wails became shrieks of agony as the pigs blazed up and began burning the upper floors of the keep. The people inside were burning to death, thought Eleanor in horror, too stunned to take it all in. By the end of the following day the cries had ceased, and one corner of the keep collapsed with a deafening noise that shook the ground.

The few defenders left alive finally surrendered. The crossbowman, who had fired the fatal shot against the King's man on the first day of the siege, was hanged before the entire camp.

John mounted his horse, bade the caravan to follow, and went on to the next battle.

Chapter Thirty-Five

O nce again, the caravan moved slowly from Rochester to the northernmost tip of England where it meets Scotland. With winter on the horizon, the travelers were ill-equipped for the cold weather of the north, and they resorted to wrapping themselves in horse blankets to keep warm. Eleanor learned along the way that Queen Isabella had given birth to another girl—which greatly irked the King.

"A girl!" he spat out angrily, speaking with Eleanor one day on the journey north. "We don't need any more girls."

Eleanor remained silent and stood in the King's presence with her head bowed. She felt cold, and her head ached from the many weeks of travel. Perhaps she wasn't eating well, since her weight was beginning to drop. She needed to take better care of herself if she was going to be on this extended war caravan with the King and his army.

"So, woman, what do you see next for our efforts to defend the realm?" The King sat snugly in a padded chair brought along for his comfort. His belly spilled out over its sides. He was inside a tent that had a warm fire blazing.

Eleanor coughed, then spoke. "Sire, I apologize, but I see nothing. I am unsure of your plans. I only know that the rebel barons have invited the French to march against you, which you already know. Prince Louis of France has accepted the barons' offer of your crown. You have many battles ahead. I am so sorry, Your Majesty, but … your rejection of the Great Charter has inflamed the barons, and now the French are preparing to invade England."

He stood and pounded his fist into his open palm. "Never!" he shouted. "Never will I allow the French to rule this island! You've become worthless to me, woman. You have made no prediction of any value for weeks, and the few you have made are so vague they could be made by a common fishwife. Be gone, woman, be gone I say!"

She scurried away, wrapping her cloak about her and covering her face. She felt wretched, tired, weak, and desperately cold. She carefully wandered to the edge of the woods and slipped inside. When, after about forty-five minutes, she could not find Thomas, she realized she must be lost. Tears burned behind her eyes. She came to a large tree and leaned up against it, panting, her head swimming, and her vision going dim. Thomas, Thomas where are you? I need you. Did she think it or say it out loud?

She collapsed on the forest floor, unconscious. She heard a pounding on the ground, like horses running, and saw a large stag approach, bearing heavy white antlers. It gave a snort and pawed at the ground. It shook its antlers dangerously close to her face. Then there were more stags, all of them rearing up, pawing the ground angrily and snorting steam into the cold air. They encircled her.

One of the stags opened its mouth and spoke. "Who are you?" it asked Eleanor.

"God?" Eleanor responded. "Is that you?"

"God!" It replied with a derisive laugh, "There is no god here."

Another one spoke. "I know who this is. It's the King's necromancer. She's a sorceress."

"She's a witch," said another.

"She's the King's whore, you mean."

"No!" cried Eleanor, "That's not true!"

"Leave her alone," said another stag. "Enough of your blasphemy. Can't you see she's ill? She's the Queen's midwife, you fools."

The stags danced around her, like children dancing around a maypole, but then they lost their shapes and turned dark, transforming into gray puffs of smoke that swirled and blended into one another until the entire forest became pitch black.

Then there was daylight, and she was with Patrick, her fiancé. They were walking through New York City's Rockefeller Plaza at Christmas after seeing the famous Christmas show with the Rockettes and the live nativity.

"That was wonderful, wasn't it?" Patrick said to her. His arm was wrapped around her as they walked through the busy streets, both bundled up against the cold.

He was so handsome, she thought, with his dark wavy hair and broad shoulders. On a street corner they sat on a bench and ate roasted chestnuts. It was a perfect day—but something nagged at her.

"Patrick," she began, "I have something to tell you."

"Yes, Eleanor," he said, looking at her with affection and kissing her cheek. "What is it, dearest?"

"Patrick, I don't know how to say it, so I'll say it quickly. I'm in love with someone else. I met him in England, his name is Thomas, and he's a stone mason working on the King's castle."

Patrick was looking at her with confusion and worry etched on his face, but he did not speak. As Eleanor watched him, his face became dark and blurry, and he made clucking noises with his mouth. "Tut tut," he said, "there, there missy, ye'll be right as rain in no time. It's the fever that's taken hold of ye."

"What are you talking about, Patrick?" she answered. "What fever?" But it was now too dark to make out his face.

Slowly, Eleanor's vision cleared and she saw a woman leaning over her, offering soothing words of comfort. The old woman, who reminded her of Agnes, had a scarf tied around her head and was dabbing at Eleanor's forehead with a wet cloth. Eleanor shivered and closed her eyes. Was she still dreaming, or was this real? She fell asleep again, and this time she did not dream.

———◆———

It would be more than a week before Eleanor was fully conscious and aware of her surroundings. At first, she believed she had taken ill and was being cared for by the King's servants. But she soon realized she had passed out in the woods and was taken captive by none other than Baron Fitzwalter and his fellow nobles, whose army was fighting the King's forces.

When she awoke again, Baron Fitzwalter was looking down at her. He was in his late forties, tall, well built, with a dark beard. He carried a sword that dangled from a belt on his hip. "My men found you half dead in the woods, covered in filth. You would have been food for the wolves had we not taken you with us, and now we've nursed you back to health."

"Thank you," she said, a little sheepishly. "I appreciate your efforts. I'm free to leave?"

"Well, not exactly," he said, taking a stool and sitting beside her. "We know who you are, and we know the King is anxious to recover you for your … assistance in matters of state. We know that you've been predicting the future for him, and with fair accuracy, I add."

"Sir Robert," began Eleanor, her head pounding with a headache, "I have been able to give him some idea of future events, but I am not a soothsayer and do not ever, I repeat, ever communicate with evil spirits. I believe God puts these events in my mind, but I can't on my own foresee anything."

"Alright," said Fitzwalter dismissively. "What do you see for our efforts? For the barons who have taken up arms against the King's tyrannical rule?"

Eleanor did not hesitate. "You will fail," she said bluntly. "The French you have invited into England will wreak havoc and take over much of the realm, but they will ultimately be driven out. England will stand and will never be a vassal state of France."

Robert Fitzwalter looked shocked, and he could not respond for several moments. Eleanor continued. "I don't know or foresee many details. I don't know what victories or defeats you will have, and I don't know your fate, Sir Robert. I know that England only becomes stronger in time."

"How can you know these things?" he demanded. His voice became harsh, and his brows furrowed threateningly. "I don't believe you. The French are already here, with a huge force of men on their way to add to those. They are indestructible, while King John is weak and without much support. Our spies tell us he's preparing to push into southern Scotland, but he'll be greeted with a big surprise when he does," added Fitzwalter.

"What do you mean?"

"Why should I tell you, woman? As a fortune teller, don't you know already? I'll tell you this much. King Alexander of Scotland has joined our cause. His clansmen warriors are the fiercest fighting men on earth.

The King will be routed."

Eleanor had no idea what would happen next. King John will not die at the hands of the Scottish king, she knew that, but she had no memory of these northern battles from her reading. She asked, "Where are we now? Where is this camp?"

"We're close to the battle," was all he would say. "Rest up, woman. I want you healthy, and I want your visions for the future. Understand? Good or bad, I want them." He gave her a stern look, and she could only nod.

Chapter Thirty-Six

After spending several weeks in the camp of the barons, Eleanor was roughly dragged from her straw bed one morning by a group of soldiers. She was undressed, save for a rough linen shift given to her by one of the servants.

She was in a daze, not knowing what was happening and why she was being taken away. Was she being kidnapped again? Was it even possible to be kidnapped this often?

"Take the witch away!" a man yelled.

She remembered that voice from her dream in the forest; it was one of the stags. She was dragged into the cold morning air, her feet bare, her hair wild and unkempt, and her shift paper thin. A man, one of the barons, walked up to her. As she stared at him uncomprehending, he spat in her face. "Thou shalt not suffer a witch to live!" he said, loud enough for the assembled soldiers and camp followers to hear. "You've been accused of witchcraft, woman, and you will stand trial immediately."

"What are you talking about? I'm not a witch!" She was trembling with fear and cold. Accusations of witchcraft in the Middle Ages were serious. They burned witches, didn't they? Yes, she answered herself. They burned them at the stake. Perhaps she was still dreaming, but soon her head cleared, and she knew it was really happening. Dear God, she prayed silently, please protect me, please give me the right words, please give my accusers ears to hear. Please, please, please, dear Lord.

A blanket was thrown around her by a servant, who had darted through the crowd. "Here are yer shoes, miss," she said, bending down to place them on Eleanor's feet as she was led away. "Give her a minute, ye filthy animals!" the servant woman shrieked to the crowd.

Inside one of the large baronial tents, Eleanor was forced to stand in the middle while twelve men surrounded her, all seated, hurling accusations at her.

"You are accused of being a witch, woman, and giving the King of England false advice based on communion with Satan himself," said one of the barons.

"Where is Sir Fitzwalter?" she asked, looking around the table, a tortured look on her face.

"We are asking the questions," said the man. "How do you answer the charge?"

She felt the pressure to defend herself like a noose around her neck. "I … I have never, ever had communion, as you put it, with the Devil. I believe in God Almighty. I am a Christian, sirs."

"How do you predict the future if not through perverse communion with the forces of darkness?"

"I simply get ideas, pictures of future events, from God. I have never made any prediction that came from the voice of God that did not come true."

"That's a lie!" The baron, whose name, she learned, was William de Clare, leaped to his feet and pointed an accusing finger at Eleanor. "Through your sorcery you have doomed our leader, Robert Fitzwalter, to failure by selling your soul and the soul of the King to the prince of darkness."

"What?" demanded Eleanor. "That's absurd."

"Furthermore," continued de Clare, "through your sorcery, the King was able to defeat the rebel forces at Rochester Castle. That castle was an impenetrable stronghold that could only have succumbed to the darkest forces."

"He beat your rebels by spending more than a month battering the castle," she answered, "then burning it from the bottom up."

"Silence! You will not speak until we give you permission."

"I won't be silent during this ridiculous inquisition," she insisted, her anger rising. "Of the few predictions I have made, all have come true. If they had not, that would have been the true mark of a false prophet."

"Oh, you have the mark, alright," hissed de Clare. "The witch's mark, right there on your back." Two men came forward and pulled down the back of her shift, ripping it down the middle, to reveal a large birthmark on her upper back. "There!" said de Clare. "There it is! The mark of the Devil, a permanent mark made when Satan raked his claws across your flesh during one of your nocturnal rites."

Eleanor could not help laughing at this. "That's a birthmark, you idiot. I've had it since I was a baby."

A soldier came up and slapped her so hard across the face it caused her to fall to the ground. De Clare and the other barons erupted in anger, rising to their feet and pointing at her accusingly, some making the Sign of the Cross to ward off evil spirits.

Eleanor sobered up quickly, got her anger under control, and said another silent prayer, pleading with God to give her peace of mind and the right words to convince the men of her innocence.

"We have a witness to your witchcraft," said de Clare. "Bring him in."

The curtains of the large tent parted and—to Eleanor's astonishment—Simon the Seer, the only one who could possibly be in league with Satan, walked in. At first, she didn't recognize him. He had shaved off his beard, and his hair was closely cropped. He still had his ink-black eyes, which she would recognize anywhere. Why would he accuse her now? What did he have against her? she wondered for the hundredth time. She had never done him any harm.

"You!" she exclaimed. She addressed her accusers. "This man was turned out from the King's castle for being a false prophet." She pointed a finger at him. "He is a witch, a false prophet, and a liar, not me. He gave the King a false prophecy, not me. He fled for his life after the King accused him of being a sorcerer, not me. You must not believe his lies!"

"Quiet!" shouted de Clare. "Restrain her." A guard bound her hands behind her back and gagged her. She fought him, but to no avail. "Proceed, sir," de Clare encouraged.

Simon walked into the center of the room. He was conservatively dressed; gone were the flamboyant magician's robe and hat. He wore dark hose and a heavy coat over his tunic. He bowed solemnly to the men. "Sirs, I did, indeed, meet with the King, but he was so enchanted, or should I say, entranced by a spell put on him by this witch here that he could not think straight. He would only listen to this woman, this witch."

Eleanor tried to object through her gag but could only make grunting noises. "I, sirs, am a magician. Indeed, I am known far and wide for weaving wonders wherever I travel. But," he continued, punctuating his words with a dramatic gesture, "let it be known that my craft is pure and untainted by the shadows of dark arts. Every enchantment I perform is but a clever sleight of hand, a spectacle designed solely to entertain and amaze. My magic tricks are only that, tricks and gimmicks and nothing more."

"What evidence have you that this woman practices the dark arts?" asked de Clare.

"I saw her, in a moment when she believed herself to be alone, praying to that old serpent, the Devil himself. She had stolen away from the King's chambers to recharge herself with communion with her lord, Satan. I followed her to a secluded corner of the castle and watched her bow low to the ground and plead with her dark master to send her prophecies to trick the King. 'I will serve you for the rest of my life,' she told the serpent, 'if you will only grant me this.' Then," said Simon, pausing for dramatic effect, "she pulled out a knife secreted beneath her skirts, sliced her wrist with it and held the wound up above her head. I heard the most foul sound, as of a beast licking something, and though I could see no beast, I saw the blood disappear from her wrist before my eyes, licked away by the prince of hell."

Eleanor was aghast. She hung her head, finally giving up her protests. The guard removed her gag but kept her wrists tightly bound.

"If you will give me a moment alone with the witch, perhaps I can get her to confess," said Simon. The men conferred before leaving the tent. "Stay close," added Simon, "lest she call upon the Devil to aid her in breaking her bindings and claw me."

Once alone, Simon led her to a chair and sat her down. He pulled out another chair and sat in front of her, leaning in close enough to her face that only she could hear him. His breath was foul, and she turned her face away from him. "I want the jewels, Eleanor. Wherever you have them, tell me, and I'll recant my testimony. I'll save you from burning at the stake."

She pulled back, eyes wide, and looked deep into his eyes. "What jewels? What are you talking about? How could you tell such a crazy story?"

His eyes narrowed, and his mouth tensed. "Don't play stupid. I know you have the crown jewels, or at least some of them."

"The crown jewels? How would I have them? The King always keeps them with him, under guard. Are you telling me that's what this is all about? You, sending me to this time, following me to the castle, accusing me in front of the barons? You think I have the crown jewels of England? Are you mad?"

Simon looked confused. He stammered, "You do have them. I've … I've seen you with them, in the future. You …" At that moment, the barons returned.

"Did she confess?" asked de Clare.

Simon did not answer. Eleanor could see he was struggling with his thoughts, trying to decide if he believed her. Before moving away from her, Simon leaned down, close to her ear, and whispered, "Get them. Get the jewels."

If only Baron Fitzwalter was here, she thought, he would be reasonable, he would be her champion. Champion … champion. The word unlocked something in her memory. She recalled the story of *Ivanhoe*, set in medieval England during the reign of King John. What was it about a champion that was taking shape in her memory? Then it came to her.

"With God as my judge, I claim combat by champion." she blurted out to the barons. "I demand a trial by combat with the champion of my choosing. I call upon the might of Sir William the Marshal to champion my cause." In the epic tale of *Ivanhoe*, the heroic Rebecca finds herself unjustly accused of witchcraft. Defiantly, she invokes the ancient custom of trial by combat, entrusting her fate to Ivanhoe. With a swift stroke, Ivanhoe defeats her accuser in a joust, winning Rebecca's freedom.

Whether or not such a practice existed in medieval England, or only on the pages of *Ivanhoe*, mattered little as the notion leaped from her mind and burst from her lips in a moment of determination.

The barons were taken aback and remained silent for a moment. De Clare stood and spoke. "You will burn for your devilish ways, woman," he said. "There will be no trial by combat. Witches don't have any rights."

"Wait a minute," spoke up another baron. "Anyone in the realm may request trial by ordeal."

"She isn't even an Englishwoman," said another. "She's a Frenchie.

She has no rights here."

"I nominate Sir Bertrand," yelled one baron.

"Even Bertrand cannot defeat William the Marshal," said another, in a more sober voice. "The Marshal was undefeated every year he competed in a joust, with more than 500 victories on the field."

"Yes, but he's an old man now. He can't possibly defeat Bertrand."

While the men were debating Eleanor's fate, she noticed that Simon had slipped away. Another escape.

"Take her away," de Clare said with a dismissive wave of his hand. Eleanor was dragged away to her tent with two guards posted outside.

That evening, Robert Fitzwalter strode into the tent and stood facing her. "I'm greatly distressed by the proceedings today," he said directly. "I was not present to intervene. Yet the barons have made their decision, and I must abide by it. You are to be allowed combat by champion. As soon as both champions are located, we will commence the joust. If Sir William defeats our knight, you will be released and the charges dropped. If he loses, you will be burned. I'm sorry woman, I cannot change the outcome."

The next morning, she awoke to loud noise in the camp. Fearing she would be dragged from her bed yet again, she jumped up and wrapped a blanket around her. Peering outside she saw a large white steed enter the camp followed by two other horses. Sir William! She felt a surge of hope. Was that Alfred with him? Yes, and who was the third rider? Was it—yes, it was her Thomas!

The men entered the center of the camp, their horses stomping the ground as if they, too, were angry at the false charges brought against her. She dressed quickly and was soon led outside. She cast a quick glance toward her champion. The Marshal was clad in armor from head to toe. Even his white charger was covered in armor. Together they were a majestic, indomitable sight.

Fitzwalter walked out to meet him. "Our champion has not yet arrived," he said. "You will be safe here until he does, but you may not communicate with the accused."

"We'll wait here till the mornin'," said Sir William. "If your so-called champion does not arrive by dawn, we will take the woman—the innocent woman—with us and be gone. If he arrives in time, I shall dispatch him without mercy quickly, and we'll be on our way. Either way, Sir Fitzwalter, we're leavin' with the woman. Ye've greatly angered the King yet again by yer deeds here."

Eleanor did not sleep at all. Finally, at dawn, she learned that the barons' champion, Sir Bertrand, never arrived. She supposed he was too afraid to fight the great Sir William the Marshal. Within the hour, they had all assembled outside and prepared to depart. Eleanor mounted behind Thomas on his horse as the barons assembled, grim faced and seething with anger.

Fitzwalter spoke. "You best be gone quickly," he said to the Marshal. Sir William bowed his head as he sat on his horse and, without a word, turned around, and they rode out of the camp.

Once out of sight, Sir William turned around and said, "Be quick, both of ye. I don't trust these churls for a minute not to follow us and try to take us down in the forest. Make haste!" And they spurred their horses to gallop.

Chapter Thirty-Seven

As the year 1216 dawned upon England, Eleanor found solace once more nestled in the comforting embrace of the Adelfrids. It proved a soothing salve for her weary soul and frail body to be reunited with them. Their house was chaotic at times, loud with life— but it was home, and it was safe.

After their hard ride away from the barons' camp, Sir William, Alfred, and Thomas, with Eleanor still feeling ill and bouncing along the back of Thomas's horse, arrived the following day at the King's camp.

This is the last place on earth I want to be. I'm still a little sick, weak in the legs, and now I've got to deal with yet another monster.

When she was brought before the King, he looked her up and down, a frown creasing his face. Was that worry? Could this godless, perverted tyrant actually feel such an emotion? She swayed on her feet in front of him, trying not to collapse.

"You are in no shape to continue with us," he told her after a moment, obviously annoyed. "I can see you are still weak from your illness. The barons will pay, woman, for your abduction and their threats to your life." He wagged a finger in her face. "You are my servant, and they will be sorry they laid a hand on you."

"Thank you, Sire," Eleanor said, giving a slight curtsy. She was afraid if she sank too low she might not make it back up.

"You may rest for a few weeks at the Adelfrids. Rest up, and let Thomas get you back to us as soon as you're well. I must ask before he takes you, have you any visions for me?"

She sighed. She only knew the year would see some victories and some losses, but her mind was not clear about any of them. "Sire, I do not," she finally answered. "I fear my mind is still not working well, due to my illness. If I can spend some time recovering, I will devote myself to prayer, and hopefully God will give me some knowledge to pass on. I apologize that I cannot be of more help right now."

After all his lecherous advances, the murder of poor Sabine, the brutality against his own subjects, *now* he has some sympathy for her. She didn't trust him. She knew he only wanted her healthy enough to predict his future—a bright future.

"Never mind," he said with a wave of his hand. "You may go."

Outside, preparing to depart, she asked Thomas, "How did you get your freedom back, Thomas? You seem to be in the King's good graces again."

"He hates the barons, Eleanor, and when I explained what happened, he considered that I did him a service, eliminatin' one more baron. Of course, the King is not above rape hisself; he's violated too many women to count. He's also thankful I brought ye back to him. I'm grateful I'm able to live out in the open again."

"Me, too." She squeezed his hand.

The Marshal met them as they prepared to leave for Graston. "Well, ye've done it again, missy," he said with a scowl on his face.

"Sir William, you can't possibly think any of that was my fault. I was ill, kidnapped, falsely accused of being a witch, and almost burned alive. How did I bring that on myself?"

"Ye seem to bring trouble wherever ye go, girl. Ye're like a wounded hare attractin' the wolves. Be gone, both of ye. Thomas, the King wants her back, though God knows why; she's nothin' but trouble. Keep her safe, and get her back soon. We'll get word to ye where we are."

She couldn't help smiling at the Marshal's words. He's like a father to me, like a substitute father. His dressing down of her carried more affection than anger.

———

Several weeks later, she was feeling fit, and her color had returned. Lavinia remarked on how well she looked. "Almost too well, Eleanor, for ye'll be goin' back to the King's camp soon."

"I know, but I must return. I gave my word, and Thomas will be coming back soon to fetch me. How are you doing, Lavinia?"

"Very well," she said with a huge smile. "My darlin' little Richie is my joy." The baby was bouncing on Lavinia's knee, grabbing one of Eleanor's fingers and trying to suckle it. "I can't imagine life without him now, not carin' at all about how he got his beginnin'. And Dicun is the best husband a woman could ask for. I tell ye, Eleanor, everythin' has worked out well, as ye said it would. And now that Thomas is free from the law, we can all rest easy. The only dark cloud hangin' over us is the war. Will we all become French? I don't know that I could bear it."

"No," answered Eleanor with a laugh. "You will not all become French." She corrected herself. "We will not become French."

Thomas showed up the following week with a small horse tied to his own. "This one's for you, Eleanor. The King hisself sent it, so that you'd not have to ride on my horse behind me. Though I must admit, I wouldn't mind that at all."

"Thomas!" exclaimed Beja, stepping outside. She swatted him with a kitchen rag. "Show Eleanor a little respect, and don't speak to her like she were a common dairy maid."

He smiled broadly as he climbed off his horse. "Sorry, Ma. I'll not disrespect the lady again." And he winked at Eleanor, who smiled back at him as her cheeks reddened.

The next day, they began their trip to Windsor Castle. The idea of being alone with Thomas, even if all they did was ride hard for most of the day, was exhilarating.

Thomas explained as they rode, "There's been a temporary truce. The King is headed to Windsor now, and he wants us to meet him. I have some other news for ye. The King of Scotland, Alexander, invaded the north and sides with the barons. What's more, the King's own bastard brother, William Longespée, who'd been commandin' the King's army here in the south, has gone over to the barons. It's a terrible blow to King John, for sure. I fear the French invasion is comin' quickly, and we'd best be watchin' the Channel for their fleet. I don't know how long this truce will last, but the King is puttin' together his own naval fleet to stave off the invasion. I fear we'll be overrun by the French."

"In the end, it won't happen," she answered with confidence. "But there will be bloody battles, and the French will invade." She felt like a broken record, saying the same thing over and over. Even knowing the final outcome—that England would not fall to the French—Eleanor feared the battles and bloodshed ahead.

———

"Miss Eleanor, it's glad I am to see ye!" said Agnes when they arrived at the castle, throwing her frail body around Eleanor in a big hug. "I've worried so, I have. And I heard about yer trials. Dear me, it's all the talk. But here ye are, safe and sound, lookin' fit if ever ye was!" She hugged her again and wiped tears from her eyes.

After visiting the Queen, Eleanor was summoned to the King's privy chamber. Present were several other men, including the King's closest advisers. She curtsied as she entered the room and remained standing in front of the men with her head slightly lowered. These men wielded immense power, and they greatly frightened her. But she had been thinking and praying about what to tell the King, and she hoped he would approve of what she was about to say. After all, she was only remembering what actually happened, or will happen.

"Be seated," said the King. "Bring her a chair, quick!" He snapped his fingers, and a guard slid a chair behind her. "She's ill from mistreatment at the hands of the traitorous barons. Tell me, now, has God given you any visions of what will transpire? What do you see, woman? Be plain and honest."

The men leaned forward to hear what Eleanor would say. He said he wanted honesty, but she knew he only wanted good news. She chose her words carefully. "Your Majesty, my thoughts are much clearer now, and I can tell you several things that will occur. First, the French under Prince Louis will invade the realm with the support of the barons and many mercenary soldiers on their side. This much you already know. They will do a lot of damage and will retake Rochester Castle." The King bristled, but she continued, "They will also take your royal castle at Canterbury." The men gasped, but John waved them to be quiet. "They will then set their sights on Dover Castle, but they will *not* succeed there. You should consider sending your soldiers to Dover quickly to fortify that stronghold. But I assure you, the French will not take Dover. And in the end, Rochester and Canterbury will be retaken by the realm."

What Eleanor could not say was that John would be dead by the time England won back many of its holdings. It would be another leader who would retake these castles. It was not all good news, but it was the truth.

One of the King's advisers spoke up. "Sire, you must not listen to this charlatan. She has predicted a future that cannot be believed, the French taking over your castles? It cannot happen."

"Quiet," shouted John. "She has not been wrong yet. I believe her, and if she is wrong, it's to the fire for her." His threat did not frighten her. Eleanor was certain of her memories. Since praying that God would allow her to remember her history studies, these events were coming back into sharp focus. She had complete and total faith that God was helping her.

"When will this occur?" demanded another adviser. They all turned to stare at her again.

"That, I cannot say with certainty," she answered. "But since we are already heading into spring, it will be soon. It would be prudent to prepare now for these sieges."

Eleanor wondered vaguely if predicting the future for the King could change history. Not possible. Not with this King. His behavior has only become more reckless.

The clock, she reminded herself, is winding down for King John.

Chapter Thirty-Eight

They entered the King's camp in the late afternoon. The sun was low in the sky, casting a red glow in the valley over hundreds of tents, soldiers, and servants—a cauldron bubbling with activity. The King's army had swelled to thousands. This was one encampment of many soldiers scattered throughout the realm, fighting the French and barons. Two guards escorted Eleanor to meet with John. Thomas refused to leave her side.

She stepped into the dimly lit tent, its interior filled with the scent of parchment and candle wax. King John sat at a makeshift table surrounded by his advisers, including Sir William, their heads bent over a large map. The King looked much older, with gray sprinkled throughout his beard and his hair thinning on top. His once-piercing eyes were now dulled by the weight of responsibility, and he restlessly tugged at his unkempt beard like a man oppressed. He wore no crown, nor was he wearing any of his other jewels. She knew well his penchant for wearing them even in the most incongruous of circumstances. But she was certain they were nearby. His jewels went everywhere with him, so fearful was he of losing control of even one of his baubles.

Suddenly, it hit her. The crown jewels. Simon the magician's comments, "I know you have the crown jewels—get them!" A memory was trying to form in her mind, but it wasn't gelling properly, remaining a hazy vision of chaos and death that somehow involved the King's jewels. Why did Simon believe she would somehow acquire the jewels? How was it possible? They were securely locked up, always under guard. Even if they weren't locked up, she would never steal even one coin. If the King's army lost to the French, she assumed the French or the barons would seize the treasure. She could not make a coherent memory out of the swirling images in her mind, but she could at least give the King something to ponder.

With Thomas remaining outside the tent, Eleanor curtsied to the King as he turned his attention to her. All his advisers, save for William the Marshal, left the tent. Eleanor had racked her brain for something to tell King John, fearing he would want to see her immediately with a new prediction. She prayed, asking for a clear mind.

"I'm in need of your premonitions," the King said. The Marshal was studying her intently.

"Sire," she began, "I hope the Queen and the children are well?"

"Yes, yes" he answered curtly, "they are hidden away and under guard, while the cursed French invade our land at the invitation of the pox-ridden barons!" Spittle flew from his lips as he worked himself into a black rage. "They will all pay for their treason, I swear it by God!" He calmed himself, but not without effort. "Out with it, woman. What have you to say that can help me?"

"Sire, I can only say again that in the end, the French and the barons will not succeed in taking the realm. England will remain independent, though weakened by the bloodshed and destruction. It will survive." You'll be in your grave by then, she thought. "However," she added, "I have one more memory, prediction, regarding the crown jewels and the royal treasury."

"What?" he straightened himself, looking alarmed. "What about the jewels?"

She forged ahead. "I believe there will be an incident, perhaps a battle, where there will be an attempt to take the jewels from you. I advise you to keep them close, locked up, and under guard at all times."

"Of course!" he shouted, irritated that she was stating the obvious. "They are safe and secure right now, under guard, locked up, and close at hand." He signaled for a guard to enter and ordered him to immediately ensure that the wagons that held the jewels were well fortified.

"That's good, Your Majesty," she responded, lowering her head. "I only meant to warn you that the jewels will be threatened in some way. If I can recall anything more about this … vision, I will tell you immediately."

He sighed, clearly exasperated with her. "Anything else? Anything new about the French plan to take Dover Castle? I've sent reinforcements there."

"Sire, they will not succeed, as I stated before. But it will be a long siege."

He seemed somewhat mollified and, waving his hand, bade her to leave.

"Thomas, I assure you, the King hasn't got long to live," she told him, voice lowered so that no spies outside the tent could overhear. "We need to make plans to get away from this entourage, or we could be defeated with the King."

"I thought you said England would stand?"

"Yes, it will, but the King will not survive, and many with him will fall to the …" She didn't know how to finish. She wasn't sure what happened or why so many people surrounding the King would die, but her memory was that death and destruction were coming—and coming soon.

"Don't ye worry, Eleanor," he said. "We'll think of somethin', and we'll be waitin' for our way of escape."

———

The King's army arrived at Dover Castle a few days before the French and baronial forces struck. After weeks spent fruitlessly besieging the castle, Louis called another truce in mid-October and returned to London, where his support was still strong.

Watching the retreating French army from the King's encampment on a northern hill, Thomas gave a whoop of delight. "I knew they would never breach the castle!" he said, giving Eleanor a crushing hug of joy. "We spent many months fortifyin' the outer defenses, at yer own suggestion, mind ye, and it served the King well."

Eleanor was proud of him. "You oversaw the construction. It will go down in history as a tribute to your hard work." She hoped it was true. Eleanor would never forget that Thomas Adelfrid of Graston, England, had been instrumental in saving Dover Castle.

"Never ye fear," said Thomas. "I'll be beside ye at all times. I swear it."

As the entourage wound several miles through the countryside, Eleanor developed a nagging feeling that they were in imminent danger, despite the truce.

Danger is all around. It's in front of us, behind us, but I can't see it … yet.

Chapter Thirty-Nine

That same day, the King's forces—a grand spectacle of hundreds of wagons, horses, soldiers, servants, guards, and camp followers— embarked on their journey northward. Their departure was swift and purposeful, a strategic maneuver to evade the looming threat of Prince Louis's army, encamped outside London. Amidst the flurry of activity, Eleanor, riding with the entourage, struggled to maintain the pace, her body fatigued from the relentless rhythm of the journey. They camped that night near the village of Wicken and continued north early the next morning.

The day dawned bright and windy, and Eleanor wrapped her cape around herself as she mounted her horse to begin the day's travels. She had briefly seen the King as they all ate a quick meal before beginning their travels. The King had been eating a bowl of sugared plums, but he looked unwell. He was bent over and appeared to be in pain. He awkwardly mounted his horse with the aid of one of his guards, and the procession began. Within a few hours, they passed through the town of King's Lynn, south of the great Wash—a large bay on the coast fed by a snaking web of roiling estuaries. The bay was at low tide as they approached, and the King, appearing frailer than ever, urged the train forward.

"This is not a good idea," commented Thomas, who had not budged from her side since they began their journey at dawn. "The tide's about to come in, and I doubt all these wagons can get across quickly enough. Eleanor, don't move from here; I'm goin' to ride up to the front to talk with the Marshal."

<hr>

She could not see Thomas up ahead since the train was so long, but within thirty minutes he reappeared, galloping toward her at top speed. "The Marshal agrees, but he says the King won't stop. He wants to get across now. It'll take us at least an hour or two for all these horses, wagons and men to make its across, and we're both fearin' that the tide will rise to a dangerous level. Look how the water bubbles even now. Eleanor, be sure to hold on tight to yer horse and remember, I'll be with ye all the way."

Slowly the train, with its hundreds of wagons, lumbered into the Wash. As the time approached for Eleanor and Thomas to urge their horses into the water, the estuaries had begun to churn and swirl as if the water was simmering on a giant stove and getting ready to come to a full boil. She and Thomas were toward the end of the train, with about a dozen carts behind her. Some of them, she suspected, were the wagons containing the King's jewels and all his money, probably trunks filled with gold and silver coins. They were the only wagons heavily guarded by the King's personal guards.

Carefully, her horse stepped through the water, which was rising high on the horses' legs, almost to their stirrups. She gripped the reins tightly but rocked back and forth sideways on her horse as it struggled to make its way through the turbulent, churning water.

Up ahead, men shouted, "Steady, men, steady!" Some of the King's men jumped off their horses and reached up to stabilize the wagons as they swayed dangerously in the Wash. As the water continued to rise, one cart, then another, was pulled over and dragged into the water. She could not believe what she was seeing: horses struggling and toppling over, their legs flailing, emitting pitiful shrieks as the swirling water sucked them under.

To her horror, her own horse foundered, and she realized that she was caught not just in a tidal whirlpool, but a bog of quicksand. She screamed as her horse fell over and she was thrown into the churning quagmire.

Behind her, the horse-drawn wagons toppled over, like toys tossed aside by a tantrumming child. They slowly sank into the quicksand. Then the guards were pulled under, along with their horses. Panicked, she flailed her arms in a windmill motion, trying to grasp anything that could keep her from being pulled under. The wailing and screams of men and horses made her eardrums thrum. The wagon train surrounding her was slowly disappearing beneath the boggy Wash.

Her arms thrashing, Eleanor finally felt a hard surface, a large chest, sitting atop a slowly sinking wagon. As the cart tipped, the chest fell sideways and knocked her back into the quicksand. The lock broke, spilling silver and gold goblets and coins into the Wash. They quickly disappeared in the quicksand. The crown jewels! Where was Thomas? She desperately looked around as the bubbling bog drew her down, pulling her as if there was a weight tied to her legs preventing her from moving.

Soon the quicksand was up to her waist. Her arms felt like she was moving through drying cement, only this cement continued to swirl and move like water being sucked down a drain in slow motion. Looking around, desperately trying to find something to grab hold of, she saw that nearly all the wagons, as far as she could see, were gone. One pathetic horse struggled to move, its nostrils expanding and contracting rapidly to take in air. Then it appeared to give up, and its head disappeared beneath the thick swirl and the quicksand below.

She would give up, too. She was too weak to keep struggling. Thomas had probably been dragged under already. There was no way to survive this, no one to help her, so she would ask God to make it quick. She closed her eyes. She would let the quicksand draw her down. She was panting, breathing harder than ever before, and her heart beat so rapidly inside her chest that it made her choke. Or was that the quicksand making her choke? Soon, my heart will stop beating once I'm pulled under completely and my lungs fill with quicksand. How long will it take? How long before suffocation and death comes? Lord, please make it a fast death, and wherever Thomas is, please make it fast for him too. Lord—

Then she heard a voice calling her. "Eleanor! Eleanor!" It was Thomas! The quicksand was up to her chin. She struggled to even turn her head, and there was Thomas, a thick rope tied around his waist, with the other end tied about fifty yards away around a large, pointed rock toward the edge of the Wash. He had created a means of escape for the two of them. But would it work?

"Eleanor!" he yelled again, untying the rope from his waist, "grab hold of this rope when I toss it to ye, and I'll pull ye in. Quick, Eleanor; can ye get yer hands free?"

She moved her shoulders slowly. Her arms felt as if they were caught in plaster, but with great effort she was able to push her hands up toward the surface. She sank lower, her mouth covered by the swirling quicksand, her eyes wide with terror. Thomas threw the rope toward her, but it landed barely out of reach. He pulled it back in and threw it again. This time she could barely touch the rope but could not get a grip. She tilted her head back, but it was too late. She gave a last desperate gulp of air as her nose and eyes were covered, and her head went under. Only her hands remained, waving wildly in the air trying to find the rope.

Just as she could hold her breath no longer, fearing she would be forced to fill her lungs with quicksand, the rope landed on one of her hands. She grabbed it fiercely and tugged on it. Slowly she was being pulled out of the bog. It was painfully slow going, and when her eyes emerged, she saw Thomas grimacing as he pulled her inch by inch toward him. She gave a huge gasp and breathed in air as her mouth finally surfaced. She coughed out a mouthful of muck. She was moving slowly toward Thomas, but her left foot was too heavy, as if a pair of hands had a grip on it, pulling against Thomas's efforts. Her mind wasn't working right, she thought wearily. Were they the hands of King John, dragging her into hell with him? Would he never let her go? She panted and groaned with the effort, but after nearly thirty minutes of being slowly dragged out of the marshy estuary, Thomas grabbed hold of her hands and dragged her into his arms.

"Great gad, Eleanor, what an effort! If feels as if ye weigh a ton."

"Thomas," she said between gulping breaths, "there may be something caught on my leg. It feels so heavy."

"Nothing to be done right now, Eleanor. I need to get us both over to that rock and to safety on the bank of this estuary. That daft King John forcin' all of us to go into a whirlpool of quicksand! I tell ye, he's a madman."

They struggled for the better part of an hour to pull themselves toward the bank, resting occasionally with Eleanor clinging to Thomas's back while his arms moved one over the other to pull them forward. Finally, collapsing on the bank as the cold water still covered her to her waist, Thomas pulled her by her arms out of the Wash and onto a dry spot. She looked back and surveyed the scene. All of them gone. Every wagon, every soldier, every horse. She assumed some of the party, including the King at the head of the train, had survived and made it across, but she could not see them.

"Well, look at this," Thomas said. He was standing above her, looking at her leg. Tangled in her long skirt, tied up with something that looked like seaweed, was a large satchel about fifteen inches square, tightly sealed at one end, sopping wet, and filled with something hard and heavy.

Still panting, she sat up and gazed at the bundle wound around her leg. "This is what was dragging me down," she said. "Whatever is inside is heavy."

Thomas took out the knife he kept tucked into his waist and cut the strands of seaweed away. He cut off the tight bindings on the top of the satchel and opened it, peeling away some of the padding inside. He gasped.

"What is it?" she asked.

He pulled out a large golden hand, studded with jewels. "Why, I heard tell about this." He gazed at it. "It's the Hand of Maud. And there's more in here, as well." He looked around quickly and said, "Eleanor, can ye stand up and walk? We need to make haste and get out of here. We're the only survivors at this end of the Wash, but there will be others at the front of the train." He helped her up, and they quickly put distance between themselves and the Wash. They headed northwest, avoiding King's Lynn to the south with the satchel and the Hand of Maud tucked safely under Thomas's arm.

Chapter Forty

"**W**here are we going, Thomas?" asked Eleanor, panting from the effort to keep up with him. Grime from the Wash clung to her like a shell of dried clay, hardened and flaking at the edges.

"I'm exhausted, Thomas, and I need to clean up." Eleanor was brushing off the flaking quicksand as she traveled. "Can we stop and spend the night in the woods?"

"'Tis not safe," he answered. "The rebels are everywhere. They're wreakin' havoc among the people. Try to keep goin', dear. I'll get ye settled as quick as I can."

They traveled on, with Eleanor needing to stop every fifteen minutes or so to rest. As the sun was setting in front of them, they saw signs of a town up ahead, but they stayed off the main road to hide themselves. A few villagers warily opened their doors to glare at the filthy travelers, and Thomas engaged one couple at their front door.

"We've been travelin' all day," he began. "Can ye tell me where we are? We're lookin' for a place to lay our heads for the night."

"Aye," said the man. "Ye're in Stephens Gate, and there's an inn up ahead. Called the Ram's Head. Ye'll find a good meal there and a room, nothin' fancy but a comfortable bed." He glanced over Thomas's shoulder and appraised Eleanor's mud-covered appearance. "What happened to ye? The lass looks a fright."

Thomas looked back at Eleanor, huddled beneath her sodden cloak, covered in Wash mud. "She was caught up in the tidal currents back near

King's Lynn. She's in desperate need of dryin' out and a good meal."

Taking pity on them, the man handed them both a piece of bread and offered them a glass of water, which they consumed greedily. Thanking him and feeling fortified, they made their way into Stephens Gate as darkness descended. Thomas rented them a room for the night and asked for a meal to be brought to their room on the third floor. Beneath them was the welcome sound of travelers and locals enjoying a hearty meal. Occasionally, lively music was heard, played on flute and some kind of stringed instrument. Eleanor heard feet stamping on the wooden floor below, people dancing and enjoying themselves even with war raging all around them.

A maid brought several basins of water for them to clean up and a brush for their clothes. As Eleanor stripped down to her underclothes, not caring if Thomas saw her, she ate and drank contentedly. While she tended to herself, Thomas carefully looked over the satchel containing the Hand of Maud and several other items.

"Eleanor," he said, "ye've got to see what else is in this bag. Look here." He held up a delicate crown encrusted with small, precious stones, rubies, emeralds, sapphires, and diamonds. He laid out a necklace studded with tiny gems, a simple cross on a chain ornamented with flowers, and a gold ring with a large ruby in the center, surrounded by gold leaves, diamonds and pearls.

"I've seen this ring on the Queen," Eleanor said, carefully examining the pieces. "It was one of her favorites. This crown," she continued, "is one of the King's favorites. But I noticed he wasn't wearing any crown this morning when we crossed the Wash." She picked up the Hand of Maud and marveled at the beauty of it. "It's unbelievable; it must be worth a fortune."

"Aye," said Thomas. "I've heard the Empress Maud brought this along with a wagonload of other jewels when she returned from Germany to claim her throne. Ye know she was the grandmum of King John?"

"Yes," said Eleanor. "I remember now. So, these are her jewels?" Then she remembered the words of Simon the magician. "I want the jewels, Eleanor. I know you have the crown jewels."

His words had come true. She had the crown jewels of England.

Chapter Forty-One

The next morning, they awoke and prepared to begin their journey to the Adelfrids. Thomas was hoping to locate at least one horse. He had some coins with him, and said he could afford to purchase a horse, though not a good one.

The night before, Eleanor had stretched out on the straw bed, piling her still-dusty dress beneath her head for a pillow. Thomas made himself a bed on the floor. She watched him struggle to get comfortable and finally told him to get into the bed with her. "It's not much better," she told him, "but we've been through an exhausting day, Thomas, so please sleep in the bed and be comfortable."

He eagerly joined her and wrapped his arms around her from behind. Despite her fatigue and aching muscles, she was acutely aware of his presence, his breath on her neck, the aroma of soap on his body from washing up, mingled with hers. She breathed more deeply, wanting to turn around and kiss him but fighting the urge. There was only this moment; nothing else that had happened mattered, not the danger, the death, the kidnapping, the King. She felt him roll her over, his hand moving behind her head and into her loose hair, bringing her lips to his quickly. There was no finesse or gentleness to his kiss, only a fierce ardor that locked them together. He kissed her over and over, stroking her face, nuzzling her neck, then back to her lips. Despite the exertions of the day, they both became excited, their breath coming in gasps and pantings. Finally, he released her, almost pushing her away, breathing hard as he did.

"I cannot control myself when I'm near ye, Eleanor," he said, "and I'll not have ye this way." He slipped off the bed back onto the floor. "The next time we lay together in a bed, I pray it's as man and wife."

She did not answer him. She watched him slowly regain his breath as he lay on the floor, then he rolled over. Within minutes they were both asleep.

"Eleanor, I have some news." Thomas helped her onto the pitiful horse he'd purchased. Its back was swayed and it had a gray muzzle. "I heard from the innkeeper that the King is ill. He and a small band of men made it to Newark Castle, but it's said he's on his deathbed. The rumor is that nearly all the King's army and horses drowned in the Wash, and his wagons were sucked down in the muck. Only a handful of those in the front of the train got to safety, but the King's treasure, they're sayin', was lost. Already there's people scouring the area lookin' for his loot."

"We'd best hurry," said Eleanor. "We don't want anyone figuring out that we survived the Wash. They may guess we have some of the treasure. Did you hear anything about the Marshal?"

"No," he answered, "but since he was near the front of the train, I'm guessin' he made it to safety." Eleanor was sure of it.

They traveled all day and arrived at the Adelfrids late in the evening. "Pa!" called Thomas, banging on the locked door. "Ma! Open up, it's Thomas!" They heard noise inside and saw a candle pass by the front window. The door flew open, and Beja stood in the center of it, her gray hair in long braids, wearing a nightdress and shawl.

"Thomas!" she exclaimed, throwing her arms around him. "My darlin', I've missed ye so, and worried for ye." She looked over his shoulder and saw a disheveled Eleanor behind him. She cast her son aside and lunged at Eleanor. "Oh, my dear," she said, grabbing her by the shoulders and pulling her inside. "Get in here, both of ye. Tell me what's happened. Are ye hurt? We heard about the loss of the King's army and his people, and we've been sick with worry."

"We're alright, Ma," Thomas said as she and the maid, Mary, who had arisen with several of the children at the tumult, fussed over them both, bringing them food and drink.

"Tell us everythin'," said Richard, his expression deadly serious. "How did ye survive it, and what happened to King John? We've heard bits and pieces. Did Sir William survive?"

"I don't know about the Marshal," said Thomas.

"I'm sure he survived," chimed in Eleanor. She knew his time had not yet come. "He was in the front of the train with the King. He must've been with him."

Thomas told them everything, about their escape from the Wash and the gossip they'd heard about the King's illness. Finally, exhausted again, they were gently led to their beds, Eleanor with her hair brushed out and wearing a clean nightdress.

She fell asleep quickly and dreamed. She was back home, back in 1964 with Patrick. They were on their honeymoon, visiting London and riding on a double-decker bus through the city. Passing Windsor Castle, she marveled at how old it looked, yet also how much larger and more expansive. As she strained to make out the window where the Queen used to stand and peer at the gardens, she suddenly saw the Queen come into view. Wearing her crown atop her long blonde hair, loose and waving in the wind, she leaned out the window and waved to Eleanor as she passed, her ruby ring visible on her hand. The Queen retreated, and King John came to the window, glaring at Eleanor as the bus drove by. His head was bare and his eyes dark with anger.

Wake up, Ellie, wake up!

She awoke to find the sun already up and the family assembled for breakfast. "We've got news," Richard said as Eleanor made fast work of her breakfast.

"Oh, let me tell it," cut in Beja, and Richard smiled and waved her to continue. Eleanor glanced at Thomas, but he only gave her a little smile. "The King is dead. There, I've blurted it out. But 'tis true. Died of dysentery, they say, possibly after eatin' some tainted fruit. Some say he was poisoned." Eleanor remembered the bowl of plums she'd seen him eating the morning they crossed the Wash. "Died at Newark Castle, and his body is returnin' now to Worcester Cathedral, where the Queen and children will meet for his funeral."

"Many of the townsfolk are quietly celebratin'," Thomas said. "He was a devil, that one was. Not like any of the other kings we've had to put up with." Thomas paused and cleared his throat, then he stood and held out his hand toward Eleanor. "Eleanor, would ye take a walk with me? There's somethin' I'd like to talk with ye about."

She was apprehensive, but she grabbed a wrap and walked outside in the cold October air. As they strolled through the back field Thomas took her hand in both of his and turned her to face him.

"Eleanor, my dearest, ye know my feelin's for ye," he began. His eyes were moist, and she wondered if he was going to cry. What was making him so unhappy? she wondered. "I don't want to drag this out, but there's much I'd like to say." He pulled out a small parchment from his vest and handed it to her. "I'll leave ye alone to read this, but what I'm sayin', Eleanor, what I'm askin', is that I pray ye'll agree to be my wife. I don't want ye to go back to yer time. I believe we could both be happy together here, livin' in our own home with Ma and Pa nearby. I'll care for ye and protect ye with my life, Eleanor. I'll leave ye now, and hope for an answer to my question."

He walked away, back into the house, leaving Eleanor standing in the field, stunned, surprised, happy, and worried, all at the same time.

She opened the letter and read. He had written to her in his finest prose. "My heartily beloved Eleanor," it began, "whose name is most dear to me and reminds me of our beloved Queen Eleanor. I pray you accept this token from me, a ring of royal heritage, fit for the Queen of my heart, thee!" Inside the letter was the ruby ring, the ring worn by the Queen which had been inside the satchel entangled around her foot in the Wash. She read the letter to the end. "Wouldst thou grant me my greatest desire: To be thine husband? Say yes, my love, my life, my sweet Eleanor. Say yes!"

Eleanor placed the ring on her finger and walked inside. All the Adelfrids were in the kitchen, staring at her expectantly as she approached Thomas. "Yes, Thomas, I'll marry you. I'll be your wife."

Chapter Forty-Two

They were married less than a week later. Wearing a green linen dress with a red tunic and belt, topped off with a fur collar hand-stitched by Beja and Lavinia, Thomas and Eleanor stood before a local priest and exchanged their vows.

"I'll be buildin' us our own home soon, beloved," Thomas said as they retired that evening to one of the empty cottages on the Adelfrid's estate. "Till then, this'll do nicely."

He opened the cottage door and Eleanor squealed with delight. There were only two rooms, a living area with fireplace, table and chairs, and there was the bedroom.

"It's beautiful, Thomas!"

"'Twas Lavinia and Mary. They slipped away from the banquet and prepared this for us."

They'd left a bowl of oil and spice on the table to create an inviting fragrance. The bed was a straw bed with a feather mattress on top. The sheets were linen, and the feather pillows were covered in linen cloth. Above the bed was a spray of dried herbs, for fragrance and to bless the newly married couple. There was a fire lit in the main room, and wine with two goblets was laid out, along with some food and drink for the morning.

Inside, Eleanor and Thomas drank wine and tried to relax after the hectic day, but Eleanor found she could not wind down. She had changed into a delicate linen nightgown stitched by Beja, while Thomas wore a long tunic shirt with ties along the front. This would be the first time for both of them, and she was, she admitted to herself, scared to death.

"I'm afraid," she told him with a shy smile, taking his hand. What if he doesn't like the way I look. What if …

"I, as well," he replied, kissing her hands. "We can be afraid together."

Then they prayed, asking God to bless their marriage. Eleanor opened her eyes and gazed into husband's shimmering eyes. How she loved him! She spoke nervously. "In my time, most of the girls are not virgins when they marry. They call it free love."

"Free love?" he repeated, tilting his head with a baffled look.

"Yes, they believe in having sex with whoever they want, whenever they want. For the pure pleasure of it. Sex that is free of commitment or consequences."

He leaned forward and kissed her gently on the lips. "I want commitment, and I want consequences with you, Eleanor."

"Consequences?"

"A child."

She was startled. She hadn't considered having a baby, but she smiled at the thought.

"You have captivated my heart, beloved," he said. "How beautiful you are, in every way."

He stood and took her hand, leading her to the bed. She could feel her heartbeat and put her hand on her chest to calm it. He turned down the covers for her and she slipped inside, pulling the sheet up to her chin in a display of genuine bashfulness. After all they'd been through together, she should not be shy with him now. And yet, she was more nervous than she'd ever been. He blew out the candles. The moonlight coming through the window cast a soft glow over the room.

"Now that we're wed, I can touch ye and kiss ye wherever and whenever I please," he said. "Free love."

She smiled.

"I hope ye're prepared for my advances, Eleanor." And he gave her a most lascivious grin, causing her to giggle and pull the sheets up even higher beneath her chin. "Are ye cold, dear wife?"

"A little."

"Let me warm you."

He got into bed with her. Lying beside her, both on their sides facing each other, he wrapped his arms around her. He raised up on one elbow, leaned over and began kissing her on her neck, raising a tingling sensation all over her body. He kissed her cheek, her forehead, then worked his way over to her welcoming lips. Eleanor felt warm as their kisses intensified. She wrapped her arms around his shoulders and drew him close, kissing him back with growing excitement.

"I'm warming up."

"So much clothin' for a warm room on our weddin' night."

They embraced. Clothing against clothing. "I love thee, Eleanor, oh how I love thee!"

"I love thee, as well."

Clothes loosen, fabric falls away. Cool air meets warm skin. Bare against bare, they draw closer—slow, unhurried. Hands wander gently, learning, seeking. Lips brush, then press, mouths open in silent need. Their bodies ache, wanting, giving. Heat builds with every breath, every touch—smooth curves, firm lines, the shape of each other memorized in movement.

Limbs tangle, his rough beard traces paths along her cheek, her neck, her body. They move together, slowly at first, then faster, need sharpens. Skin damp, breath quickens. Then stillness, suspended in the moment, the world falls away. Only touch remains—only them.

Breathing slowly, but they hold on, unwilling to part. Tears well. He kisses them, licks them away. They stay like that—quiet, close, loving.

"Good heavens, Eleanor, that was somethin'," he finally said with a grin. "I wasn't sure I'd survive it, but here I am. Did I hurt ye?"

She laughed and kissed him. "It's nothing. I don't think I've ever felt anything that delicious before."

"Ah yes, delicious is the right word!" he said, and gnawed at her neck and face as she laughed. "I'm hungry again, wife, for more of that delicious food ye just served up. Let's do it again; I bet I can do it even better!"

"I doubt it," she said. They both laughed, and they did, and it was.

Chapter Forty-Three

I f she could have frozen time, it would be this moment.
A soft fire flickered in the hearth. Eleanor, newly wed and now grounded in this unfamiliar time, moved with ease through the cottage. She wore the belt Beja had given her, the Book of Psalms, always close, was in the little purse that hung from the belt—unaware that this was the last ordinary moment she'd know for some time. She should have known peace wouldn't last.

Slipped inside the Book of Psalms given to her by the Archbishop were Thomas's engagement letter and her sketch of him. As always, she tucked a knife beneath her skirt. Inside her bodice, for safekeeping, was the ruby ring. She rarely wore it, knowing it would draw too much attention, but around the cottage, she loved to look at it sparkling on her hand.

I'm happy here, happy *now*. In this time, this place, with Thomas. The King is dead, and this war will wind down soon. Life is already blessedly routine. She decided she'd better finish cleaning up since she would be assisting with a birth today in the village. One of the women had started laboring early in the morning; it won't be long now.

She picked up one of Thomas's torn tunics, which she needed to repair. She thought about him, anticipating his return that evening. He was busier now than when he worked for the King, with so many buildings in need of repair since the start of the war.

There was a knock on the door. She tucked the tunic into her belt. Eleanor assumed it was Beja, arriving with her carriage to bring her to the home of the expectant mother. But it wasn't Beja.

The moment she saw him, her breath caught—Simon. But this time, not in a crowded fair or in a room full of castle advisers. No, now he stood in the doorway of her cottage. A few weeks into her marriage, with her heart full and guard lowered, Eleanor was about to learn that danger can find you even when you think you've outrun it, or outlived it. He was still tall and thin but his hair was white. He had no beard and was wrapped in a cloak.

I remember now! I remember! I remember seeing him like this, disguised, I remember—like waking from a hazy dream—that fair in New York, the one I attended with Carol. It had to be in the early 1970s. I already had a baby. That man, that man at the jewelry booth, the tall man with the white hair and no beard—Simon.

At that fair, Simon had stared at the ring she was wearing, the Queen's ruby ring. He asked a lot of questions about it. Then Eleanor had filled out a card at his booth and given her name and address. He told her she could win a drawing of some sort, some piece of fake medieval jewelry, and that's how he knew where she lived.

I finally understand. He saw the ring and recognized it as one of the crown jewels. He assumed I had more. He had to send me back so I could get them. He must've been the one who mailed me the invitation to the fair in Bouvines. I made it easy for him; I showed up. How stupid could I have been.

Simon seems able to travel through time at will, back and forth whenever, wherever, he wants. He'd seen me wearing the Queen's ring *after* I'd come back from the past and was able to be at the fair in Bouvines *before* I went into the past. How did he do it?

These thoughts machine-gunned around her head so quickly she could barely keep up with them. Eleanor tried to slam the door on him, but he forced his way in and put his hand over her mouth. Though she kicked and screamed, he easily subdued her, pushing her onto the floor. No, no, no! He took out a bottle with liquid in it, poured some onto a cloth, and held it over her mouth. He never said a word to her.

She was becoming dizzy, sleepy. What is this? Chloroform? She tried to scream, and Simon hit her in the face. She blacked out.

When she awoke, she was bouncing on the back of his horse. She had a rope tied around her neck. He held the end of the rope in his hands as he rode the horse into the woods. In a small clearing, Eleanor saw his magician's wagon. He dumped her on the ground, holding tight to the rope around her neck.

"Don't make a sound or I'll kill you," he said, leaning over her. She was too groggy to speak. "If you haven't got the jewels with you, you know where they are. I saw you with some of them in the future. I know you have them. If you won't tell me where they are right now, I'll send you back to your time and get you to tell me then. Maybe you've hidden them somewhere in the future. I'll get them, Eleanor, one way or another."

He added ominously, "I know where you live. I know who your daughter is."

Eleanor could not speak. *My daughter? I have no daughter.*

He was going to take her back to the future and kill her. A wave of panic crashed over her, stealing her breath. *I don't want to leave here, not anymore. I don't want to leave Thomas.* Yet Eleanor did not want to tell Simon where they'd hidden the jewels. All she had with her was the ruby ring, tucked inside her bodice. The other jewels—the crown, the other baubles, and the Hand of Maud—were hidden. But not in the future. They were hidden here, in this time, in Graston. Thomas and Eleanor had decided to bury them until the war was over. Then they would decide what to do with them.

Eleanor finally found her voice. "No, please. Don't send me back. I don't have them; I don't have the jewels. They were lost in the Wash."

Lying on the ground, her feet tied up, Simon first rummaged through the little purse around her waist and found the Book of Psalms with Thomas's letter and Eleanor's parchment sketch tucked inside. He threw them on the ground, disgusted. Still groggy from the chloroform, she scooped up the Psalms and the scattered pages and stuffed them back in the purse around her waist.

Simon opened the back of his wagon and pulled out some objects. One was a wooden platform. He brought out what looked like a tent and some poles, then he assembled curtains around the platform. She recognized the same setup he'd had at the fair in Bouvines, the curtained chamber that sent Eleanor to the past. There was another device that looked almost like a large battery or generator.

That may have been what flashed the light at the fair in Bouvines right before I was sent back in time. This time.

Simon dragged Eleanor across the clearing to his time machine. "Alright," he said, "Let's go back together, and you can show me where you have the jewels."

Eleanor recoiled in terror. Maybe I should tell him where Thomas and I hid the other jewels before he sends me to the future. Maybe then he won't send me to the future. But if he gets the jewels, will he kill me? Yes, Ellie, he'll have to kill you. And then he'll kill Thomas.

She was paralyzed, unable to think clearly, trapped between two unbearable choices with no way out. There was no more time; Simon dragged her onto the platform. He stepped alongside her, wrapping his arms around her to keep her from jumping off. He turned on the generator and immediately there was a bright light, followed by a spinning sensation.

The knife! She felt it jabbing at her thigh beneath her skirt. With Simon's arms around hers, she slid her right hand beneath her skirt and found the knife. She reached up as far as she could and stabbed him in his side. He shrieked in pain, let go of her, his hands flying to the wound in his side. He saw the knife in her hand and tried to grab it, but her arms were both free now, and with a quick arcing motion, she stabbed him in the neck. For a split second she recalled Archie, the filthy ruffian who'd attacked her in the woods when she first arrived in this time, how she'd stabbed him, too, in the neck.

This time, she struck the magician with so much force, two-handed, that he fell backward, screaming, blood spraying.

The white light was flashing in a circular motion. As Simon fell back, half outside the curtain, the two of them began to move through time. Everything spun, and Eleanor was dizzy. Simon had one hand clutched at his bleeding neck and the other on one of the support poles that held up the curtains. His upper body was leaning outside the curtains.

Eleanor saw with horror that his face had begun to dissolve and twist, like it was boiling. His arms were dissolving and twisting, like he was covered in oozing sores. She watched dumbfounded as his skin moved and bubbled. His face was contorted, his mouth was open, and his eyes were wide. He let go of the support pole and fell completely out of the tent. Everything went black.

Eleanor screamed. She was traveling away from her home and

Thomas. "Thomas!" she screamed, and her voice echoed.

She passed out, like the first time, and it was over.

PART THREE

Present Day

"Do not boast about tomorrow, For you do not know what a day may bring forth."

Proverbs 27:1

Chapter One

Time had taken so much from her—her home, her youth, her love. But not her memory. Never that.

"The time machine was gone, the magician was gone, I was gone. And Thomas was gone."

Eleanor's voice, though barely more than a breath, shattered the silence of the room. She leaned back slowly, her head resting against the fabric of her chair as though the story itself had left her hollowed out. Her eyes fluttered shut, and for a moment, she looked fragile, like her memories were too fragile to be spoken out loud.

Donna leaned forward, her young hand wrapping gently around Eleanor's weathered fingers. "Grandma, it's okay if you want to stop. You look tired."

When Eleanor opened her eyes again, they were distant, as if she'd only just returned from another time. George stood nearby, offering her a glass of water. She didn't take it.

"No, no, I'm almost finished." She waved them off with a frail insistence. "Let me tell you the rest."

Drawing in a slow, deliberate breath, she straightened just slightly, though the weight of what remained pressed against her. Remembering was painful. But to forget would be worse.

To forget would mean letting go of Thomas. And that, she could never do. As she spoke, Donna held her hand, while George sat close by.

"When I woke up, I was back in the future. It was 1966, and I was in the middle of an outdoor shopping mall where Graston used to be. I had the purse around my waist, and I had something else in my hand." Eleanor stood stiffly and shuffled slowly into bedroom and began rummaging through her closet. When she came back, she held a small object in her hand wrapped in a handkerchief. She sat and laid it out on the coffee table, opening the handkerchief. Inside was a plastic bag containing a blood-stained knife.

They all stared at it. The blade was spotted with a haze of dried, brownish blood. Then Eleanor spoke.

"When I woke up in 1966, a crowd gathered around me as I got sick on the pavement. I saw the bloody knife in my hand and stuffed it in my purse. Some cops arrived. I was injured. Remember, I was banged up from my battle with the magician, so they took me to a hospital. Lying on the hospital bed, still dizzy and a little sick, I remembered the ring. I reached into my bodice, and thank goodness it was still there. Thomas's tunic was still tucked into my belt, so I stuffed it and the ring into the bag hanging from my belt.

"Here," she said, handing the small Book of Psalms to George. "I brought this back with me, too. It's got a verse in the front written by Archbishop Langton."

George was astounded. "Eleanor, why didn't you let me see this before? I could've done some DNA testing, could've let my colleagues look at it weeks ago."

"Go ahead and take it. I wasn't ready to part with it before. It gives me comfort to read it every day. And it reminds me of the good people I knew in the past."

At the hospital, Eleanor said, resuming her tale, she started to feel better and wanted to leave, but had no place to go. "So, I called Patrick—your grandpa—and he flew to England to take me back home," she said. "The story I told him, and everyone, was that I'd had an injury that caused amnesia, so I couldn't get in touch with anyone. I said that once my memory came back, I'd already gotten married, but then my husband died. It was a lame story, and I don't know if your grandpa believed me. But if he didn't, he never challenged me. After all … I'd come back to him."

Eleanor paused. "I was wearing hospital scrubs when he picked me up. The nurses allowed me to shower and gave me the scrubs because my clothes were a mess. When your grandfather arrived, I was sitting in the hospital lobby, clinging to my little purse with my treasures inside.

"As much as I loved your grandfather, I regretted killing Simon because he was my only way back—back to Thomas."

"Eleanor," said George. "I can do some DNA testing on this Book of Psalms and the blood residue on the knife. It might tell us who the magician was."

"I guess it doesn't matter now," Eleanor answered. "He's long gone, but if you want to, go ahead and take both of them."

Donna gave Eleanor a hug. "I'm glad you stayed here," said Donna. "If you hadn't, you'd never have married Grandpa, my mom would never have been born, and neither would I."

Eleanor looked at Donna, hesitant to tell her the rest.

"What is it, Grandma? Is something wrong?"

"Donna, dear, there is something else. When I was in the hospital, they did some tests, some blood work. Before I left the hospital, they told me I was pregnant. I was pregnant with Beth, your mother."

Donna gasped, her eyes wide. "Then that means …"

"Yes, Thomas was your real grandfather, not Patrick. Thomas was your mom's real father."

Eleanor paused, smiled, and added, "You have his eyes."

Donna sat back heavily.

When Simon died in the time machine, Eleanor never saw him again, she told them. She never went to the fair in New York. "I guess his death changed history," Eleanor told them. "Maybe I should say it changed the future. And yet, I remember going to that fair, but like I dreamed it. I asked my friend Carol about it, and she just laughed at me. 'We never went to that fair, silly,' she told me.

"When I returned and learned I was pregnant, I knew that God had a new plan for me and that Thomas would not be my husband for life." Eleanor, holding Donna's hand, looked at her granddaughter with a soft expression. "He would be the father of my child and grandfather to you. Your grandfather Patrick was the only reason I was able to live a full and happy life after losing Thomas. He raised another man's child because he loved me. And I loved your grandpa. Don't ever doubt that.

"But …" Eleanor paused, her mouth trembling slightly and her eyes becoming moist and red. "In a way, after all these years, I still love Thomas."

Eleanor had begun to cry a little and dabbed at her eyes. Her hands were wringing her handkerchief into a knot.

"I still love him, though he died centuries ago. God brought us together for a reason and separated us for a reason. Sometimes, I feel that he's still alive, but in a different time. He might be an old man back in medieval England, just like I'm an old woman now, in this time. In a way, I like to imagine that we've aged together, as we had planned when we got married."

Donna and George exchanged a glance, laced with concern and the unspoken weight of disbelief. Eleanor saw it. She knew how impossible it all sounded. But this was how she kept Thomas close—by imagining him not gone, but merely elsewhere, alive in another time, just out of reach.

George had been quietly recording, the soft hum of his device barely audible over the hush that had settled. He looked up, his voice careful. "I have an idea," he said, breaking the silence.

Donna and Eleanor turned toward him.

"The DNA from Thomas's tunic still hasn't found any matches. But what if we try comparing it to yours, Donna—and your mother's? We might be able to retrieve your mom's DNA from her clothing, a hairbrush, anything personal. If there's a connection to Thomas, that will confirm if he was truly your grandfather."

He paused, then added, "We'll also test the DNA from the Book of Psalms and the knife. Then we'll feed everything into the ancestry databases, cast as wide a net as possible. Would that be all right with you, Eleanor?"

Eleanor gave a faint smile, her fingers brushing the edge of the chair, as though steadying herself against what lay ahead.

"Yes," she said. "Go ahead."

Why not? she thought. She already knew the truth. But Donna— Donna needs proof. She needs to see it spelled out in blood and bone to believe what I already know.

Chapter Two

"It's a match!"

It was two days later when Donna's phone rang. Seeing it was from George, she answered quickly. "Hi George."

"It's a match!"

She hesitated, not sure what she had just heard.

"The DNA matches, Donna. Thomas and your mother are related. Donna? Are you there?"

"Yes, yes, I'm just stunned."

"And your DNA matches both. But before you get too excited, this only proves that the wearer of the tunic, presumably Thomas, and your mother are related. And you're related to both of them. It doesn't prove that Thomas is from medieval England or that time travel was involved."

"I understand, but Grandma's story is … could it all be true?"

George said, "So far, we've had no matches to the blood on the knife. But there's more. And I can hardly believe it."

Donna's throat tightened. What's coming next?

"There is no DNA available for Stephen Langton, the archbishop, but we have DNA from ancestors of the Langton family that we compared it to, and it's a likely match. Donna, your grandmother's little Book of the Psalms really did belong to Langton, and he did write the Bible verse inside with his own hand."

That night, Donna and George ate dinner together at a restaurant close to the university. Something invisible yet powerful kept tugging them toward one another as they listened to Eleanor's story over the past weeks. Their conversations, often sitting on the front-porch swing at Eleanor's home, rocking slowly back and forth, in the campus coffee shop, or over the phone, flowed effortlessly. They exchanged smiles for no reason, every glance charged with the thrill of something new, something precious. Time stretched and compressed all at once.

In the restaurant, Donna asked George, "Do you believe my grandmother's story?"

"Do you?" he asked.

"Yes. I believe most of it. It feels true, George. Do you know what I mean? It's utterly fantastic, but it all seems to fit. And now the DNA fits the story, too."

"Yes, it feels true," said George. "And to answer your question, the best I can say is that I'm not fully convinced, not yet. You know—this is going to sound a little out there—many scientists believe in time travel, in theory, at least. That was a component of Einstein's theory of relativity. But time travel like what your grandmother describes has never happened. Or I should say, it's never been documented. I read about a physicist in Georgia who's been working on a time machine."

Donna tilted her head, one eyebrow arched.

"I'm serious, Donna. Why don't we try to meet him—see what he has to say about your grandmother's story?"

She thought for a moment. "Okay. I want to know the truth, wherever it leads. When can we go?"

He laughed. "Maybe we should finish our dinner first?"

She laughed, too, and across the table, their eyes locked and held—charged, unyielding, impossible to look away. With dozens of diners around them, chatting in a low hum, they both leaned forward and kissed softly, holding hands, their surroundings dissolving like a watercolor painting left out in the rain, a gently drifting, indistinct blur around them.

When they pulled away, they realized with a start that they were in a restaurant and the waiter was standing over them with their next course. He was rolling his eyes.

They both sat up straight. When the waiter left, they started to laugh.

"Let's go tomorrow, George," said Donna, still laughing. "Let's head to Georgia."

Chapter Three

The next day, Donna and George drove to Georgia to meet with Dr. Anton Mellick. An aide ushered them into his office, a room filled with books, papers, and stacks of files. Donna looked around, amazed. How can anyone work in such a cluttered room?

Mellick entered his office with a burst of energy. "Hello, hello!" he said to Donna and George, shaking their hands enthusiastically. "I'm so glad to meet you!"

Donna was immediately drawn to this odd man. He was middle aged, with graying hair and a slight paunch. Eccentric, she thought, but with a kind smile and loads of energy.

"Sit, sit," he said, moving the piles of papers off the chairs. "I can't wait to hear your story about your grandmother."

"You'll find it hard to believe," Donna began, and she told him everything, ending with her grandmother's trip back to her time in the magician's time machine.

"You say the time machine that your grandmother described had some kind of light in it? Did it sound like she was describing a laser light?"

"I don't know," George answered. "It may have been a laser beam, but she only saw light, a spinning light, she said. She also said there was something like a generator or battery that turned the machine on. Is that relevant?"

"I don't know. But lasers can be used to create a circulating beam of light that theoretically twists space and time. To put it in a nutshell, these circulating beams use magnetic fields to warp time. You can walk through time as you walk through space. Theoretically."

Donna laughed. "That's what you call 'putting it in a nutshell'?"

"Dr. Mellick," George said, "I read that you've experimented with time travel yourself."

"I'm working on it, yes," he said. "The principle is sound, but I haven't had success yet. I've heard rumors—they're only rumors, mind you—that some people have created machines that have moved people back and forth in time. Never officially documented, though. That's why I'm fascinated by your grandmother's story. She says she went back about 750 years?"

"Yes, from her time, which was 1964." said Donna.

She and George told Mellick about the DNA matches. Dr. Mellick's eyes grew round with amazement, and he stretched out his arms as if to capture and embrace the words that Donna had just uttered. "My dear Miss Westbrook, you must have no doubts; your grandmother really traveled to the past, exactly as she described. The genetic evidence is irrefutable."

"But Dr. Mellick," said George. "The genetic link between Donna, her mother, and Thomas doesn't prove time travel. Only a family connection."

"Oh, poo!" he said. "Did your grandmother lie about this Thomas fellow?"

"Well, no," said Donna. "I'm certain she didn't. I'm sure there was a Thomas, though when they met I can't be certain."

"Well," Mellick continued, "did she not bring back a ring from medieval England? A ring connected to the royal family? Did she not show you a Book of Psalms with the handwriting of Stephen Langton himself? *The* Stephen Langton. Did not the parchment come from an extinct animal? Did not the DNA evidence line up with her story exactly? Have faith, Miss Westbrook. Time travel has been my life's work, and you've given me real hope that I'm on the right track."

Then he added, "If only your grandmother's time machine had survived her trip back to 1966."

—•—

On the drive back to Virginia, Donna's phone pinged. "It's a hit from the ancestor web site," she told George. She scrolled through a few screens. "Here's one from England. It says, 'Hi cousin. I assume we're cousins of some type. Didn't know I had any connections in America, so I'd be interested in knowing if you have a family tree I can look at to pinpoint our relationship. Thanks, hope to hear from you. Meg.'"

Donna responded to Meg immediately, tapping away on her phone as George drove. "Hi Meg, no family tree, sorry. Your relationship to me came from my grandfather's DNA. His name was Thomas Adelfrid. He died many years ago. He was raised in the UK, in a town called Graston near Canterbury, and that's all I know about him. He had many sisters and brothers, but I don't know what happened to any of them, or even if Thomas had other children besides my mother." After thinking about it for a moment, she typed, "His family goes back to medieval England."

Mere minutes later she received a reply from Meg. "Donna, that name isn't ringing any bells," she wrote. "But my family line goes back to medieval England, too. What a coincidence. I've traced our family to English baronage, the family of de Malet."

Was she seeing things? She read the message again. Donna's mind could not process it. The child conceived by Lavinia, Thomas's sister, after she'd been raped by Baron de Malet, had created a match. Lavinia's little boy somehow made his way into the family tree of the baron. The child's DNA, which closely matched Thomas's, was passed down through the centuries to Beth, then to her daughter Donna, and to Meg, an obscure relation in England.

Donna and George drove directly to see Eleanor to tell her the news.

"If I understand you correctly," Eleanor said, "you're saying that Lavinia had DNA that closely matched Thomas's, which passed to Lavinia's baby. The baby eventually matched with my daughter, Beth, and then Donna. And also to this woman in England."

"Yes," said George. "It's a definite match. Meg is related to the de Malet family, and Meg is related to Thomas. The only way to put Meg and Thomas together is through Lavinia's baby."

Eleanor closed her eyes. Donna watched her as a brief smile showed on her face, like a rain cloud melting away to reveal a small ray of sunlight through the mist.

Eleanor opened her eyes and said, "Donna, I want you to go back and find out what happened to Lavinia's boy. I believe God's plan to carry on the Adelfrid line was not through me and Thomas, but through Lavinia's boy. Baron de Malet was killed by Thomas, so how did the child wind up in the baron's lineage?

"And … I need you to find out what happened to my Thomas. All these years, I pictured him falling in love, getting married, maybe even having children. I told myself I'd be happy for him, even from afar. But if the only DNA match came from his nephew … then what if something awful happened? What if he never got that chance to live a full life? I need to know—I *have* to know. It's the only way I'll ever find peace … the only way I can face whatever life I have left."

Her eyes, clear and blue, focused on Donna, then on George, then back on Donna. "Both of you, go back. Find Thomas, find out what happened to him. And find the Hand of Maud. Get it, and the other jewels, back to their rightful owners—the royal family of England."

———

George drove Donna home, both exhausted yet elated at learning of the DNA match to Meg from England and the match to the wicked Baron de Malet. As they approached her front door, they were holding hands.

"George, what do you make of what my grandmother said, about going back?"

"Well, Dr. Mellick was correct when he said the DNA evidence is irrefutable. Now we have more evidence—the DNA link supplied by Meg connecting you, your mom, the baron's family, and Thomas.

He paused, then aded, "We don't need any other proof. But the idea of finding the jewels, especially the Hand of Maud, fascinates me. She told us where they're buried."

"And what if we could find out what happened to Thomas?" Donna added. "But how could we go back? The magician's time machine is gone."

"That's the million-dollar question."

George leaned in, holding Donna's face in his hands. He first kissed her cheek then her lips, softly, and she responded, wrapping her arms around his waist.

Reluctantly, they pulled apart. Before she went inside, George touched her arm. "I think we should give it a try."

"What?"

"Let's go have another talk with Dr. Mellick."

THE STORY CONTINUES

Want to know what happens next?

The Heir to the Hand, coming in 2026, continues the adventures of Eleanor, Donna, George, and the Hand of Maud.

Please enjoy the excerpt from *The Heir to the Hand* on the following page: ▶

Donna landed with a thud.
  Perhaps landed wasn't the right word … *came to* would be more accurate.

When she came to, it was as if one moment she was plummeting through space—gravity, or something else, clawing at her stomach, no ground in sight, only the inevitable impact. The next moment, she was awake, her body jolting, her heart hammering in her chest, her breath coming in shallow, rapid pants. For a brief, disoriented moment, reality felt unsteady.

Soon her mind caught up with the illusion that she was falling, and the clawing feeling in her stomach intensified until she was sick in the grass.

Grass. She was lying in a field. The grass was soft beneath her, cool, a light breeze dancing along her skin. Rolling on her back, she looked up at the sky, which stretched wide and endless.

This is not my sky. This is a sky from centuries ago. Am I dreaming this? Did I really wake up in medieval England? Did it work?

Birds called in the distance, along with the rustling of grass.

Someone was approaching.

Unsteadily, she rose to her feet, remembering her mission: Tell anyone you meet that you're lost. Ask for directions to Graston, to the home of the Adelfrids. And stay calm.

The sound of footsteps stopped abruptly as she wobbled to her feet. Then a man called to her.

"Eleanor! Eleanor! Praise God, ye've returned to me!"